Critical Acclaim for Alan Spence

'One of Scotland's most accomplished literary talents'
The Times

'Brilliant . . . in all of the stories there is some sense of epiphany, a moment of acceptance even in the hardest of circumstances. They are all exquisitely and beautifully written stories' LIZ LOCHHEAD, *The Herald*

'The gulf between Spence and [his] contemporaries is underlined by the craftsmanship and profound humanity of his new volume . . . He magically evokes the tremulous terrain of family affection and foreboding' *Scotland on Sunday*

'Brilliant . . . taut and elegant' *Harpers & Queen*

'Memorable, not because of what happens, but on account of the mood that is created and the shifts of feeling that are revealed. They are memorable because they ring true. They are rather like Chekhov's stories. Spence, too, takes a little moment of ordinary experience and transforms it, in the simplest possible manner, into something significant . . . In an age of ugly preoccupation with violence, he draws attention to moments of beauty and stillness. He is a gentle writer, but never sentimental. The beautiful moments have always been earned . . . He is a writ⸱ to cherish, one offering deep and fulfilling pl⸱⸱
The Scotsman

'Reflects the brittle, strun⸱
perfection . . . formidabl⸱

'The magnetic attraction ⸱
to be the way he draws o⸱   ⸱⸱ood
experiences to add life to   ⸱⸱ . . This is a
mixture of real, and imagine⸱, ⸱⸱mories woven with simplicity and Spence's wonderful sense of humour'
Stirling Observer

Alan Spence was born in Glasgow in 1947 and now lives in Edinburgh where he and his wife run the Sri Chinmoy Meditation Centre. He has also written for theatre, television and radio.

By the same author
The Magic Flute
Stone Garden & Other Stories

Its Colours They are Fine

ALAN SPENCE

PHŒNIX

To Nityananda and Shantishri
(Tom and Maureen McGrath)

A PHOENIX PAPERBACK

First published in Great Britain
by William Collins Sons & Co Ltd in 1977
This paperback edition published in 1996
by Phoenix, a division of Orion Books Ltd,
Orion House, 5 Upper St Martin's Lane,
London WC2H 9EA

A CIP catalogue record for this book
is available from the British Library.

ISBN: 1 85799 753 0

Typeset at The Spartan Press Ltd,
Lymington, Hants

Printed and bound in Great Britain by
Guernsey Press Co. Ltd,
Guernsey, C.I.

Contents

ONE

Tinsel

The swing-doors of the steamie had windows in them but even when he stood on tiptoe he couldn't reach up to see out. If he held the doors open, the people queuing complained about the cold and anyway the strain would make his arms ache. So he had to be content to peer out through the narrow slit between the doors, pressing his forehead against the brass handplate. He could see part of the street and the grey buildings opposite, everything covered in snow. He tried to see more by moving a little sideways, but the gap wasn't wide enough. He could smell the wood and paint of the door and the clean bleachy smell from the washhouse. His eye began to sting from the draught so he closed it tight and put his other eye to the slit, but he had to jump back quickly as a woman with a pramful of washing crashed open the doors. When the doors had stopped swinging and settled back into place he noticed that the brass plate was covered with fingermarks. He wanted to see it smooth and shiny so he breathed up on it, clouding it with his breath, and rubbed it with his sleeve. But he only managed to smear the greasy marks across the plate, leaving it streaky and there was still a cluster of prints near the top that he couldn't reach at all.

He went over and sat down on the long wooden bench against the wall. His feet didn't quite reach the ground and he sat swinging his legs. It felt as if his mother had been in the washhouse for hours.

Waiting.

People passed in and out. The queue was just opposite the bench. They queued to come in and wash their clothes or to have a hot bath or a swim. The way to the swimming baths was through an iron turnstile, like the ones at Ibrox Park. When his father took him to the match he lifted him over the turnstile so he didn't have to pay.

Unfastening his trenchcoat, he rummaged about in his trouser pocket and brought out a toy Red Indian without a head, a pencil rubber, a badge with a racing car, a yellow wax crayon and a foreign coin. He pinned the badge on to his lapel and spread the other things out on the bench. The crayon was broken in the middle but because the paper cover wasn't torn the two ends hadn't come apart. It felt wobbly. He bent it in half, tearing the paper. Now he had two short crayons instead of one long one. There was nothing to draw on except the green-tiled wall so he put the pieces back in his pocket.

The coin was an old one, from Palestine, and it had a hole in the middle. He'd been given it by his uncle Andy who had been a soldier there. Now he was a policeman in Malaya. He would be home next week for Christmas. Jesus's birthday. Everybody gave presents then so that Jesus would come one day and take them to Heaven. That was where he lived now, but he came from Palestine. Uncle Andy had been to see his house in Bethlehem. At school they sang hymns about it. Come all ye faithful. Little star of Bethlehem.

He scraped at the surface of the bench with his coin, watching the brown paint flake and powder, blowing the flakings away to see the mark he'd made.

The woman at the pay-desk shouted at him.

'Heh! Is that how ye treat the furniture at hame? Jist chuck it!'

He sat down again.

Two boys and two girls aged about fifteen came laughing and jostling out of the baths, red faced, their hair still damp. One of

4

the boys was flicking his wet towel at the girls who skipped clear, just out of reach. They clattered out into the street, leaving the doors swinging behind them. He heard their laughter fade, out of his hearing. For the moment again he was alone.

He stood his headless Indian on the bench. If he could find the head he'd be able to fix it back on again with a matchstick. He pushed the Indian's upraised arm through the hole in the coin, thinking it would make a good shield, but it was too heavy and made the Indian fall over.

He shoved his things back into his pocket and went over to the doorway of the washhouse. The place was painted a grubby cream and lightgreen and the stone floor was wet.

Clouds of steam swishing up from faraway metaltub machines. Lids banging shut. Women shouting above the throbbing noise.

He couldn't see his mother.

He went back and climbed on to the bench, teetering, almost falling as he stood carefully up.

A woman came in with a little girl about his own age. He was glad he was standing on the bench and he knew she was watching him.

He ignored her and pretended to fight his way along the bench, hacking aside an army of unseen cut-throats, hurling them over the immense drop from the perilous bench-top ridge. He kept looking round to make sure she was still watching him, not looking directly at her but just glancing in her direction then looking past her to the pay-box and staring at that with fixed interest and without seeing it at all.

The woman had taken her bundle into the washhouse and the little girl sat down on the far end of the bench, away from him.

His mother came out of the washhouse pushing her pram. He jumped down noisily and ran to her. As they left he turned and over his shoulder stuck out his tongue at the girl.

Once outside, his mother started fussing over him, buttoning his coat, straightening his belt, tucking in his scarf.

'There yar then, ah wasn't long, was ah?' Gentle voice. Her breath was wheezy.

She was wearing the turban she wore to work in the bakery. Today was Saturday and she only worked in the morning, coming home at dinnertime with cakes and pies. He'd gone with her to the steamie because his father was out at the doctor's and he couldn't find any of his friends. They'd probably gone to the pictures.

He had to walk very quickly, sometimes trotting, to keep up with the pram. The snow under his feet made noises like a catspurr at every step. The pramwheels creaked. In the pram was a tin tub full of damp washing which was already starting to stiffen in the cold. It was the same pram he'd been carried in when he was a baby. His mother's two other babies had been carried in it too. They would have been his big brothers but they'd both died. They would be in Heaven. He wondered if they were older than him now or if they were still babies. He was six years and two weeks old. His wellington boots were folded down at the top like pirate boots. His socks didn't reach up quite far enough and the rims of the boots had rubbed red stinging chafemarks round his legs.

They rounded the corner into their own street and stopped outside the Dairy.

'You wait here son. Ah'll no be a minnit.'

Waiting again.

Out of a close came a big loping longhaired dog. The hair on its legs looked like a cowboy's baggy trousers. Some boys were chasing it and laughing. All its fur was clogged with dirt and mud.

His mother came out of the shop with a bottle of milk.

There was a picture of the same kind of dog in his Wonder Book of The World. It was called an Afghan Hound. But the one

6

in the book looked different. Again the steady creak of the pram. The trampled snow underfoot was already grey and slushy.

They reached their close and he ran on up ahead. They lived on the top landing and he was out of breath when he reached the door. He leaned over the banister. Down below he could hear his mother bumping the pram up the stairs. Maybe his father was home from the doctor's.

He kicked the door.

'O-pen. O-pen.'

His father opened the door and picked him up.

'H'Hay! Where's yer mammy?'

'She's jist comin up.'

His father put him down and went to help her with the pram. He went into the kitchen and sat down by the fire.

Dusty, their cat, jumped down from the sink and slid quietly under the bed. The bed was in a recess opposite the window and the three of them slept there in winter. Although they had a room, the kitchen was easier to keep warm. The room was bigger and was very cold and damp. His father said it would cost too much to keep both the room and the kitchen heated.

He warmed his hands till they almost hurt. He heard his mother and father coming in. They left the pram in the lobby. His father was talking about the doctor.

'Aye, e gave me a prescription fur another jar a that oint-ment.' He had to put the ointment all over his body because his skin was red and flaky and he had scabby patches on his arms and legs. That was why he didn't have a job. He'd had to give up his trade in the shipyards because it was a dirty job and made his skin disease worse.

'An ah got your pills as well, when ah wis in the Chemist's.'

His mother had to take pills to help her breathing. At night she had to lie on her back, propped up with pillows.

'Never mind hen. When ah win the pools . . . '

'Whit'll ye get ME, daddy?' This was one of their favourite conversations.

'Anythin ye like sun.'

'Wull ye get me a pony, daddy? Lik an Indian.'

'Ah'll get ye TWO ponies.' Laughing. 'An a wigwam as well!'

He could see it. He'd ride up to school, right up the stairs and into the classroom and he'd scalp Miss Heather before she could reach for her belt.

He'd keep the other pony for Annie. She was his friend. She wasn't his girlfriend. That was soft. She was three weeks older than him and she lived just round the corner. They were in the same class at school. She had long shiny black hair and she always wore bright clean colours. (One night in her back close – showing bums – giggling – they didn't hear the leerie coming in to light the gas-lamp – deep loud voice somewhere above them – sneering laugh – Annie pulling up her knickers and pulling down her dress in the same movement – scramble into the back – both frightened to go home in case the leerie had told, but he hadn't.)

The memory of it made him blush. He ripped off a piece of newspaper and reached up for the toilet key from the nail behind the door where it hung.

'Jist goin t' the lavvy.'

From the lobby he heard the toilet being flushed so he waited in the dark until he heard the slam of the toilet door then the flop of Mrs Dolan's feet on the stairs. The Dolans lived in the single end, the middle door of the three on their landing. The third house, another room and kitchen, was empty for the moment because the Andersons had emigrated to Canada.

When he heard Mrs Dolan closing the door he stepped out on to the landing and slid down the banister to the stairhead. In the toilet there was only one small window very high up, and he left the door slightly open to let light seep in from the stairhead.

A pigeon landed on the window-ledge and sat there gurgling and hooing, its feathers ruffled up into a ball. To pull the plug he climbed up on to the seat and swung on the chain, squawking out a Tarzan-call. The pigeon flurried off, scared by the noise, and he dropped from his creeperchain, six inches to the floor.

He looked out through the stairhead window. Late afternoon. Out across the back and a patch of waste-ground, over factory roofs and across a railway line stood Ibrox Stadium. He could see a patch of terracing and the roof of the stand. The pressbox on top looked like a little castle. When Rangers were playing at home you could count the goals and near misses just by listening to the roars. Today there was only a reserve game and the noise could hardly be heard. Soon it would be dark and they'd have to put on the floodlights.

For tea they had sausages and egg and fried bread. After they'd eaten he sat down in his own chair at the fire with his Wonder Book of The World. The chair was wooden and painted bright blue.

His father switched on the wireless to listen to the football results and check his pools.

The picture of the Afghan Hound had been taken in a garden on a sunny day. The dog was running and its coat shone in the sun.

'Four draws,' said his father. 'Ach well, maybe next week . . . '

'There's that dog, mammy.' He held up the book.

'So it is.'

'Funny tae find a dog lik that in Govan,' said his father.

'Right enough,' said his mother. 'Expect some'dy knocked it.'

Nothing in the book looked like anything he had ever seen. There were pictures of cats but none of them looked like Dusty. They were either black and white or striped and they all looked clean and sleek. Dusty was a grubby grey colour and he spat and scratched if anyone tried to pet him. His mother said he'd been kept too long in the house. There was a section of the book about the weather with pictures of snow crystals that looked like flowers and stars. He thought he'd like to go out and play in the snow and he asked his mother if he could.

'Oh well, jist for a wee while then. Ah'll tell ye what. If ye come up early enough we kin put up the decorations before ye go tae bed.'

He'd forgotten about the decorations. It was good to have something special like that to come home for. It was the kind of thing he'd forget about while he was actually playing, then there would be moments when he'd remember, and feel warm and comforted by the thought.

He decided he'd get Joe and Jim and Annie and they'd build a snowman as big as a midden.

Joe was having his tea and Jim felt like staying in and Annie's mother wouldn't let her out.

He stood on the pavement outside the paper-shop, peering in through the lighted window at the Christmas annuals and selection boxes. The queue for the evening papers reached right to the door of the shop. The snow on the pavement was packed hard and greybrown, yellow in places under the streetlamps. He scraped at the snow with the inside of his boot, trying to rake up enough to make a snowball, but it was too powdery and it clung to the fingers of his woollen gloves, making his hands feel clogged and uncomfortable. He took off his gloves and scooped up some slush from the side of the road but the cold made his bare fingers sting, red. It felt as if he'd just been belted by Miss Heather.

Annie's big brother Tommy was clattering his way across the road, trailing behind him a sack full of empty bottles. He'd gathered them on the terracing at Ibrox and he was heading for the Family Department of the pub to cash in as many as he could. Every time the pub door opened the noise and light seeped out. It was a bit like pressing your hands over your ears then easing off then pressing again. If you did that again and again people's voices sounded like mwah . . . mwah . . . mwah . . . mwah . . .

He looked closely at the snow still clogging his gloves. It didn't look at all like the crystals in his book. Disgusted, he slouched towards his close.

Going up the stairs at night he always scurried or charged past each closet for fear of what might be lurking there ready to leap out at him. Keeping up his boldness, he whistled loudly. Little Star of Bethlehem. He was almost at the top when he remembered the decorations.

The kitchen was very bright after the dimness of the landing with its sputtering gas light.

'Nob'dy wis comin out tae play,' he explained.

His mother wiped her hands. 'Right! What about these decorations!'

The decorations left over from last year were in a cardboard box under the bed. He didn't like it under there. It was dark and dirty, piled with old rubbish – books, clothes, boxes, tins. Once he'd crawled under looking for a comic, dust choking him, and he'd scuttled back in horror from bugs and darting silverfish. Since then he'd had bad dreams about the bed swarming with insects that got into his mouth when he tried to breathe.

His father rummaged in the sideboard drawer for a packet of tin tacks and his mother brought out the box.

Streamers and a few balloons and miracles of coloured paper that opened out into balls or long concertina snakes. On the table his mother spread out some empty cake boxes she'd brought home from work and cut them into shapes like Christmas trees and bells, and he got out his painting box and a saucerful of water and he coloured each one and left it to dry – green for the trees and yellow for the bells, the nearest he could get to gold.

His father had bought something special.

'Jist a wee surprise. It wis only a coupla coppers in Woollies.'
From a cellophane bag he brought out a length of shimmering rustling silver.

'What dis that say, daddy?' He pointed at the label.

'It says UNTARNISHABLE TINSEL GARLAND.'

'What dis that mean?'

'Well that's what it is. It's a tinsel garland. Tinsel's the silvery stuff it's made a. An a garland's jist a big long sorta decoration, for hangin up. An untarnishable means . . . well . . . how wid ye explain it hen?'

'Well,' said his mother, 'it jist means it canny get wasted. It always steys nice an shiny.'

'Aw Jesus!' said his father. 'Ther's only three tacks left!'

'Maybe the paper-shop'll be open.'

'It wis open a wee minnit ago!'

'Ah'll go an see,' said his father, putting on his coat and scarf. 'Shouldnae be very long.'

The painted cut-out trees and bells had long since dried and still his father hadn't come back. His mother had blown up the balloons and she'd used the three tacks to put up some streamers. Then she remembered they had a roll of sticky tape. It was more awkward to use than the tacks so the job took a little longer. But gradually the room was transformed, brightened; magical colours strung across the ceiling. A game he liked to play was lying on his back looking up at the ceiling and trying to imagine it was actually the floor and the whole room was upside down. When he did it now it looked like a toy garden full of swaying paper plants.

Round the lampshade in the centre of the room his mother was hanging the tinsel coil, standing on a chair to reach up. When she'd fixed it in place she climbed down and stood back and they watched the swinging lamp come slowly to rest. Then they looked at each other and laughed.

When they heard his father's key in the door his mother shooshed and put out the light. They were going to surprise him. He came in and fumbled for the switch. They were laughing and when he saw the decorations he smiled but he looked bewildered and a bit sad.

He put the box of tacks on the table.

'So ye managed, eh,' he said. He smiled again, his eyes still sad. 'Ah'm sorry ah wis so long. The paper-shop wis shut an ah had tae go down nearly tae Govan Road.'

Then they understood. He was sad because they'd done it all without him. Because they hadn't waited. They said nothing. His mother filled the kettle. His father took off his coat.

'Time you were in bed malad!' he said.

'Aw bit daddy, themorra's Sunday!'

'Bed!'

'Och!'

He could see it was useless to argue so he washed his hands and face and put on the old shirt he slept in.

'Mammy, ah need a pee.'

Rather than make him get dressed again to go out and down the stairs, she said he could use the sink. She turned on the tap and lifted him up to kneel on the ledge.

When he pressed his face up close to the window he could see the back court lit here and there by the light from a window, shining out on to the yellow snow from the dark bulk of the tenements. There were even one or two Christmas trees and, up above, columns of palegrey smoke, rising from chimneys. When he leaned back he could see the reflection of their own kitchen. He imagined it was another room jutting out beyond the window, out into the dark. He could see the furniture, the curtain across the bed, his mother and father, the decorations and through it all, vaguely, the buildings, the night. And hung there, shimmering, in that room he could never enter, the tinsel garland that would never ever tarnish.

13

Sheaves

The patch of wasteground had always been called the Hunty. Nobody knew why. Nobody even knew what the name meant. It was roughly rectangular, the same length as the tenement block that backed on to it. There had once been a line of walls, railings and middens separating the Hunty from the actual back courts, but progressive decay, wind and rain, and several generations of children had eroded this barrier almost completely.

Aleck and Joe had crossed into the Hunty and were crouching down playing at farms. Aleck had a toy tractor and a few plastic animals, and Joe had a Land-Rover and trailer, and some soldiers to use as farmworkers.

Using bits of slate, they scraped up a patch of dirt and divided it into fields which they furrowed with lollipop sticks. Joe crammed some scrubby grass into his trailer and Aleck made a primitive farmhouse out of a cornflakes packet.

They were both wearing T-shirts and khaki shorts, and for the first time since the start of the endless summer, Aleck suddenly shivered. The wind was cold. His clothes were too thin. That morning his mother had said it was the first day of autumn.

'Gawn tae Sunday school this efternin?' asked Joe.

'Ach aye,' said Aleck. 'Mightaswell. Anywey, it's harvest the day.'

There had been a harvest service on the wireless that morning.

Aleck had been half listening to it during breakfast. That was probably what had made him think about farms and bring out the toys they were playing with.

'We aw slept in fur chapel,' said Joe. 'Huv tae go the night.'

Apart from the rough grass, all that grew on the wasteground were nettles and dandelions. Aleck plucked a dandelion clock. Fluffy ball that had once been a bright yellow flower. Peethebed. He began blowing on it, sending the seeds drifting through the air, counting to tell the time.

One . . . Two

Each seed would hang, parachute down, land somewhere else and grow again.

Three . . . Four

Joe had grown tired of farming and he was using his soldiers as soldiers. They took over the cornflakes packet and killed some of the animals for food.

Five . . . Six

Joe made aeroplane noises and dive-bombed the farm with stones and clods of earth. The soldiers and animals were scattered, the fields churned up, laid waste.

Seven . . . Eight

Aleck wondered why dandelions were called peethebeds. Maybe you wet the bed if you ate them.

Nine.

Aleck's mother opened the window and shouted him up. That meant it must be time to get ready for Sunday school. About half past one.

He gathered up his things.

'Mibbe see ye efter,' said Joe.

'Prob'ly,' said Aleck.

As he crossed the back court towards his close, he decided that the time told by a dandelion clock was magic. That was why it was different from ordinary time. If you caught one of the seeds you could make a secret wish. That proved they were magic.

Only special people knew how it worked. Like Jesus and witches and medicine men. Magic time.

He could see his mother working at the sink, the window slightly open. He stopped and cradled his toys against him with one arm, almost dropping them as he waved up at her.

The theme music for the end of *Family Favourites* was crackling out above the rush of the tap. Behind the sports page, his father absently was singing along, adding the words here and there.

> 'With a song in my heart
> Da da dee, da da dee, da da dee . . . '

His mother, at the sink, was washing and cutting vegetables for soup, a pot with a bone for stock simmering away on one gas ring. On the other, a kettle of water for Aleck to wash himself was just coming to the boil.

'Ah'll let ye in here tae get washed in a minnit son.'

'Och ah'm quite clean mammy. Ah'll jist gie ma hands'n face a wee wipe.'

'A cat's lick an a promise ye mean! Naw son, ye've goat tae wash yerself right. Ah mean yer manky. Ye canny go tae Sunday school lik that.'

> 'Da da dee da doo
> I will live life through
> With a song in my heart
> FOOOOR YEW!'

On the last line of the song his father stood up, arms outstretched, still holding the newspaper, hanging on to the long nasal concluding note, crescendo drowning out the radio, hearing himself as a miraculous combination of Al Jolson and Richard Tauber and Bing Crosby.

'Whit a singer!' he said, patting his chest.

'Whit a heid ye mean!' said his mother.

'Ah'm tellin ye, ah shoulda been on the stage.'

'Aye, scrubbin it!' they replied, in unison, and they all laughed.

She shifted the vegetables on to the running board, emptied the basin and unclogged the sink of peelings. Then she cleaned out the basin and poured in hot water from the kettle.

'Right!' she said, handing him a towel.

Stirring the water with his hands, he made ripples and waves, whirlpools and storms. He squeezed the soap so that it slipped up and out of his grasp and blooped into the basin. He slapped the water with his palm, ruffled it up till its surface was a froth of bubbles. Then he washed his hands and arms, face and neck.

'Aboot time tae!' said his mother. 'Yirra mucky pup, so yar.'

She laid a sheet of newspaper on the floor in front of the fire and lifted the basin on to it.

'Feet an legs!' she said. He looked down at his grubby knees and didn't bother to complain.

Sometimes he didn't mind being clean. It could give you a warm feeling inside, like being good. It was just so much of an effort.

His mother laid out his shirt and his suit, his heavy shoes and a pair of clean white ankle socks.

This was the horrible part, the part that was really disgusting. The clothes made him feel so stiff and uncomfortable.

Slowly, sadly, he put them on.

The shoes were solid polished black leather and he consciously clumped round the kitchen. He found it impossible to feel at ease. Clumpetty shoes and cissy white socks. He glowered down at his stupid feet, his shirt collar chafing his neck. He put away his blue socks and white sandshoes. They were what he liked to wear. When he wore them he could run fast, climb dykes, pad and stalk like an Indian. Playing football he could jink and dribble without making one wrong move. Blue and white flashing. A rightness. A sureness of touch. The feel of things.

Clump!

'Whit's the matter?'

'Eh?'

'Yer face is trippin ye.'

'Nothin.'

'Yer no gonnae start aboot thae shoes'n socks again ur ye?'

'Naw. Ah'm awright mammy, honest.'

He knew he couldn't explain and he knew if he tried she would just go on about how lucky he was to have a decent set of clothes to wear. Then his father would chip in about when he was at school – bare feet or parish boots.

His father had laid down the paper, so he picked it up and looked for the jokes and cartoons. Oor Wullie. The Broons. Merry Mac's Fun Parade.

Oor Wullie, Your Wullie, A'body's Wullie. That always made him snigger because of the double meaning.

Wullie and Fat Boab were being chased by PC Murdoch because they'd knocked off his helmet. As usual, everything ended happily. As usual, Murdoch had a kindly knowing twinkle in his eye. As usual, Wullie was on his bucket in the last frame, slapping his thighs and laughing.

Real policemen didn't wear helmets any more. They wore caps with black and white checks. They swore at you and moved you on for loitering and booked you for playing football in the street. Joe had been booked about three weeks before and he was waiting for a summons to go to court. There had been about eight of them playing, but only Joe had been caught. He'd been using his jacket as a goalpost and when he'd stopped to pick it up he'd fallen behind. The others had charged through closes and escaped across the Hunty. Aleck had torn his knee on some barbed wire and he'd worn an ostentatious bandage for a week. When anyone had asked what was wrong he'd tried to look sinister like a gangster and spat out his reply.

'Ah goat it runnin fae the polis.'

And he'd hoped it conjured up a picture of himself, gun-toting masked desperado in a running shoot-out across Govan. Wanted. Hunted.

Clump!

'An mind an keep thae shoes clean an don't go gettin them scuffed playin football.'

'Ah kin jist see me playin football in Sunday school!'

'Less a your cheek boy! Yer mother's right. We canny be forever buyin ye new shoes wi you kickin the toes outy them.'

In one frame, Wullie was skulking, head hung, shoulders hunched, and above his head was the word GUILTY.

That was the name of one of Aleck's comics. It had JUSTICE TRAPS THE in small letters across the top, with GUILTY in big red print above blue-uniformed American policemen machine-gunning their way into a roomful of gangsters. Into a plastic bag his mother put a little of each of the vegetables she was using for the soup. Carrot, turnip, potato, celery, onion, leek. This was to be his offering for the service. She added an apple and laid the bag on the table, together with his Bible and a penny for the collection.

'There. That's you.'

He was over at the stove, looking in the pot. The broth was coloured red-gold and the fatty stock made the surface shine, globules bubbling, catching the light.

'Smells good.'

'Well, ye kin get intae that when ye get back. Noo c'mon or ye'll be late.'

On his way out of the close he was about to take a running kick at a tin can but he remembered about the shoes and he stopped, restrained. At the next corner were three or four boys he knew, boys his mother was always telling him to stay away from, because every time he got into trouble, it just happened to be with them. They saw him crossing the road and they whistled and shouted at him.

'Waell!'

'Gawn yersel!'

'Heh Aleck, yer luvly!'

'Ah'll get ye!'

One of them began singing and clapping his hands in time.

> 'Will ye come to the mission
> Will ye come will ye come
> Will ye come to the mission
> Will ye come.'

Aleck laughed back at them but he was blushing and he felt hot and confused. He wanted to go to Sunday school, but at the same time he envied them their freedom and their dirt. His walk was suddenly clumsy and awkward and he was happy to take a short-cut through a close, away from their taunting.

The mission hall was a converted shop, stuck between a close and a HANDY STORE. The flaking paint on its front was an indeterminate colour – a dirty green or brown. Above the door was the name GLASGOW CITY MISSION and on one of the boarded-up windows was a list of the week's activities. Sunday School. Bible Class. Christian Endeavour. Band of Hope.

Mr Neil was at the door to welcome everybody in, grinning, nodding, pushing up his glasses which kept slipping down his nose. He was not much taller than most of the older children.

'Hello Aleck. Hello. Comeaway in.'

Inside, the place was cool and dark, the only sunlight getting in through the open door. Aleck could smell the different fruits and flowers and vegetables that most of the children had brought, above the usual smell of damp and polished wood and musty old books. The seats were arranged in groups of five or six, the children grouped according to age. At the far end was a small raised platform, with a piano, a lectern and a table draped with a white cloth. On the table stood a wooden cross and a vase of mixed flowers – yellow and red.

At the piano was Mrs Neil, a big woman with greying hair. She wore a white hat and glasses with frames that turned up at the side, like wings. She was talking to Jim, the teacher for Aleck's group, who waved to him as he came in.

Aleck went and sat at his place, making too much noise with his chair. There were four other boys in the group – David, Robert, Martin and John. They all looked up and said hello.

'Learned yer text Aleck?' asked David. David was the only one of the group that Aleck really thought of as a friend. The others had returned their attention to their Bibles and were soundlessly mouthing the text over and over.

'Jist aboot,' said Aleck. He opened his Bible at the place, which he'd marked by inserting his attendance card and his membership card for the Life Boys.

He went over the words into himself.

'Mark 4:28 and 29 – For the earth bringeth forth fruit of herself; first the blade, then the ear, after that the full corn in the ear. But when the fruit is brought forth, immediately he putteth in the sickle, because the harvest is come.'

'Quite a long wan this week, intit,' said David.

'Aye, so it is,' said Aleck. 'An ah canny get ma tongue roon that "putteth in the sickle".'

'Aye it's hard right enough. Whit is a sickle anyway?'

'It's wan a they things fur cuttin grass. Lik a big knife wi a blade lik that . . . ' and Aleck drew an arc in the air with his forefinger.

He went on, 'D'ye remember they kerds ye goat wi FLAGS bubble-gum?'

'Aye.'

'Well, d'ye remember the Russian wan ah hid, the wan ah widnae swap?'

'Ay, aye it wis a red flag.'

'Well, thoan wee things in the coarner wis a hammer an sickle, croassed lik that.' He crossed his forefingers in front of him.

'Aw aye, ah remember. Huv ye ever seen a real wan?'

'A red flag?'

'Naw, a sickle.'

'Naw. Huv you?'

'Naw. Bet it wid be some chib, eh?'

They hadn't heard Jim coming up behind them. He tapped David on the head with his Bible.

'What would be some "chib"?' he asked, sitting down at the head of the group.

'A sickle,' said David, slicing the air to demonstrate. 'Schuk!'

'Bloodthirsty shower!' said Jim.

Aleck asked him if he'd seen a real sickle.

'Och yes,' he replied. 'We've got one at home. In the toolshed.'

Aleck had forgotten that Jim lived in a house with a garden. He only came to Govan to teach at the mission. He was about twenty-five and he always had a redfaced, clean and scrubbed look. He smelled of soap and haircream, and he always wore a sports jacket with a Christian Endeavour badge in the lapel.

'Ah'm glad you all managed to bring something for the service,' he said. 'Have you all learned the text?'

He got five different replies, from Yes through Silence to No.

'Ach well, we'll see anyway. Would you like to pass me your cards?'

While he was taking in the attendance cards, David turned again to Aleck.

'Didye go tae the pictures last night Aleck?'

'Naw. Ah jist steyed in. Did you?'

'Aye. Ma big brurra took us tae the Lyceum. It was a war picture. Aboot Korea. Terrific! Ah'll tell ye aboot it efter.'

Jim took each of them in turn, and with varying degrees of assurance and hesitancy they intoned the text for the day in the same monotone of incantation that characterized the way they would recite the alphabet or the multiplication tables or any other memorized litany. Then he marked their cards, once for attendance, once for reciting the text. He also marked Aleck's Life Boy card.

The Junior Division of the Boys' Brigade. Sure and Steadfast.

'That's fine,' said Jim. 'Now if you'd all like to open your Bibles at the place, we'll have a wee look at it. Mr Neil's going to talk about it after, so I won't spend too much time on it. Right, well what's the text about then?'

'Harvest,' said Robert.

'Right, and what's that?'

'Time a year when aw the crops ur ready,' said David. 'Corn an wheat an stuff.'

'Fine,' said Jim. 'In fact all the crops we need to make food. To live. And that's why we celebrate harvest specially. To give thanks for our food. Now. Do you remember what a parable is?'

'A story,' said Aleck.

'That's right, but it's a special kind of story that Jesus told. If you look at the top of the page it says The Parable of the Sower. Now Jesus told stories like this when he wanted to explain something in a way people could understand. This one starts at verse 3.

'. . . Behold there went out a sower to sow . . .' And Jim read them the whole story, about some seed falling by the wayside and some on stony ground and some among thorns and some on good soil, and when nobody understood, Jim explained about the sower being Jesus.

'If you could look at verse 14,' he went on, 'it says "the sower soweth the word". So Jesus is trying to make something grow from his words. Now, what do you think it is?'

Everybody shrugged or looked at the floor.

'Look at verses 30 and 32.'

Five heads scanning the books.

Silence, except for rustling pages and shuffling feet and creaking chairs.

'No? Oh well. It is quite difficult I suppose. It's talking about the Kingdom of God, growing up like a tree.

'So if Jesus is the sower, trying to make it grow by spreading his words, what d'you think it means about the different kinds of soil?'

Another silence. Then Aleck said, 'Different kindsa people?'

'Yes!' said Jim. 'Good. Good. We're getting there!'

When he finished explaining he said, 'I suppose these things'll be easier when you're older,' and smiled and added, 'like me.'

The singing of hymns left Aleck feeling strange, though he didn't know why. Sometimes he felt like crying. Sometimes he felt his face flush. Everything seemed very real but far away, as if he was watching it on a film.

Above the platform hung a single light bulb with a pink plastic shade. Aleck was looking at it as if he'd never seen it before. There was a dark crack on the shade, running from the rim about half way up. Aleck hated pink. The colour was like the sound of the word, like the taste of the pink pudding they sometimes had in the school dinnerhall.

Mr Neil with his wife at the piano had led them in singing the hymns. Heavenly sunshine. This little light of mine. This is my story. Give me oil in my lamp.

Cracked pink plastic shade. Sickly insipid pink.

Now Mr Neil was talking, about harvest and parables, about the day's text. The miracle of the growing corn. Man's labour in tending and growing. He putteth in the sickle, because the harvest is come.

'And I know,' he was saying, 'that it's difficult for us in a place like Glasgow, and especially in a place like Govan, to appreciate what harvest really means. I mean it's only in the country that people can really be aware of the changing seasons and what they mean, because there it matters, and so much of your life is bound up with these changes and the actual growing of the food we eat depends on them. Now as you know, the food you eat is just bought by your mothers from the shops. More than likely it comes in packets and tins. The whole process of getting the food from where it's produced to your table is so ... so vast and complicated that it's easy to lose sight of the fact that it all still depends on those same basic changes. On the sun and the rain. On the goodness of the soil. On human effort, and patience, and skill. And you know, I've been thinking about all this and about these parables that Jesus told. Like the one you've been talking about today – the Parable of the Sower. And I've been thinking especially about the way Jesus used parables – with one meaning on the surface that is obvious and easy to see, but with another far deeper, far greater meaning which is there for us to find.

'And in this parable of the Sower – at one level it's just a wee story about a man planting his seeds, and what happens to them. But when we see that the Sower is Christ, then we see that other meaning, and we think of the harvest that He will reap. And there are so many passages from the Bible, so many hymns that tell us the same story, that "All the world is God's own field". And you are that harvest, boys and girls. You are his children. And if you grow in his light, you will

"stand at the last accepted,
Christ's golden sheaves for evermore
to garners bright elected."

And you will be gathered to Him, to dwell with Him in Heaven.

'And no matter what happens to you, even if the dirt of the world seems to have settled on you and made you forget what you really are, deep inside you are still his golden sheaves. And no matter how drab and grey and horrible our lives and this place may sometimes seem, remember that this is only the surface. And even the muck of hundreds of years cannot hide that other meaning which is behind all things. The meaning that we are here to celebrate. That God is love and Christ is Life.

'And now boys and girls, if you will pray with me in the name of our Lord Jesus Christ, The Light of the World, The Sower of the Word, who taught us when we pray to say . . .

'Our Father . . .'

And everyone stood and joined in –

'whichartinheaven
hallowedbethyname
thykingdomcome
thywillbedone
inearth
asitisinheaven
giveusthisday
ourdailybread
andforgiveusourdebts
asweforgiveourdebtors
leadusnot
intotemptation
butdeliverus
fromevil
forthineisthekingdom
andthepower
andtheglory
forever
amen.'

'Now then,' said Mr Neil, 'whose turn is it to take the collection?'

A small girl from one of the younger groups raised her hand.

'Ah yes, Cathy. Here you are then.' And he handed her the collection bag.

Another two girls from the same group were appointed to

gather in the harvest offerings. These they collected in a large laundry basket made of bright yellow plastic, which Mr Neil brought out from behind the table. And as the girls performed the little ceremony with as much slow solemnity as they could, Mrs Neil played Bringing in the Sheaves.

With Mr Neil's help, they raised the basket on to the table, between the flowers and the cross. Then he gave thanks once more and everyone stood as he led them in the closing hymn – We plough the fields and scatter.

This was one of Aleck's favourite hymns. It had the same kind of thumping triumphant feel as the tunes they sang at the match or played in the Orange Walk.

> 'We plough the fields and scatter
> The good seed on the land
> But it is fed and watered
> By God's almighty hand;
> He sends the snow in winter
> The warmth to swell the grain
> The breezes and the sunshine
> And soft refreshing rain.'

And Mr Neil conducted some vast imagined angelic choir, clenching his fists and jabbing the air, raising high his cupped hands, stretching wide his arms. And the voices rose with each wobbling note on the piano, up and out across the back courts and the tenements, the puddles and the rubbish, and the broken walls and railings and the sad sparse tufts of grass and nettle that encroached regardless.

> 'All good gifts around us
> Are sent from heaven above;
> Then thank the Lord, O thank the Lord,
> For all His love.'

27

As David and Aleck crossed the back court, David was describing and acting out scenes from the Korean war film he'd seen at the Lyceum.

'Anywey ther's this Yankee pilot gets shot doon bi the communists, an ye see um fightin is wey oot the cockpit wi aw these flames roon aboot um. 'Nen e manages tae bale oot. An ye jist see is face lookin up, really shitin is sel. Then ye jist see um gawn lik that . . . Nyaaa!' And with his finger he indicated the spiralling fall.

'But did you say they wur fightin communists?'

'Aye.'

'An the yanks ur the goodies?'

'Aye.'

'But your da's a communist.'

'Aye. Ah know. Ah couldnae understaun that either. But ah didnae bother. It wis a great picture.'

Aleck left David at his own close and carried on down the road. At the corner were the same boys he'd passed earlier. They were kicking a ball about. He wondered if they would be gathered to Heaven too. They didn't go to Sunday school. He didn't know.

In his mind the whole day was a confusion; of dandelions and playing and hymns, of soldiers and communists and golden sheaves, harvest and parables and magic time.

The ball bounced across towards him, and instinctively he trapped it and chipped it back. One or two of them gave a sarcastic cheer. The ball went to Shuggie, who was in Aleck's class at school. He shouted across to him.

'Come doon efter if ye want a gemm. We'll be playin roon the Hunty.'

'Thanks,' said Aleck. 'Ah might dae that.' And he started off towards home. Suddenly he laughed and began to run. His dinner would be ready. He would change into his old clothes, and after he'd eaten he would go to the Hunty and play till it was dark.

In his path was a piece of stone chipped from a brick and without slowing down he booted it hard across the road and went charging on towards his close.

The Ferry

The cane arrow rose in the still warm air. Aleck and Joe shielded
their eyes from the sun and watched its flight. It seemed to rise,
clear of the tenements that enclosed them and hang for a
moment against the sky before turning back to complete its arc
and fall to land with a jar that staved and shuddered its whole
length on the hardpacked dirt and brick of the back court.

'It's a goodyin!' said Joe, grinning and flexing the bow that
Aleck had just made. The bow had fired its first shot, and it was
good. Aleck nodded and set about making a bow for himself as
Joe ran across to pick up the arrow.

They had bought six bits of bamboo cane. Each was long
enough to make a bow or be broken in half to make two arrows.

Aleck was stringing the bows, notching each end for the string
to fit, and Joe was making the arrows. If he had simply snapped
the canes in half the pieces would have split, leaving each arrow a
loose mess of fibres and split ends. So he used an old hacksaw
blade to cut carefully through each cane before breaking it and
binding each end with black insulating tape.

They played at their craft with seriousness. They were
crouched in a clearing. The grey buildings were their jungle and
the fragments of stone and broken glass they had gathered and
laid out were imagined arrowheads of flint and bone.

The hacksaw blade cutting through the cane sometimes made
a harsh rasping noise that set Aleck's teeth on edge. Like the

squeak of polystyrene rubbed on a window. Like the scrape and squeal of the teacher's chalk on the blackboard.

(Guide-lines for her chalk against the black – like the lines on the pages of his jotter – date in the left hand margin – NAME in the middle of the top line – below that (miss two lines) the title of the composition – 'What I want to be' – sun shafting in through the window, lighting on dancing particles of dust – dust of chalk in the air – sunlight – what I want – to be.)

At the beginning of the long summer holidays it had seemed as if they could never end. Eight weeks was an eternity stretching before them. Now, incredibly, five of those precious weeks had passed.

'Imagine huvin tae go back tae school 'n a cuppla weeks,' said Aleck.

'You're no sa bad,' said Joe. 'Youse Proddies uv goat a week merr than us.'

'Ach well,' said Aleck. 'Youse ur always gettin hoalidays a obligation. Jist wan saint efter another. Ah think we should get an extra two weeks tae make up fur it.'

Joe stuck out his tongue and gave Aleck the V-sign. Then he grinned.

'Heh Aleck, comin wull no bother gawn back tae school? Wull jist run away an dog it forever.'

'That wid be brilliant!' said Aleck. 'Wherr could we go?'

Joe held up his arrow.

'We could go tae America an live wi REAL Indians. Ah've goat an auntie in Canada.'

'Ach thur's nae real Indians left,' said Aleck. 'They aw get pit oot 'n daft wee reservations.'

'How aboot India then?' said Joe. 'Or Africa? We could live in a tree hoose.'

'Pick bananas 'n oranges,' said Aleck.

'Hunt animals.'

'Make pals wi some a them but,' said Aleck. 'Lions 'n tigers an that.'

'Make pals wi the darkies tae.'

'Great white chiefs.'

'Me chief Joseph.' He pouted his lips and spoke in as deep a voice as he could, beating his chest with his fist.

'Me chief Alexander,' said Aleck, raising his bow. 'We wid huv tae gie wursels better names but.'

'Walla Walla Wooski!' said Joe.

'We could paint wursels tae,' said Aleck. 'Werr feathers an bones.'

'Imagine bein cannibals,' said Joe. 'We could jist eat white men that got loast in the jungle.'

'Fancy gawn intae the chippy,' said Aleck, 'an askin fur two single fish an a whiteman supper!'

'Sausage rolls wi pricks in them,' said Joe, laughing.

'At's horrible!' said Aleck, making a face as if he was going to be sick.

(Louie in the chip shop – like Sweeney Todd – cutting people up for pies – rubbing his hands and gloating over the carcass of a fat schoolboy – ambushed in the back court.)

'People ur supposed tae taste like pork,' he said at last. 'Think ah'll stoap eatin meat.'

'Ach don't be daft,' said Joe. 'If we didnae eat animals we'd get ett wursels.'

'Suppose so,' said Aleck.

He put the finishing touches to his bow. Joe taped the last arrowhead. They went padding off across Congos and Zambezis of their own making, to see what was to be hunted.

Aleck lay with his eyes closed on the flat roof of the midden, the warmth of the sun on his bare arms and legs, his face against the stone. And nothing existed outside himself in that moment. (Colour, mainly red, behind his eyes – warm, warm – low sounds, a feeling, a murmur – flies, drone – voices far away – a dream, faint breeze – laughter, a car, tin can dropped in a bin – warm, he lay like some great slow lizard, coiled and lazing on a warm rock – he could almost remember it.)

He sat up suddenly and looked around. The colours were still behind his eyes. He focused on Joe on the ground below, stalking a pigeon. Joe. The back court. Hunting. It was real. He was Aleck. His whole life had actually happened.

Joe shot his arrow and the pigeon flustered off to circle round and perch on a railing.

'Bastard!' said Joe.

The arrow skimmed the wall where the pigeon had sat and landed on the other side in the next back court.

'Gonnae nik doon an get that Aleck?' said Joe, looking up.

From his high perch on the dyke Aleck could see both back courts.

'Ther's some fullas watchin yer doo,' he said. 'Thu'll prob'ly huv the perry us fur tryin tae shoot it.'

Aleck climbed down on to the wall.

'If ye hear me gettin mangled yull know whit's happened,' he said.

'Ach well,' said Joe, 'it wis nice knowin ye.'

Aleck dropped down on to the other side of the wall.

The men gave no sign that they had even noticed him but he hesitated to move for the arrow, which had landed almost at their feet.

It was funny to think of them as bird watchers. Most of them were in their twenties or thirties, one or two were older. Men without jobs who seemed to spend their whole time loafing or shambling around, always in a cluster, scuffling and shabby, always finding ways to fill the time till the glorious weekend when there was money for wine and they were loud and alive and glowing, singing and fighting and sick.

Watching the pigeons was a mystery with its secrets, its

initiates, a language of its own. They would cup their hands to their mouths and echo the bird's own call. They used strange words like fantail and others that Aleck could never quite make out or understand. Some of them even built wooden doocots, box-hutches where the birds could feed. Doocot meant dovecot because doo was short for dove. Dovecot. Cot for a dove. But the pigeons were mostly grey, although if you could look closely you might see colours. Like an oilstain on the road under the light. Gurgling and strutting and grey. Doves should be soft and graceful and white. Like the dove sent from the ark, to find land where it could rest. Miss Riddie had told them the story and taught them the song.

(The words chalked on the blackboard – teacher with her pointer – repeat after me –

> O that I had wings like a dove
> Then I would fly away and be at rest
> Lo then would I wander far off
> And remain in the wilderness

di dum diddy dum diddy dum/diddy dum diddy dum didum.)

One of the men picked up the arrow. He looked straight at Aleck and snapped the arrow in two. He was grinning.

'Aw . . . izzat no a shame . . . ah've went an broke it!'

The others laughed and he threw the pieces aside.

'Get tae buggery wi yer bows 'n arras or ah'll snap yer fuckin neck!'

Aleck ran and scrambled back across the wall.

The pigeon rose and soared over the rooftops and out of sight.

The afternoon sticky and hot and the pavement tar soft and melting. Aleck and Joe were scraping their initials with their arrows.

(The way the tar opened under the pressure – glistening black scar on the pavement's dusty grey – initials – names.)

'Tar's brilliant stuff, intit,' said Joe.

'So it is,' said Aleck. 'See the smell aff it when it's jist been laid! Makes ye wanty sink yer teeth inty it!'

'So it dis. Ah love smells lik that.'

'The smell a the subway!'

'New shoe boaxes!'

'Rubber tyres!'

'Terrific!'

Joe dug into the tar, wound the arrow till its end was coiled and clogged.

'Looks lik a big toly disn't it!'

They dug out lumps with their hands, kneaded and stretched and smeared it.

'Really dis make ye wanty eat it.'

'D'you remember eatin sand when ye wur wee?' asked Aleck.

'Naw, ah don't think so,' said Joe. 'How, d'you?'

'Aye. Sandpies it wis. Looked great. Tasted horrible but.'

(Mouthful of dirt – becoming mud – grit between the teeth.)

'Jesus!' said Joe. 'How ur we gonnae get this stuff aff?'

Aleck looked at his blackened hands. 'Margarine's supposed tae take it aff,' he said.

'We could always leave them,' said Joe. 'Cover wursels in it so's we look lik darkies.'

'Fur gawn tae the jungle,' said Aleck. He picked up his bow and arrows.

'Ach look at that!' said Joe. His arrow had split digging into the tar. He threw it away, disgusted.

'Never mind,' said Aleck. ''Mon wull go up tae mah hoose'n clean it aff.'

Margarine smeared on their tarry hands, a greasy mess, the fat and the tar merging to make a mucky green as they rubbed and scraped and tried to clean it off.

'Horrible, intit,' said Joe, looking at his hands.

'Imagine seein thaym comin ower yer shooder'n a dark night,'

35

said Aleck. He wailed and thrust gnarled slimy claws towards Joe. They stalked each other round the kitchen, menacing the furniture with green and trembling werewolf paws.

'Smelly,' said Aleck, stopping in mid-growl to sniff his hands. He went to the sink and tried washing them clean under the tap but the cold water couldn't dissolve the grease which still clung in globules and streaks.

'Ah canny really be bothered bilin up a kettle a watter,' he said.

'Gie's up that auld towel aff the flerr, wull ye.'

With the towel they managed to rub off most of the dirt.

''At's no bad,' said Joe. 'Prob'ly werr aff in a day ur two.'

They looked at the dirt still ingrained in the skin and under their nails.

'Dead quiet,' said Joe, unaccustomed to the emptiness of the house. Joe had brothers and sisters and his house was always loud with their noise.

'Suppose so,' said Aleck.

The tick of the clock. Stillness. Noises from the back court.

'Think ah'll jist stey in,' said Aleck. 'That's hauf four the noo, an ma mammy'll be hame fae ur work at five.'

'When dis yer da get in?' asked Joe.

'Aboot hauf five ur somethin.'

Joe lifted his bow and moved towards the door.

'Fancy gin doon tae the ferry efter tea?' he said.

'The ferry?'

'Aye, we could nik acroass tae Partick an play aboot therr 'nen come back. Disnae cost anythin.'

''At's a great idea,' said Aleck. 'See ye efter tea then.'

He handed Joe one of his arrows.

'Here,' he said. 'That's us git wan each.'

Past a pub with a cluster of neon grapes above the door, past a mission hall called Bethel, left off Govan Road and along a narrow lane, through the docks to the ferry steps.

Ferry steps. They were often invoked as part of a prophecy, against the drunk and incapable. Spat out like a curse – 'That yin'll finish up at the fit a the ferry steps.'

Aleck and Joe sat at the top of the steep slippery wooden steps, waiting for the ferry to cross from the Partick side.

'Imagin slippin fae here,' said Joe. 'Ye'd jist tummel right in.'

They looked in silence, down to where the steps disappeared into black invisible depth, the oily river lapping softly.

'Here it comes!' said Aleck.

They stood up and watched as the squat brown ferry chugged across towards them.

The water swirled up the steps as it bumped and thudded to rest.

The ferry had the same kind of low dumpy bulk as a tug, though it was much smaller. It had a long low deck with sides to a height of about three feet running along its whole length and open at each end. Spanning the middle section was a canopy. This gave shelter for the passengers in the rain and also covered the pilot's wheel-house. The whole ferry, including the canopy, was painted the same dull brown.

Aleck and Joe went to the front and leaned over the side. Smoke phutted from the chimney as the ferry chugged its way out. Joe had left his bow at home but Aleck had brought his with him, the one remaining arrow tucked under his belt. He trailed the bow in the water, watching the wake ripple out behind it, the boat rocking gently beneath them, the feel of the deck through their thin-soled shoes.

Towering along both banks were the great jutting cranes of the shipyards, a tanker further downstream, gulls circling overhead.

They'd been told a little about the river in school. How it began as a trickle away in the southern uplands and wound its way down through sheepfarms and mining towns and eventually flowed through Glasgow and beyond to the firth and the open sea.

'Funny tae think'n aw this watter comin fae a wee stream up'n the hills,' said Aleck.

'Intit,' said Joe.

'Ah mean, the same watter,' said Aleck.

They were silent, looking down at the oily flow. Grey with colours. Like the pigeon.

The journey was too quickly over. At the Partick side they charged up the steps then stopped and looked around them. The ferry started back across.

Miss Riddie had told them about Partick and Govan growing side by side. The deepening of the river. Shipbuilding. Cheap houses for the shipyard workers. She had said they were like reflections, Partick and Govan, with the river like a mirror in between.

The grey buildings looked the same, but they were not their own. They felt lost and threatened. The strange streets and unfamiliar faces were hostile. At the corner opposite, a group of men loafing. Boys their own age, playing, looking towards them. They would have to go past them to get clear of the ferry.

'D'you know anywherr tae go?' asked Aleck.

'Naw. No really,' said Joe.

'D'ye fancy jist gawn back?'

'Comin?'

'Right, c'mon!'

They squatted on the steps waiting. If Partick and Govan were on opposite sides of the mirror, only one side was real. It depended on where you had been brought up. And for Aleck and Joe, Govan was the only reality they knew. When they were back once more on the steps at the Govan side, Joe turned to Aleck.

'Hey! D'ye fancy jist steyin oan the ferry an gawn back an furrat a coupla times? Jist fur a wee hurl?'

'At's a great idea!' said Aleck. They jumped back on to the ferry just in time before it moved off.

The low sun was bright on the water and the shadows it cast were long. 'Heh Aleck,' said Joe. 'Ye could haud up the driver wi yer bow'n arra an get um tae take us tae America or Africa or wherrever it wis.'

'Imagine!' said Aleck. He looked at the bow. 'Och wid ye lookit the state ae it!' The string had split the cane at one end and the split had continued half way down its length.

'Never mind,' said Joe.

'Disnae really matter, ah suppose.'

At the Partick side they decided to jump off and join the oncoming passengers for the journey back, just for the sake of the leap from the deck to the steps. But when they tried to get back on the pilot blocked their way.

'Right!' he said. 'Yizzur steyin aff. Yizzuv bin up an doon aff this boat lik a fuckin yoyo. D'ye think it's jist fur playin oan? Noo goan! Get!'

They stood helpless, watching as the ferry moved off towards their home shore.

'Whit'll we dae noo?' asked Aleck.

'Ther's another ferry up at the Art Galleries,' said Joe. 'We could walk it up.'

'Wull that no take us a while?' said Aleck.

'Nothin else we kin dae.' Joe looked out after the ferry, now almost at the Govan side.

'Bastard!' he said.

'Cunt!' said Aleck.

He threw his split bow and his last arrow into the water and watched them being swirled out by the current. He wondered how far they would be carried. Out past the shipyards, past Greenock and Gourock to the firth, past the islands, out past Ireland, out to the Atlantic, out . . .

Aleck suddenly shivered. The sky was beginning to darken.

The river was deep and wide. They were far from home, in an alien land.

'Fuckin Partick,' said Joe.

They began the slow climb to the top of the ferry steps.

Gypsy

'Gypsies ur worse than cathlicks!' said Shuggie to Aleck. 'Nae kiddin. They havnae a fuckin clue.'

Les the gypsy said nothing. He just laughed and carried on tearing open packets of jotters and stacking them on an old table. The storeroom was thick with dust and a yellow winter light filtered in through the one window, which was small and grimy with bars on the outside. There was a single light bulb but it had fused and the janitor hadn't got round to replacing it.

Shuggie and Aleck were savouring the few minutes of freedom from the classroom, clambering over packing-cases and ancient desks, all chipped and battered, scrawled on and carved. They climbed and rummaged, poked and dug, from the highest shelf to the darkest grubbiest corner, expecting always to unearth some fabled, long-lost treasure.

But Les insisted on going on with the work they'd been sent to do. That was what had rankled Shuggie, though he hated the gypsy anyway.

'Wotcha think yer gonna find?' asked Les.

'Wojja finkya gonna foind?' said Shuggie, mocking his English accent.

'Very funny,' said Les.

'Vewy fanny,' said Shuggie. 'Anywey, never you mind whit. Jist you wait an see.'

'Some'dy funn a stuffed owl wance,' said Aleck. 'In a gless case it wis. An some'dy else funn a dead dead dead auld fotie a the Rangers.'

'Whit ye talkin tae that cunt fur?' said Shuggie.

'Ach c'mon,' said Aleck. 'E's no daein any herm. Ah mean wu've goat tae soart oot the jotters sometime.'

'Aw ah'm sayin is thur's nae hurry,' said Shuggie. 'We kin take wur time. Nae need tae belt intae it as if wur daein piecework.'

'Ach well,' said Aleck. There was a silence. Then he went on, telling Les, 'An thur's supposed tae be gasmasks, an fitba strips, an bladders, an loads a great books, an jist . . . hunners a things!'

'Must be pretty well hidden!' said Les, looking round the room and laughing.

'Smartarse!' said Shuggie, then, turning to Aleck, 'D'ye wanty gie tit-features a haun then?'

'Aw right,' said Aleck, jumping down from the desk-top where he was squatting.

'Freezin in ere, innit,' said Les.

For answer, Aleck nodded and shuddered, blowing on his hands and rubbing them together. 'Nae radiators in here,' he said. He lifted down a packet of jotters and tore it open.

'F2,' he said.

'Over ere,' said Les, indicating two of the piles he'd made. 'These other ones are FO and C2. Anythin else we've just t'leave ere.'

The jotters were all a dingy brown colour with the Highway Code on the front. On the back were the multiplication tables and lists of weights and measures, to be memorized. Aleck was reading over the rules for road safety. He had never really thought about them before, though he must have looked at the words a million times. DANGER! DANGER! DANGER! At the kerb HALT! That was like the Life Boys. By the left, Quick MARCH! Aleck hated the stupid marching and drill. He really went to the Life Boys for the football. NEVER play games on the street. Where else was there to play? Mrs Stone their teacher was always on about keeping them off the streets. She was new at the school and she wanted to organize sports for them. She said it was good for them to be in the Life Boys or the Cubs. Healthy. Shuggie had been in the Cubs once but he'd been put out for stealing a scout-knife and fighting over it in the hall. Now whenever he saw Aleck with his Life Boy uniform he had a good laugh at it. Called him sailor-boy. NEVER follow a ball, hoop or playmate into the street. Playmate was a funny word. He tried to imagine himself using it, calling Shuggie his playmate. The thought made him laugh. I say, playmate!

'Aleck!' Shuggie's voice was muffled as if he was shouting from down a hole. He had crawled along under the desks to get at a low cupboard in a far corner of the room. He had no room to crouch or turn. To get out again he would have to crawl backwards. He was kneeling there, hunched, coughing and choking on the dust he'd stirred up.

'Gonnae see if ye kin find a stick or somethin,' he said.

Aleck looked around the room. 'Wid a ruler dae?' he asked.

'It wid prob'ly brek,' said Shuggie. 'Somethin a wee bit heavier.'

Aleck looked again and this time found a broken pointer. He held up the two bits. 'Prob'ly cracked ower some'dy's skull!' he said.

'Likely enough,' said Les.

'See if this'll dae,' said Aleck, passing the pointed end in to Shuggie.

'Great!' said Shuggie. He wedged it in at the jamb of the door and tried to prise it open. There was a loud crack as something splintered and broke, and he ducked his head from another shower of dust, and the door flapped back on its hinges.

When the dust had settled he began scrabbling and groping in the cupboard. Then he let out a yell. 'Aleck! C'mere an . . . Jesus! Wait tae ye see this!'

Aleck hurried over, stooping down to peer under the desks as

Shuggie came struggling out, backwards, feet first. He was dragging with him a cardboard box. Aleck tried to see what was in it. He could make out some colour, red and white, a streak of yellow. Then Shuggie was out and up on his feet, lifting the box clear, into the light.

'Therr!' he said, laying it down on the floor.

Aleck looked and couldn't believe it. The box was full of football jerseys, the old style, with collars. They had red and white stripes. On top was a goalkeeper's jersey, yellow. Aleck kneeled down, open-mouthed, bright-eyed. He touched one of the jerseys, softly. It didn't disappear. It was real. He let out a long slow breath, full of amazement and wonder.

'D'ye think ther's a full set?' he said at last, grinning up at Shuggie.

'Mibbe,' said Shuggie, grinning back. 'Mon wull count them.' He began, lifting them out and passing them to Aleck. They handled each one gently, lovingly, fearful in case such a treasure should crumble away.

'Ten,' said Aleck, 'an a goalie's jersey!'

'A whole fuckin team!' said Shuggie.

'They've git numbers an everythin!' said Aleck, laying them down beside the jotters.

Shuggie searched through the pile till he found the number nine jersey. He draped it over his shoulders, the sleeves hanging down at the front, then he side-stepped past Les and dribbled the cardboard box across the floor.

'Jist a minnit,' said Aleck. 'Whit ur we gonnae dae wi thum?'

'Ah wis thinkin,' said Shuggie. 'Listen. Ye know how auld Stoney's always oan aboot sports an that. Ah think we could get ur tae let us huv a team.'

'God,' said Aleck. 'D'ye think she wid?'

'Sure!' said Shuggie. 'Wu'll take thum back up wi us an you kin ask ur.'

'How me?' said Aleck.

'Och c'mon!' said Shuggie. 'She likes you. You're good at compositions an that. If ah ask ur she'll tell me tae go an take a running fuck.'

'Jist imagine ur sayin that!' said Aleck, laughing.

'That's whit she'd mean aw the same,' said Shuggie.

'Aw right,' said Aleck. 'Ah'll ask ur. C'mon, we better get back up before ther's a search-party oot lookin fur us.'

Shuggie placed the jerseys carefully back in the box.

'Tellt ye we'd find somethin din't ah!' he said to Les.

'We better not forget the jotters,' said Les.

Ach!' said Shuggie. 'Whit did ah tell ye Aleck? Gypsies ur ignorant. Pure fuckin ignorant.'

'So you just happened to find them on a shelf while you were looking for the jotters?' said Mrs Stone.

'Yes miss!' said Shuggie and Aleck, together. She didn't look convinced.

'How did you get yourself so dirty Hugh?' she asked Shuggie. He had dusted himself down, but he still looked far from clean. Somehow he had managed to smear a lopsided moustache across his upper lip.

'Ther wis a lot a dust 'n tap a the boax, miss,' he said.

'On TOP of the BOX,' she said. 'Not on tap of the boax! Some of these days I'll manage to teach you children some English!'

But she was glad that the jerseys had been found. And it was agreed, they were to have a team. She would arrange a few friendly games for them with other schools and youth clubs. Then later she would see the headmaster about getting them into the schools league. But first they were to have a trial match. They were to pick two teams, a first and a second. The trial was fixed for the coming Saturday.

But for now they had to give out the jotters. They had grammar to learn.

The rest of the afternoon dragged. Aleck kept looking out the high window at the grey sky, dreaming, not really hearing Mrs Stone's droning voice, wishing they were free so he could talk to the others about the team. He glanced across the passage at Shuggie. Inside the cover of his new jotter, he was drawing a football player, in a striped jersey, with a number nine on the back.

They were not real gypsies, only people who travelled with the shows, moving from fairground to fairground, all over Scotland and England, and sometimes across to Ireland. But theirs was a wandering life and they lived in caravans, so people called them gypsies or tinkers.

When they came to Glasgow, they lived on a rise of wasteground, backing on to a railway line, across the road from the school. Here they stayed for two or three months every winter, when the shows were at Kelvin Hall or Glasgow Green.

The rise of ground had come to be called Gypsy's Hill. Along the crest of it was a high wooden fence, each section about a foot wide and thick enough to stand on, dark wood, rotted and weathered by the years. The fence ran right round the gypsies' encampment like a great stockade, enclosing it.

At the foot of this stockade, Aleck and Shuggie were playing. The ground had frozen over and they had been trying to smooth a part of the slope, taking turns at sliding down it on a makeshift sledge, a chunk of linoleum they'd dragged out of a midden. But now the sun was growing warmer, thawing out the ground. Only the part of the hill in the shadow of the fence remained frozen, hard. There was practically a straight line, the line of the shadow, dividing this part from the rest, already growing soft and muddy.

Aleck noticed it, the strangeness of it, and pointed it out to Shuggie.

'Weird that, intit,' he said.

'So it is,' said Shuggie.

Neither of them had ever seen the like. The line was so definite, the division so sharp.

'Bet ye that's thae gypsies,' said Shuggie.

'How d'ye mean?' said Aleck.

'Hauf ae thum's witches an that,' said Shuggie. 'They know aw aboot magic an spells an stuff.'

'Fortune tellin,' said Aleck.

'Tell'n ye,' said Shuggie, 'therr's prob'ly aw kinds a bad magic aboot here. That's how the grun's still aw frozen here an naewherr else.'

They looked up at the fence, looming, the thick upright sections like standing stones against the bright, watery sky.

'Ma da says gypsies wid cut yer throat for a penny,' said Shuggie. 'Thur always kidnappin weans tae.'

Aleck didn't really believe it. He shivered, but only from the cold. He remembered from somewhere a bit of a poem.

> My mother said I never should
> Play with gypsies in the wood.

Never play games on the street. Never follow a ball, hoop or playmate.

'Think wur gonnae go up in a puff a smoke any minute?' he said, laughing.

'Naaa!' said Shuggie. 'Ah'm no feart fae gypsies ur tinkers ur naebody!' and he went to the foot of the fence, Aleck following. They went to where there was a knot-hole a couple of feet from the ground. The hole had been worn away and was big enough for a foot-hold. Aleck crouched down and peered through.

'Therr's wee Valerie,' he said. Shuggie crouched down beside him.

Valerie was another reason Shuggie hated the gypsies, especially Les. She too was in their class at school. She had blonde hair, long and soft, parted in the middle and tied back from her face.

Shuggie had always fancied her, but she had no time for him. She preferred Les, another gypsy, English like herself. They watched her now, framed by the rough oval of the hole in the fence. She was playing at shops, by herself. She had a few old bottles, filled with dirt and small stones. She was emptying these on to scraps of newspaper, wrapping them into small parcels and arranging them along the wooden steps leading to the door of a caravan. They watched her, moving before them, lost in her own world. Then Shuggie put his fingers to his lips and let out a piercing whistle. She looked up but couldn't see them. She was too far away and the hole was too small. She went back to her game.

Shuggie climbed up on to the fence and reaching down helped Aleck up after him. They sat, straddling the fence, their legs dangling down on either side. From here they could see the whole camp spread out, huge vans and lorries, caravans with windows and doors and smoke rising from tin chimneys, gruff-looking men and women, going about their mysterious business, everywhere children and dogs.

Shuggie called out Valerie's name in a high-pitched, mocking voice. She looked up, saw them and turned her back, very deliberately going on playing. He called out again. This time she went up the steps into the caravan and a moment later a man came out. He had a thick sandy moustache. He was dressed in dungarees. He waved his fist and shouted at them.

'Gaan! Get dahn ourra that!'

Shuggie gave him the V-sign, a last act of bravado, but as he started towards them they were glad to scramble down from the fence, down to the foot of the hill and clear across the back courts, scared that the man would strike them down with a curse, shrivel them to ashes as they ran.

Saturday morning was clear and cold. Shuggie and Aleck were the first to arrive at the pitches, at the far end of Bellahouston Park. Four or five other games were already under way and the sounds carried over, the sounds that were always so strangely empty in such an open space. Voices shouting. Leather against leather. Shuggie had brought his ball, specially dubbined and laced, blown up hard. They tapped it about to each other while they waited and gradually the others arrived, singly and in small groups. Mrs Stone was there to act as referee, and a few girls from the school, to watch. The teams had been picked from their class, which was the qualifying, and the one below. The first team had already been issued with the jerseys and they all wore their strips under their other clothes which they just had to slip off to be ready. Some had boots, others made do with heavy shoes.

Among the girls was Valerie, who had come with Les. Les was at left back for the second team. Although he lacked a fanatical devotion, he sometimes liked a game, and he had put down his name and been picked. Shuggie was at centre forward for the first team, Aleck at outside right. The jerseys were all the one size so Aleck's was too big for him, the sleeves coming down over his hands, and Shuggie's was a bit tight, the cuffs stopping short of his big bony wrists. They laughed at each other. Aleck pranced up and down like a male model and Shuggie threw the ball after him, both performing for the girls watching as well as for each other.

At last they were ready, the coin tossed for choice of ends, everybody more or less in their positions. At the centre, Shuggie rubbed his hands together, flexed his legs, jumped up and down on the spot. Then he hunched over the ball, ready, and at the first blast of Mrs Stone's whistle, he kicked off and the game began.

They played half an hour each way, stopping for five minutes at half time. The frozen bone-hard pitch was rutted and uneven, the grass rough and sparse, and the ball difficult to control, especially for the bigger, heavier defence of the second team, who floundered and grew more shaky and haphazard as the game went on. The other team were generally more nimble, surer on their feet, and in the end they won easily by six goals to two, Shuggie scoring three. At the final whistle they leapt in the air, threw up their arms, rushed to hug and slap each other on the back. It didn't matter that it was just a stupid trial. They had won. They were entitled to strut and parade in their glorious red and white.

Mrs Stone had to go then. That was why the game hadn't been a full ninety minutes. But most of the boys decided to stay and play on.

'Wonderful game, boys!' said Mrs Stone. 'Wonderful! I'll be seeing you all on Monday morning then. And don't forget to bring back the jerseys.'

They watched her go. Some of the girls went with her, but a few stayed, to go on watching, a giggling huddle on the touch-line. They re-shuffled the teams, to make things a bit more even. Four of the boys had gone so they were down to nine-a-side.

They had been playing about twenty minutes when the ball broke to Aleck just on the half-way line. He moved infield and pushed it through the middle. Shuggie ran on to the pass. He shuffled past a defender and he was clear, moving on towards goal, but Les had moved back to cover. As he came in to tackle, Shuggie dummied to the left, expecting Les to follow, then swerved to the right again with the ball. This should have left Les stranded and off balance, but he was slow and instead of following Shuggie's feint, he lunged forwards clumsily, missing the ball, catching Shuggie below the knee with a heavy tackety boot. Carried forward by their own momentum they collided, crashing together and falling to the ground.

Shuggie was up first, hobbling, gritting his teeth against the pain in his leg, easing it by spitting out a steady rhythmic barrage at Les.

'Gan ya durty fuckin black enamel bastard ye!'

Les was just getting to his feet when Shuggie threw the first punch, catching him on the jaw and laying him out again. Then

Les was up and they were swinging at each other. A few of the other boys tried to break it up and pull them apart. The girls were shrieking with delighted horror. The ball had rolled a few yards away and lay where it came to rest, unnoticed and forgotten.

On Monday morning some of the girls had been talking to Mrs Stone. She was looking grim and righteous as she sent Aleck next door to fetch the boys from the other class who had played in the trial.

'And tell those who have jerseys to bring them,' she said. The others had been called out to the floor in front of her desk, without explanation. They waited, shuffling, awkward. She went on with some corrections. When Aleck came back with the rest she put down her pen and looked at them.

Then she began. She was horrified. The girls had told her about the scuffle, about the amount of swearing that had gone on.

'And I was disgusted,' she said. 'It seems I just can't turn my back on you for a minute but you're behaving like the lowest of animals. You've really disappointed me, boys. If that's a sample of your behaviour then you just can't be trusted. And I'm certainly not willing to make any effort for a bunch of hooligans who are just going to disgrace me. So that's it, boys. No more football, and you've only yourselves to blame.' She brought out the cardboard box and laid it down in front of her desk.

'Those of you who have jerseys,' she went on, 'put them back in the box. The boys from next door, go back to your class. The rest of you sit down and get out your arithmetic jotters. Hugh and Leslie, stay where you are. I hear you were the worst offenders.' She reached into the desk for her belt.

'Actually brawling!' she said. 'Just think yourselves lucky I don't send you to the headmaster. Right Leslie, you first. Cross your hands.' She belted them both twice. She sent Les back to his seat and told Shuggie to pick up the box of jerseys.

'You will take these jerseys,' she said, 'and put them back where you found them, and I will hear no more about football from any of you.'

They were numbed. She had pronounced sentence, and they knew that it was final.

'Right!' she said, turning to the class. 'Arithmetic.'

Gypsy's Touch was a sadistic kind of tig-game that had been dreamed up by Shuggie. Somebody would accidentally or deliberately brush against Les or another gypsy, and jump back as if contaminated. The aim of the game then was to transfer the infection, by touch, to somebody else who would try to pass it on again.

Now that they all blamed Les for the collapse of their dreams of having a football team, the game was more popular.

Shuggie jostled Les in the dinner-hall queue and recoiled.

'Gypsy's Touch!' he gasped out, clutching his hand to his throat, then poking somebody else and beginning the game. The queue broke up in disorder as they chased and ran, ducked and climbed, desperate to avoid the Touch.

'D'ye know whit happens when ye get Gypsy's Touch?' shouted Shuggie.

They delighted in trying to imagine.

'Ye turn intae a gypsy an they come an take ye away!'

'Ye go aff yer heid an kill yer maw an da!'

'Ye get covered in plooks!'

'Yer skin turns green!'

'Ye get scabies!'

'Warts!'

'Worms!'

'Nits!'

'Boils!'

'Dysentery!'

'Leprosy!'

'Black Death!'

'THE DREADED LERGY!'

And at this last, the ultimate affliction, they all joined in a strangled cry and gave up trying to better each other, because no more could be added. There could be nothing worse than the Lergy. It included all the rest, and more.

And all Les could do was turn away from them, and try to let none of it touch him, for the playground was their territory, and no place for him to get into another fight.

On Friday night Shuggie and Aleck set out early for the shows. On their way down to Govan Cross for the subway, they stopped in at Louie's fish supper shop and they each bought a bag of chips for their tea. They walked on, eating greedily, the chips at first burning their fingers and their tongues.

Shuggie brought out a long skinny slithery chip, slimy with vinegar and grease. Part of it was uncooked where it had been stuck to another chip. It was green at one end.

'Look at that,' he said, dangling it between finger and thumb.

'Yich,' said Aleck. 'That's enough tae scunner anyb'dy.'

'Lik a big snotter,' said Shuggie.

'Lik a fat worm,' said Aleck.

They looked at it, Shuggie making it squirm.

'It's a poison chip,' said Shuggie. 'Tell'n ye. Louie's a Tally. Comes fae Italy. Jist the same as gypsies. An they hate us because a the war. Prob'ly shove a poison wan in every coupla bags.'

He threw it down and stamped on it, squelching it on to the pavement. Aleck felt sick. He had a few chips left. He crumpled up the bag and threw it away. But Shuggie just laughed and finished the rest of his.

'Disnae bother me!' he said.

They took the subway, two stops, to Partick Cross and walked up to the Kelvin Hall.

They paid their money, pushed open the big heavy glass panelled doors and passed through into another world. It didn't matter that the money they had was meagre and wouldn't last. They were here, and the whole carnival was spread out glittering before them. It was all theirs, and they swaggered, feeling the weight of the coins that jingled in their pockets, and their only problem was where to begin.

'C'mon wull find the Ghost Train!' said Shuggie.

The tiny greenpainted train crashed through the tin doors and trundled into the darkness and the taperecorded shrieks and sirenwails and howls. And it gathered speed and hurtled towards a succession of mechanical, wobbling figures, brightly lit for a moment as the train ran straight towards them, and always just in time lurched clear round another bend in the track, and the lights went out and the darkness swallowed the figures again, spectres and spooks, skeletons and ghouls, corpses, vampires, body-snatchers with skulls, giant spiders, bats and owls, all vanished till they were switched on again for the next train coming through. And the screams and low moans faded as the doors bashed open before them and they were back out into the brightness and noise of the main hall and the ride was over.

'Wisnae very frightening, wis it?' said Shuggie.

And they moved on. They climbed the helter skelter, had a quick glimpse of the whole fair below before spiralling back down to earth; on the dodgems, with sparks flying and a smell like burning rubber, they bumped and veered and rammed in spectacular head-on collisions; they spun on the rotor, flattened against the wall as the floor dropped away beneath their feet; they guzzled ice-lollies and lemonade, potato crisps and candy floss; they rocked almost head over heels on the ribtickler.

'Ah feel a wee bit sick,' said Aleck.

'D'ye wanty sit doon?' said Shuggie.

54

'Ach naw,' said Aleck. 'Ah'll be aw right in a minnit.'

'C'mon wull look at the mirrors,' said Shuggie. 'Ye better no take any merr shooglin aboot jist the noo.'

In the Hall of Mirrors they joined the hysterical laughing procession, convulsed and doubled up, howling with disbelief and glee at their own warped reflections. Here they were squashed to a blubbery dumpiness; here they were stretched and elongated; here their heads split into two; here eyes, noses, teeth all merged; they moved and their images rippled, changed shape, broke up and came together again, wobbled across the surface of the glass like globules of oil, like jelly, like treacle dripped from a spoon. They were still laughing as they came to the last mirror and saw there two small shabby-looking boys laughing back at them. Aleck recognized one of them as Shuggie and eventually the other as himself. It felt strange for a moment. They were still delighted and amazed at all the freak, mutated versions of themselves they had just seen, and they felt suddenly self-conscious at being confronted by their normal reflections. But they pointed at the glass and laughed again, as if this too was a distortion.

By the time they came out Aleck's system had settled a bit and he felt fit enough to venture on to the rockets. The sign said Space Trip, above painted moons and planets, and round and round it flickering fairy lights chased each other endlessly.

They ran and climbed into separate rockets, Aleck's just behind Shuggie's. The great radial metal arms began slowly to rotate and they lifted off into orbit around the central control-box, and Shuggie waved back, and their speed increased and they moved on and up and out. They spun towards the roofbeams and the rafters, the empty gloom above the hall, and Aleck wished his ship could break free from the machine, and he could sail out through a secret escape-hatch (known only to him) and zoom across the river to Govan, dip and loop; over his friends' astonished upturned faces, mad with envy as he dropped a bomb on the school. He would soar past their third-storey tenement window, waving as his mother dropped the teapot and his father gaped out from behind his newspaper, and they would call him back for his supper, but he would just laugh and go on, higher and higher, and never stop.

But as they slowed down and came to rest, his stomach was turning over again. This time he sat down on the steps and Shuggie counted out the money he had left.

'Uv you goat the same as me?' he asked.

'Jist aboot,' said Aleck.

'That means wu've goat wur subway ferrs an enough fur another coupla hurls,' said Shuggie.

Aleck was looking across at a group of stalls and at one of them he saw Valerie, taking in the money. The game she had charge of was to lob rubber balls into upturned enamel buckets. Aleck pointed her out to Shuggie.

'Fancy tryin wur luck?' said Shuggie.

'Might win somethin ah suppose,' said Aleck. They sauntered over.

'Haya Valerie!' said Shuggie, hoping others would notice his casual familiarity and think he must be well in with the show-people.

'Three balls a tanner,' she said, coldly.

Aleck paid and Shuggie watched him waste all three balls. The first went in and bounced straight out again, the second hit the rim, the third missed the bucket altogether.

'Ach!' said Shuggie, shoving him. 'Useless! C'mon ah'll show ye how it's done.' They moved on to the next stall. Wild West Aunt Sally it was called. Three balls to throw at a row of wooden faces, alternate Indians and Outlaws, scowling and mean. They both recognized the stallholder as the man that had chased them down from the fence at Gypsy's Hill, but he gave no sign that he remembered them.

Shuggie's first throw knocked over an outlaw. His second sent an Indian spinning. 'Nae bother!' he said. He spat on his hands. He had already selected his prize, a red vinyl football, nestling among the racks of teddy-bears and teasets, gilt mirrors and jigsaws, stacks of knick-knacks and toys.

He drew back his arm like a baseball pitcher and threw. The ball smacked against the Indian's flat wooden face; the face wobbled but didn't tilt and just stared back at them, meaner than ever.

'Ard luck mate,' said the man, handing him a consolation prize, a white plaster poodle.

'Wait a minnit!' said Shuggie. 'Ah hut that fuckin thing an it never went ower!'

'C'mon now sonny,' said the man. 'That's the luck o the game, innit.'

'Bet yis widnae try that wi a man,' said Shuggie. 'Fuckin carve-up! Shower a pochlin bastards!'

Valerie had called the man over and whispered something in his ear. He looked angrier as he turned to them.

'So it's you two again, eh! Bloody little troublemakers. Go on. Gerraway! Hoppit before I ave yer put out!'

There was nothing they could do so they moved off, Shuggie still angry, scowling back and muttering.

They saw Valerie crossing to a lucky-dip stall called Aladdin's Cave and there behind the counter was Les. She spoke to him and pointed over, laughing, to where they stood, and Les laughed too.

'Gonnae get that cunt on Monday,' said Shuggie, quietly.

'Ye kin gie yer maw the dug,' said Aleck.

'Look at it,' said Shuggie, disgusted. 'A fuckin poodle.'

The back of the ornament was flat, unfinished, chalky.

'Kin use it fur writin on the wa,' said Shuggie, resigning himself to it. They were standing next to the Waltzers. 'Comin oan these?' he said.

'Awright,' said Aleck. 'Then that'll be us skint an we kin go hame.'

As they climbed in, Aleck suddenly felt sad that their money was gone and they hadn't seen the circus animals; the elephants, monkeys, horses and all the rest that made up the Carnival Zoo. But he soon forgot as the Waltzers started up and the dizziness came back, the tightness in his head and the nausea rising slow. They went faster and faster, spinning and hurling and he had to cling tight, gripping the metal bar. The screams and laughter and the grinding music were suddenly more than he could bear. The journey was never going to end. He would whirl and buck forever in this brash tinny hell. He wanted nothing more than to get off.

The ride at last came to a stop and he tottered from the machine. But it made no difference. It was just another nightmare. He wanted to be home and safe in his bed without the journey back through grey dismal streets. But he was here. The fair that had seemed so beautiful and full of wonders was the foulest place on earth. The ground was unsteady beneath his trembling legs. He sweated and shook. He wanted to be home but he was here and it was real. The clanking music jarred, discordant, pounding in his head. Stupid names, Space Trip, Aladdin's Cave. Faces, laughing, hostile, every one ugly and harsh. Fairy lights stuttering round and round his brain, a persistent annoying rhythm.

As he slumped down against a litter-bin, Shuggie realized he was sick.

'Godalmighty,' he said. 'Ye look green. Green as an auld chip.' Aleck groaned.

'Shows is a terrible place fur that,' went on Shuggie. 'Ah wance saw a fulla bein sick aff the chairaplane. Jist a big stream a honk flyin oot. Folk hid tae jump oot the road so they widnae get splattered!'

Aleck turned away, retched and heaved, and up it came. The final racking misery before he could be purged and clear.

He stood up shakily, wiping away the tears from his face, and his eyes focused on Valerie and Les and the man with the sandy moustache. They were talking together and laughing and he knew they were laughing at him, and he knew they must have poisoned him with their black gypsy magic.

Shuggie saw where he was looking and clapped his arm round his shoulder.

'C'mon hame Aleck,' he said. 'Yu'll feel better oot'n the fresh err.'

Outside the pubs were just emptying. They hadn't realized it was so late. They walked down to Partick Cross in silence and subdued.

Silver in the Lamplight

Aleck dribbled an imaginary ball past hulking invisible full-backs, mouth hanging open, crowdroar noises in his throat. A final swerve sent the railings the wrong way and he smashed an unstoppable shot against the midden-wall goal daubed CELTIC before he turned, arms outstretched, to receive the silent greybrick terracing acclaim of the tenements circling his back court arena. He stood for a moment, his arms raised in salute, then let them slump to his sides.

'The custom of saluting originated in the Middle Ages, when knights, as a gesture of chivalry, would symbolically shield their eyes from a lady's brilliance.' – STRANGE BUT TRUE NO. 23, one *of a series issued with Bellboy Bubblegum.*

Salute. We who are about to die salute you. That was what Roman gladiators used to say when they turned to the crowd. Aleck had read about it in one of his library books. It was up to the crowd whether a beaten gladiator lived or died. If they gave the thumbs-up he lived; thumbs down and he died. The book was called Bread and Circuses.

Sunday morning was always funny at this time; very quiet; most people having a lie-in after Saturday night's halfpissed loudmouthed ritual. Aleck picked up an empty beercan and tried to bend it. Useless. Two slight dents where he'd pressed with his thumbs. Shuggie and Joe could always bend them.

'Shite!'

He threw the can crashing hard against a middenbin.

'Get tae buggery an make a noise in yir ain back!'

Mrs Gallacher, bleached hair in curlers. Puffy-eyed and hungover.

'Aye you! Goan, get!' Fat tits bulging under a dirty cardigan, hanging out of the three-storey window.

He gave her the V-sign and regretted it immediately. She would tell his old man he'd given up cheek.

'Jistyou wait ma lad! Jistyou wait!' Woodbine cough. Bang-shut window. We who are about to die tell you where you can stick your fucking thumb. Quiet again. Might as well go up for Joe. Crunch across the pitted lunar wasteground and into Joe's close. Stale beer and catpish smells. Gurgling closet – must have just been flushed. He rapped at Joe's door.

'Is Joseph comin oot?' Always had to remember to call him Joseph. It was Mrs Kelly that had opened the door, letting radio music and breakfast sounds come seeping out of the kitchen. Aleck thought Joe's mother was middle-aged, which meant she was about thirty-five, and she smelled of nicotine and babies and hair and scent and sweat.

'Waitnull see.' She smiled and pushed a lank strand of hair back from her tired face.

'Joseph! It's wee Aleck fur ye!'

She went inside for a moment and came back to the door.

'Joseph'll no be a minnit.'

The door was pushed to but not closed and Aleck looked absently at the chalkings and scrapings on the dingy brown wall of the close.

A.J. LOVES T.K. TRUE BY A.J. Theresa Kelly is a RIDE. 1690. Fuck the Pope. King Billy was a POOF. NO SURRENDER. Up your HOLE. And there was the inevitable CELTIC 7 RANGERS 1, but with several nothings added after each number. The falsification of history was made by angry supporters of one side or the other who couldn't bear to see an adverse score written down. So first it would become CELTIC 7 RANGERS 10, then CELTIC 70 RANGERS 10, and so on forever. At the moment it stood at CELTIC 7000 RANGERS 1000. That wouldn't do. Aleck took off his snake-belt and held up his jeans with one hand while he carefully scraped another nothing with the buckle on to Rangers' mythical score. He tried to imagine a real game with a score like that. It would have to be like a Charlie Chaplin film but even faster. 17000 goals in 90 minutes. That would be 1700 goals in 9 minutes. That was nearly 200 goals a minute. It was impossible. It always gave Aleck a funny feeling to think about things like that. Why couldn't he imagine it? It was like trying to imagine the highest number possible, or putting two mirrors face to face so that you see yourself reflected again and again and again, getting smaller and smaller forever . . .

'Haya Aleck!' Joe banged the door behind him. His greeting had cut right into Aleck's thoughts and made him jerk back.

'Haya Joe. Ah nearly shat a brick therr.'

'Muss be a guilty conscience. Don't think ah didnae hear ye scrapin at the wa!'

Joe was a Catholic and therefore a Celtic supporter and would change the score back in their favour as soon as he could be bothered.

Together they shuffled out into the street, hands in the back pockets of their jeans. They wandered along towards the corner, where they found Shuggie. He was sitting on the doorstep of the corner-shop, leaning against the locked door, his legs jutting out into the pavement so that everyone coming round the corner had to make a detour to avoid stepping on him. He'd already been growled at by a scabby mongrel and kicked by a young overalled apprentice on his way to do an overtime shift in the wireworks just up the road. But Shuggie wasn't troubled by any of it. He just enjoyed provoking people, seeing how far he could push them before they'd react. He was bigger and stronger than Aleck or

Joe and he tended to boss them. He'd been too much for his mother, ever since his father had been killed. That was about a year ago, and it had made quite an impression on all of them. Shuggie's father had been knocked down by a hit-and-run driver late one Friday night and was dead by the time they'd got him to hospital. There had even been a bit about it in the paper and they'd all experienced that strange realization that somehow their lives, and the places and people they knew, had a being and a relevance in the bigger world, the world of the newspapers. And in Shuggie's reaction, in spite of his distress, there had been pride in this simple recognition of their existence. He'd cut out the newspaper paragraph telling of the accident and kept it flat between the pages of his Scottish Football Book. Aleck remembered him cutting it out and saying, 'Jist imagine, Aleck, hunners an hunners a people readin that.' And he'd looked pleased at the thought.

Nowadays, Shuggie's mother had to rely on his older brother Davie to help her keep him in check.

When Aleck and Joe came up to Shuggie, Joe made motions like a streetsweeper, pretending to sweep the pavement and poke at Shuggie's legs.

'C'mon, c'mon, we canny huv this rubbish clutterin up the pavement.'

'Right enough,' said Aleck. 'We better get the Sanitary.'

'Oh helluva funny,' said Shuggie. 'Helluva fuckin funny!' and he struggled to his feet, pleased to see them but trying to act surly. He said there might be a game of football going on in the school playground.

'Might get a gemm, if we're lucky!'

'OK.'

So they sauntered off towards the school. They'd seen each other the night before, so they had nothing much to talk about and they walked along in silence.

Despite their occasional fights, they were really very close.

They'd once decided to become blood brothers, and there in the hallowed secrecy of a rickety homemade back court hut, they'd pricked their thumbs with the pin of Joe's ABC Minor's badge, squeezed out a drop of blood, and clasped their hands together, each to each, Shuggie to Joe, Joe to Aleck, Aleck to Shuggie. That night they'd christened themselves the Tribe and solemnly pledged allegiance.

There still weren't very many people about; a podgy woman waddling along, balanced by two bulging messagebags, one in each hand; a man in his slippers, his pyjama jacket showing under his ex-army pullover, milk and rolls and the Sunday papers clutched in his arms. There were occasional family groups, consciously on their way to church or chapel, clean and polished; and there was a noisy shuffling knot of wineys, grubby and unshaven, some of them still drunk from the night before, purple faces laughing as they passed around a bottle of wine.

A very small girl, telltale soggy knickers hanging weighted below her dress, ran across the road in front of a bike. The bike skidded to avoid her, and her mother, who'd been standing at the close, charged across and battered her with relief.

'Ye might uv' THUMP 'got fuckin' THUMP 'KILLT' THUMP THUMP.

When they reached the school, the playground was empty, but they clambered over the railings anyway and just wandered about. Aleck and Shuggie saw enough of the school during the week, but there was always something in the adventure of being there when they weren't supposed to. And for Joe, who went to the Catholic school down the road, the expedition held even more of this sense of intrusion. They crossed into what was the girls' playground and were just about to climb up on to the toilets when the janitor came out of the boiler-room opposite and bawled at them, brandishing a shovel in the air. They ran back the way they'd come, and realizing he wasn't chasing them they paused at the railings to get their breath back before climbing out.

'That janny's a wee bastard!' said Shuggie angrily. 'If he tells the heedie we'll cop it themorra.' Shuggie knew there was no real danger of this happening, but he was trying to impress Joe with the unknown, unimaginable horrors of a Protestant school.

'Naw,' said Aleck, 'e'll no bother is arse.'

Outside the school, they were once more at a loss for what to do, and they started to drift back towards the corner where they'd met up earlier. All the way down towards Govan Road were half-demolished tenements, façades exposed like dolls-houses. The whole area had been scheduled for redevelopment for years and only now had a start been made. Aleck's parents had had a visit from the Sanitary Inspector the week before, and he'd assured them they would be in a new house within the year. That probably meant a shift to one of the big housing schemes like Easterhouse. At least in Govan there were shops and cinemas, and Ibrox Stadium was just up the road. But the schemes were so bleak. No pictures. No football. It would be terrible. And what then would become of Aleck's Tribe? His Uncle Peter lived in Drumchapel, and he called it the Reservation and made jokes about catching the last wagon-train from George Square, and for Aleck that was exactly how it seemed.

But that was in the future. For the moment they were together, with nothing particular to do.

'Mon wull go roon mah back,' said Shuggie, and they trooped through the close and into his back court. It was also the back court of all the other families whose houses backed on to it. But to Shuggie it was 'Mah Back'. Joe picked up a long stick of wood and looked at it thoughtfully.

'We could make a cuppla hatchets,' he said at last.

'Good idea,' said Aleck, and he wandered off with Shuggie to look for another stick and three tin cans while Joe set about breaking his long stick in half by leaning it against the wall and stamping it till it splintered under his boot. Gathering up the pieces, he followed Aleck and Shuggie. They were lucky. In the first midden they rummaged through they found the cans they needed and another short stick. They also unearthed, among the ashes and the debris that overflowed from the bins, a bundle of old comics, mainly Beanos and Dandys, and Aleck found a tattered copy of a Billy Bunter book with a library label half scraped away. He leafed through it, reading random sentences. 'O cripes! O crikey! Yaroo! Leggo! Gerroff! The fat owl of the Remove was being bumped again.'

To Aleck, the world of these stories was just as distant, just as strange, as the worlds of the other books he read – about the gladiators, about Arthur's knights, all the Children's Classics.

The bundle of comics proved uninteresting. They'd read them all before, so they dumped them back in the midden. But Aleck kept the book, shoving it down inside his jeans. He would read it later. For the moment it could wait; there were hatchets to be made. The idea was to place the end of the stick inside the can and hammer the can with a brick till it was flattened into an axe-head which could then be secured with a nail. They kneeled down by the side of a big stagnant puddle, which covered about half of the back, and started hammering away.

It was a scarletfever puddle. Aleck's mother said so. He'd had scarlet fever once and his mother said it was because he'd been playing in a green puddle and said he'd get hammered if he did it again. The puddle was actually a very nice colour, if you looked at it, though to some of Aleck's relations it would be heresy to say such a thing, for green was the Catholic colour, the colour of Celtic. His Uncle Billy went so far as to refuse to have anything green in the house. But his Auntie Lottie was forever saying 'It takes a green stem tae haud up an orange lily', and to Aleck this had seemed like the highest wisdom, very profound and enlightened. His Auntie Lottie must have thought so too, she repeated it so often, sometimes alternating it with 'Even Rangers play on green grass', and looking very reasonable and smug.

Aleck stirred the puddle with his foot and it smelled a bit foul. It was the colour of the grass in the park, of the tufts of grass along the guttering above Aleck's window.

It was funny how you said green as grass but not green as puddles. Or how about green as snotters? Aleck laughed.

'Heh Shuggie! Imagine ye wur oan the telly, oan Come Dancin or somethin, an this perr dance past an ye say "Naow heah we hev Cynthia in a beautiful snottah-green dress".'

'Daft cunt!' Shuggie threw a stone into the puddle just beside Aleck and the water splashed up but Aleck had jumped clear. And Joe had gone into convulsions, snorting and giggling. Aleck was doing a stumbling parody of a Come Dancing woman and whining Victor Sylvester music through his nose.

'Yes, snottah-green is definitely this year's fashion colour.'

Joe jumped over and joined in and the two of them were doing a wild birling lunatic waltz, and by this time Shuggie was laughing as well. Then Joe slipped and Aleck just managed to stop him tumbling bodily into the green slime. Then they both went down in a tangle and Joe's hand slapped into the puddle. He crossed over and swirled his hand in another puddle that was mucky but not green.

'Yizzur aff yer heids the perry yiz,' said Shuggie, and the three of them were still laughing as they carried on hammering. Soon their tomahawks were battered into shape. All that was needed was a nail for each one to hold the head in place. Shuggie said he'd go up and see if there were any nails in his brother's toolbag.

'Be back in a cuppla minnits.'

Aleck and Joe watched him go and waited where they were, aimless, kicking stones, scraping their initials in the dirt. To pass the time, they stood a bleach bottle up on top of a midden and tried to knock it down with stones. They were still trying when

Shuggie came back and smashed the bottle to the ground with his stick.

'Dye get any nails?' asked Joe eagerly.

Shuggie held forth his hand and, grinning, opened the clutched fingers to reveal three shiny brand-new two-inch nails.

'Dye know that Easter joke?' asked Aleck as he and Joe took their nails. He made hammering motions, knocking in two imaginary nails about five feet apart, then stopped and looked down at the nail, held between his thumb and forefinger, his lower lip protruding in an expression of exaggerated stupidity and puzzlement.

'Heh Jimmy, dye mind croassin yer legs, wu've only goat three nails.'

'That's sick!' said Joe, trying to look disgusted, but smiling nevertheless.

Aleck didn't see what he meant, until Joe added, 'Typical Proddie shite!'

Denounced as a heretic, Aleck said it wasn't a Protestant joke at all. 'Ah mean, Proddies believe in Jesus as well, ye know.'

'Never you mind um Aleck,' said Shuggie. 'Aw thae Papes ur the same. Jist too fuckin touchy.'

There was something needling in the way he said it. He was poking at Joe. But Joe just turned away and didn't take him on. Aleck gave up trying to be the Defender of the Faith, and they all carried on with their hammering.

By the time the axes were ready, Shuggie had to go away. Every Sunday he had to take a bundle of laundry to his granny's, collect her washing for his mother to take to the steamie.

'Ah'll plank ma hatchet here,' he said, hiding it at the back of the midden in the hope that nobody would find it. Joe decided he'd go and watch the Sunday afternoon film on television, and Aleck thought he might as well go home and read his book, so they hid their axes beside Shuggie's.

'See yis efter tea then,' said Shuggie.

'Right yar,' said Joe. 'Come doontae mah hoose furst.'

'Right yar, see yis.'

'OK.'

'See yis.'

'Cheerio.'

After tea, Aleck again found himself in Joe's close, and he was feeling miserable. The book hadn't been very good and his father had bawled at him for being cheeky to Mrs Gallacher earlier on. As he rapped at the door, he noticed the score on the wall had been changed again and now read CELTIC 70000 RANGERS 10000.

It was Joe who opened the door, and he took Aleck into the small bedroom he shared with his two young brothers, where Shuggie was already waiting. The rest of the family were in the other bedroom watching TV. Joe went out of the room to get his jacket and Aleck looked around him. He was fascinated by the Catholic things in the room; the Crucifix, the Sacred Heart, the framed certificate issued at first communion. He often felt envious of all the trappings and rites of the Catholic church. They seemed much more interesting than their own drab ceremonies.

He picked up a small bottle of Lourdes water from the mantelpiece. It was made from clear plastic and shaped like the Virgin Mary. It had a blue screw-on cap which formed the Virgin's crown and the name LOURDES was printed on the base in raised letters. Joe would sometimes sip some of the water and top up the level from the kitchen tap. Aleck was examining the bottle when Joe came back in.

'D'ye fancy a slug?' he asked. Aleck hesitated. He thought perhaps it would be a terrible sin for a Protestant to drink Holy Water. But Joe persisted. 'Ach goan! Jist a wee sip'll dae ye good. We kin aw take some.'

Aleck unscrewed the cap and sipped some. It just tasted like ordinary water (which by this time it probably was). He passed it to Shuggie who gulped some down, looked pleased with himself and passed it on to Joe, who took some himself and sneaked into the kitchen to fill the bottle up with tap-water. Once he'd replaced it, they all trooped out, and Aleck felt like a conspirator in some monstrous crime. It was just starting to get dark as they went and collected their axes, which were just where they'd left them. Then they decided to try and get some wood to build a hut in the back court. The best place to try was the woodwork. It should just be a matter of avoiding being caught by the watchman, so they set out across the wasteground behind Shuggie's back court.

When they reached the woodwork they decided that Aleck should keep watch while Shuggie and Joe climbed over the wall to see what was to be found. 'Ah'll gie ye a pucky up,' said Shuggie, making a step for Joe by clasping his hands together, palms upward. Joe put his foot on this and Shuggie hoisted him up so that he could scramble on to the top of the wall.

'It looks awright,' he said. 'Ah'll dreepy doon.' He let himself down on the other side and Shuggie jumped up, gripped the top of the wall and pulled himself up. Before dropping down on to the other side he shouted down to Aleck, who was holding the tomahawks.

'Mind the Hangman disnae get ye!'

Aleck laughed but felt very uneasy. The Hangman was right next to where he was standing, up against the woodwork wall. During the day it was just a lamp-post and its gallows shape held no terrors. But by night the lamp cast a vague shadow against the wall behind, and if you once admitted it looked like a hanging corpse, it became very difficult to see it as anything else. So it had become the Hangman. (Aleck had once thought maybe it ought to be 'Hanged Man', but then Hangman was easier to say.)

The street leading up to the Hangman was flanked by tenements to within about a hundred yards of the lamp-post, but this last hundred yards was bounded on one side by a blank factory wall and on the other by the area of wasteground they'd just crossed. And at night this desolate stretch, without the comfort of lighted windows on either side, was a place to be scurried past or avoided or tentatively crossed for a dare or for the sake of splashing some colour into a drab toneless evening.

Their fear of the Hangman had been heightened and confirmed by the death of Shuggie's father, for it was only a few yards away his body had been found. Round the body the police had drawn a yellow line which hadn't washed off for days afterwards. It had just lain there like a grotesque after-image. Aleck had had a frightening, confused dream in which he was at one moment lying down on the cobbled street with a yellow line drawn round him and at the next he was simultaneously watching what was going on and hanging from the lamp-post looking down at the grinning corpse of Shuggie's father, staring up at him, starting to move.

Aleck was beginning to feel really creepy and he felt grateful and relieved to see Shuggie scramble back over the wall, followed by a length of rope and then by Joe.

'We couldnae get any wid,' panted Shuggie. 'The bastards must've loacked it up.'

'Whit ur we gonnae dae noo?' asked Aleck.

Shuggie thought for a moment.

'We could go an raid the Winey.'

'Awright. C'mon.'

Shuggie wound the rope round him like a bandolero, over his right shoulder and under his right arm.

Aleck took off the trenchcoat his mother had made him wear and fastened it round his neck by the top button, like a cape.

They let out a whoop, and brandishing their axes, they set off at a run, whipping imaginary horses to a gallop.

'Tanterryanterryanterryaaaaaaan!'

'Winey' was short for 'The Wine Alley', a small pre-war

housing scheme backing on to a railway line. Although the actual houses were better than where Aleck lived, the tenements much cleaner and each flat with an inside bathroom, the place itself had some reputation for thuggery and violence. It was a bit unfair on most of the people living there, but it couldn't be denied that there were more fights, arrests and general disturbances here than in the surrounding area. When Aleck had read about Jacob's Island in Oliver Twist, he'd thought of the Wine Alley. It had its own identity, its own isolation. Aleck had grown up knowing it as the Winally, one word, and he'd thought that was its official name; it was only recently he'd realized it was a nickname and it was two separate words.

To reach it from where they were, they had to re-cross the wasteground into Shuggie's back, go through his close into the street, and cross the main road about a hundred yards away. They crossed this road, still at a gallop, and charged through a canyon between two gable-ends. This led them into a rectangular back court.

Their first act on entering the Wine Alley was to knock down a washing pole so that the line sagged and the washing trailed to the ground. It was that kind of evening and they were in that kind of mood. Whooping and yelling, they ran off and took refuge in the doorway of one of the wartime bomb-shelters that dominated the back. These shelters made good gang-huts and they were favourite screwing places for older boys and girls.

They stayed there till they got their breath back, Shuggie and Joe squatting in the doorway, Aleck chopping with his axe at a clump of nettles.

At Joe's suggestion they decided to play KDRF. That meant Kick Door Run Fast (or Kick Door Run like Fuck!) and they trooped off to do just that. Steal into a close, choose a door, each boot it in turn and scurry away.

After they'd kicked a few doors, Shuggie unwound the rope which he was still wearing.

'Right,' he said. 'We'll tie a cuppla doors thegether.'

They chose one of the closes they'd been through already, and while Aleck and Joe kept watch at either closemouth, Shuggie stealthily tied the ends of the rope to the handles of two opposing doors. This was a variant of KDRF in which, with any luck, the people who tried to open the doors would be set heaving and straining in a ridiculous tug-of-war as the taut rope kept the doors closed.

But this time Shuggie was just in the act of booting the second of the doors when a huge woman from the landing above came lumbering down the stairs and chased him and Aleck into the street, bellowing after them as they ran.

'Gan ya durty wee bastards!'

Joe, who'd been at the back of the close, had made his escape into the back court, and when Aleck and Shuggie realized the woman wasn't after them, they stopped running and went to look for him, going through another close further up the road. When they found him he was nursing a grazed hand. In the scramble from the close he'd got his legs tangled up with his axe and he'd fallen and scraped his hand on the ground.

It had started to rain now, a thin soaking drizzle, but it didn't matter.

'Didye see that wumman's face?' said Aleck.

'Ach she fucked it up,' said Shuggie, disappointed. 'She'd loosen aff the rope afore they came tae the door.' Then suddenly, inspired again, he grinned.

'Right,' he said. 'We'll go an get a can.'

Yet another variant of KDRF was to fill a tin can with water and lean it against a door. Then, when the door was opened, the can would fall over, spilling water into the house. This was what they were going to do now and they filed off in search of a can. As they crossed the back court towards a midden, Aleck remembered a story from another of the books he'd read, and he pretended they were some of Arthur's

73

knights crossing the wasteland towards the castle where they'd find the Holy Grail.

Again they were in luck. Rummaging, they unearthed a large family-size soup can. Shuggie peeled off the label to reveal its shiny metal sides.

'Hey, look at this!' shouted Joe. He was holding up a discarded paint tin.

Prising off the lid, he found that there was still some paint left, covered by a thick rubbery skin. Also in the tin was a piece of stick which had been used for mixing, the end of it clogged with paint, once white, but now grimed and grey. He used this to puncture the surface, revealing a little white paint, still fluid, at the bottom of the tin.

They crossed over to a puddle and Shuggie kneeled down and began slowly, ritually, to fill the soup can with water, using a smaller can as a cup. This puddle too was green and stagnant, though much smaller than the one in Shuggie's back. Joe was stirring the paint and Aleck was watching, fascinated, as Shuggie scooped feverwater into the can.

When the can was about half-full, Shuggie suddenly stopped and looked up at them.

'Heh! Ah've goat a better idea. We'll aw pish in the can!'

He slopped out some of the water and urinated into the can, then passed it to Joe who did the same.

'Ah don't really need,' said Aleck, as Joe passed him the can, but he managed a trickle to swell the volume a little. Shuggie took the can in both hands, his axe tucked under his belt, and led them in procession towards the nearest close, Aleck in the middle and Joe at the rear, still carrying the tin of paint. It was raining more heavily now, but it still didn't matter. The random wantonness of what they were doing filled Aleck with exhilaration and with guilty fear, and the two were inseparable.

And all this was real. All this was actual. All this was what mattered. It was two fingers to his parents and his teachers, to the Sanitary man and the town planners, to fat Mrs Gallacher and the woman who had chased them and all adults everywhere.

Just before they entered the close, Joe stopped them with a whispered 'Jist a minnit!' He opened the paint tin and, dipping the stick into the paint, he scraped on to the wall the word TRIBE. Underneath, in smaller letters, Aleck added the word PAGAN, just because it was a good word. They laid the paint tin on the ground, pleased with their work, and took up positions as before, Aleck and Joe keeping watch at either closemouth. And they stood very still in the close, rain trickling from their hair and soaked into their clothes, their breath condensing in the damp air. A car passed on the wet road outside and the sound of its wheels faded into the distance, towards Govan Road, towards the river.

Now all they could hear were the sounds of their own breathing, and the movements of their bodies.

And Shuggie kneeled down and carefully placed the can with its rim tilted against the door.

And they were hushed and almost reverent, in awe of the moment.

And their tomahawks, like their tincan grail, shone silver in the lamplight.

TWO

Its Colours They are Fine

Billy pulled on the trousers of his best (blue) suit, hoisting the braces over his shoulders, and declared that without a doubt God must be a Protestant. It was no ponderous theology that made him say it, but simple observation that the sun was shining. And a God who made the sun shine on the day of the Orange Walk must surely be a Protestant, in sympathy at least.

From the front room Lottie mumbled responses he couldn't quite make out, but which he recognized as agreement. Over the 23 years they'd been married, she had come to accept his picture of God as a kind of Cosmic Grand Master of the Lodge. It seemed probable enough.

Billy opened the window and leaned out.

The smell of late breakfasts frying; music from a radio; shouted conversations; traffic noises from the main road. A celebration of unaccustomed freedom. Saturday had a life and a character all of its own.

Sunlight shafted across the tenement roofs opposite, cleaved the street in two. A difference of greys. The other side in its usual gloom, this side warmed, its shabbiness exposed. Sun on stone.

Directly below, between a lamp-post and the wall, a huddle of small boys jostled in this improvised goalmouth while another, from across the road, took endless glorious corner kicks, heedless of traffic and passers-by.

One of the most noticeable things about a Saturday was the number of men to be seen in the street, waiting for the pubs to open, going to queue for a haircut, or simply content to wander about, enjoying the day. For them, as for Billy, a Saturday was something to be savoured. He would willingly work any amount of overtime – late nights, Sundays, holidays – but not Saturdays. A Saturday was his. It was inviolable. And this particular Saturday was more than that, it was sacred. In Glasgow the Walk was always held on the Saturday nearest the 12th of July, the anniversary of the Battle of the Boyne. It was only in Ulster that they observed the actual date, no matter what day of the week that might be.

Billy closed the window and went through to the front room, which was both living-room and kitchen.

Lottie was laying out his regalia in readiness for the Walk – the sash, cuffs, white gloves and baton. She had laid them out flat on a sheet of brown paper and was wrapping them into a parcel.

'Whit's this?' he asked.

'Ah'm wrappin up yer things. Ye kin pit them oan when ye get tae Lorne School.'

'Not'n yer life! D'ye think ah'm frightened tae show ma colours?'

'That's jist whit's wrang wi ye. Yer never DONE showin yer colours! Look whit happened last year. Nearly in a fight before ye goat tae the coarner!'

'Look, wumman, this is a Protestant country. A Protestant queen shall reign.' He rapped on the table. 'That's whit is says. An if a Marshal in the Ludge canny walk the streets in is ain regalia, ah'll fuckin chuck it. Ah mean wu've goat tae show these people! Ah mean whit wid HE say?'

He gestured towards the picture of King William III which hung on the wall – sword pointing forward, his white stallion bearing him across Boyne Water. In a million rooms like this he was hung in just that pose, doomed to be forever crossing the

Boyne. This particular ikon had been bought one drunken afternoon at the Barrows and borne home reverently and miraculously intact through the teatime crowds. Its frame was a single sheet of glass, bound around with royal blue tape. Fastened on to one corner was a Rangers rosette which bore a card declaring NO SURRENDER.

'An you're askin me tae kerry this wrapped up lik a fish supper!'

'Ach well,' she said, shoving the parcel across the table. 'Please yersel. But don't blame me if ye get yer daft heid stoved in.'

Billy grinned at the picture on the wall. Underneath it, on the mantelpiece, was the remains of what had been a remarkable piece of sculpture. One night in the licensed grocer's, Billy had stolen a white plastic horse about ten inches high, part of an advertising display for whisky. On to its back had been fitted a Plasticine model of King William, modelled by Peter, a young draughtsman who was in Billy's Lodge.

But one night Billy had come home drunk and knocked it over, squashing the figure and breaking one of the front legs from the horse. So there it sat. A lumpy Billy on a three-legged horse.

He picked up the splintered leg and was wondering it if could be glued back in place when there was a knock at the door.

'That'll be wee Robert,' he said, putting the leg back on the mantelpiece.

'Ah'll get it,' said Lottie.

Robert came in. He was actually about average height but he just looked small beside Billy. He and Billy had been friends since they were young men. They were both welders, and as well as working together, they belonged to the same Lodge. Robert was not wearing his sash. Under his arm he carried a brown paper parcel which looked remarkably like a fish supper.

'Is that yer sash?' asked Billy.

'Aye. Ach the wife thought it wid be safer like, y'know.'

'Well ah'm glad some'dy's goat some sense!' said Lottie.

'Ach!'

Billy buttoned his jacket and put on his sash, gloves and cuffs.

'Great day orra same!' said Robert. He was used to being caught between them like this and he knew it would pass.

'It is that,' said Billy. He picked up his baton.

'Right!' he said.

'Ye better take this,' said Lottie, handing him his plastic raincoat.

'O ye of little faith, eh!' He laughed, a little self-conscious at setting his tongue to a quote, but he took the coat nevertheless.

'Noo mind an watch yersels!'

Lottie watched from the window as they walked along the street and out of sight. At least this year they'd got that far without any trouble.

As they rounded the corner, in step, Billy turned to Robert.

'Ah'm tellin ye Robert,' he said. 'God's a Protestant!'

Emerging into the sunlight from the subway at Cessnock, they could hear some of the bands warming up. Stuttered rolls and paradiddles on the side drums, deep throb of the bass, pipes droning, snatches of tunes on the flutes.

'Dis yer heart good tae hear it, eh!' Billy slapped Robert on the back.

Robert carefully unwrapped his sash and put it on, then defiantly screwed up the paper into a ball and threw it into the gutter.

'At's the stuff!'

Billy caught the strains of 'The Bright Orange and Blue' and started to whistle it as he marched along.

'Ther's the bright orange an blue for ye right enough,' said Robert, gesturing towards the assembly of the faithful.

So much colour, on uniforms, sashes and banners. The bright orange and blue, the purple and the red, the silver and the gold, and even (God forgive them!) the green.

The marchers were already forming into ranks. It must be later than they'd thought. They hurried up to where their Lodge was assembled and took their positions, Billy at the side, Robert up behind the front rank, carrying one of the cords which trailed from the poles of their banner. Purple and orange silk, King William III, Loyal and True. Derry, Aughrim, Inneskillin, Boyne. These were the four battles fought by William in Ireland, their magic names an incantation, used now as rallying cries in the everlasting battle against popery.

They were near the front of the procession and their Lodge was one of the first to move off, a flute band from Belfast just in front of them.

Preparatory drumroll. 'The Green Grassy Slopes'. Sun glinting on the polished metal parts of instruments and the numerals on sashes and cuffs.

To Billy's right marched Peter, long and thin with a wispy half-grown beard. Billy caught his eye once and looked away quickly. He was still feeling guilty about ruining the Plasticine model that Peter had so carefully made. A little further on, Peter called over to him. 'The band's gaun ther dinger, eh!'

'Aye they ur that. Thull gie it laldy passin the chapel!'

It was as if they were trying to jericho down the chapel walls by sheer volume of sound, with the bass drummer trying to burst his skins. (He was supposed to be paid a bonus if he did, though Billy had never seen it happen.) And the drum major, a tight-trousered shaman in a royal blue jumper, would leap and birl and throw his stick in the air, the rest of the band strutting or swaggering or shuffling behind. The flute band shuffle. Like the name of a dance. It was a definite mode of walking the bandsmen seemed to inherit – shoulders hunched, body swaying from the hips, feet scuffling in short, aggressive steps.

Billy's own walk was a combination of John Wayne and numberless lumbering cinema-screen heavies. He'd always been Big Billy, even as a child. Marching in the Walk was like being part of a liberating army. Triumph. Drums throbbing. Stirring inside. He remembered newsreel films of the Allies marching into Paris. At that time he'd been working in the shipyards and his was a reserved occupation, 'vital to the war effort' which meant he couldn't join up. But he'd marched in imagination through scores of Hollywood films. From the sands of Iwo Jima to the beachheads of Normandy. But now it was real, and instead of 'The Shores of Tripoli', it was 'The Sash My Father Wore'.

They were passing through Govan now, tenements looming on either side, people waving from windows, children following the parade, shoving their way through the crowds along the pavement.

The only scuffle that Billy saw was when a young man started shouting about civil rights in Ireland, calling the marchers fascists. A small sharp-faced woman started hitting him with a union jack. Two policemen shoved their way through and led the man away for his own safety as the woman's friends managed to bustle her, still shouting and brandishing her flag, back into the crowd.

'Hate tae see bother lik that,' said Peter.

'Ach aye,' said Billy. 'Jist gets everyb'dy a bad name.'

Billy had seen some terrible battles in the past. It would usually start with somebody shouting or throwing something at the marchers. Once somebody had lobbed a bottle from a third-storey window as the Juvenile Walk was passing, and a mob had charged up the stairs, smashed down the door and all but murdered every occupant of the house. Another common cause of trouble was people trying to cross the road during the parade. The only time Billy had ever used his baton was when this had happened as they passed the war memorial in Govan Road, with banners lowered and only a single drumtap sounding. A tall man in overalls had tried to shove his way through, breaking the ranks. Billy had tried to stop him, but he'd broken clear and Billy had clubbed him on the back of the neck, knocking him to the ground. Another Marshal had helped him to pick the man up and bundle him back on to the pavement.

But this year for Billy there was nothing to mar the showing of the colours and he could simply enjoy the whole brash spectacle of it. And out in front the stickman led the dance, to exorcise with flute and drum the demon antichrist bogeyman pope.

They turned at last into Govan Road and the whole procession pulsed and throbbed and flaunted its way along past the shipyards. Down at the river, near the old Elder cinema, buses were waiting to take them to the rally, this year being held in Gourock. Billy and Robert found seats together on the top deck of their bus and Peter sat opposite, across the passage. As the bus moved off there was a roar from downstairs.

'Lik a fuckin Sunday-school trip!' said Robert, and he laughed and waved his hanky out the window.

They were in a field somewhere in Gourock and it was raining. Billy had his raincoat draped over his head. He was eating a pie and listening to the speeches from the platform, specially erected in the middle of the field. The front of the platform was draped with a union jack and like the banners it drooped and sagged in the rain.

Robert nudged him. 'Wher's yer proddy god noo!'

Proddy god. Proddy dog.

(A moment from his childhood – on his way home from school – crossing wasteground – there were four of them, all about his own age – the taunt and the challenge – 'A Billy or a Dan or an auld tin can' – They were Catholics, so the only safe response would be 'A Dan' – To take refuge in being 'An auld tin can' would mean being let off with a minor kicking. Billy stood, unmoving, as they closed round him. One of them started chanting –

85

'Auld King Billy
had a pimple on is wully
an it nip nip nipped so sore
E took it tae the pictures
an e gave it dolly mixtures
an it nip nip nipped no more.'

Jeering, pushing him. 'A Billy or a Dan . . . ' Billy stopped him
with a crushing kick to the shin – heavy parish boots – two of the
others jumped on him and they fell, struggling, to the ground.
They had him down and they would probably have kicked him
senseless but about half a dozen of Billy's friends appeared
round a corner, on their way to play football. They ran over,
yelling, and the Dans, outnumbered, ran off – and as they ran,
their shouts drifted back to Billy where he lay – 'Proddy dog!
Proddy dog!' fading on the air.)

On the platform were a number of high-ranking Lodge
officials. One of them, wearing a dog-collar, was denouncing
what he called the increasing support for church unity and
stronger links with Rome.

'The role of the Order,' he went on, 'must increasingly be to
take a firm stand against this pandering to the popery, and to
render the strongest possible protest against moves towards
unity.'

Billy was starting to feel cold because of the damp and he
wished the rally was over.

'Wish e'd hurry up,' said Robert, rain trickling down his
neck.

Billy shuffled. His legs were getting stiff.

The speaker pledged allegiance. Loyal address to the crown.

Applause. At last. The national anthem.

Billy straightened up. The blacksuited backs of the men in
front. Long live our noble. Crumb of piecrust under his false
teeth. Rain pattering on his coat. Huddled. Proddy god. Happy

and glorious. Wet grass underfoot, its colour made bright by the rain.

Billy poured the dregs of his fourth half into his fourth pint. The discomforts of the interminable return journey and the soggy dripping march back to Lorne School were already forgotten as Billy, Robert and Peter sat drying off in the pub. Soon the day would form part of their collective mythology, to be stored, recounted, glorified.

Theirs was one of four rickety tables arranged along the wall facing the bar. Above them, rain was still streaking the frosted glass of the window but they no longer cared as the night grew loud and bright around them.

'Didye see that wee lassie?' said Robert. 'Cannae uv been merr than six year auld, an ther she wis marchin alang in the rain singin "Follow Follow". Knew aw the words as well. Magic so it wis.'

'Bringin them up in the Faith,' said Billy.

Over at the bar an old man was telling the same joke for the fifth time.

'So ther's wee Wullie runnin up the wing, aff the baw like, y'know. So ah shouts oot tae um "Heh Wullie, make a space, make a space!" An he turns roon an says "If ah make a space Lawrence'll build fuckin hooses oan it!"'

A drummer from one of the accordion bands was standing next to him at the bar, still wearing his peaked cap. Addressing the bar in general, he said, 'Aye, if Lawrence wid stoap tryin tae run Rangers like is bloody builders we might start gettin somewherr!'

Robert hadn't been listening. He was still thinking about children and the Faith. He turned to Peter.

'Is that wee burd ae yours no a pape?'

'Ach she disnae bother,' said Peter, and added quickly, 'Anywey, she's gonnae turn when we get married.'

'Ah should think so tae,' said Billy. 'See thae cathlicks wi weans. Fuckin terrible so it is. Tell'n ye, see at that confirmation, the priest gies them a belt in the mouth! Nae kiddin! A wee tiny wean gettin punched in the mouth! It's no right.'

'Soldiers of Christ for fucksake,' said Peter.

'D'ye know whit ah think?' said Robert.

'You tell us,' said Peter.

'Ah think it's because thur families ur that big they don't bother wae them. D'ye know whit ah mean? Ah mean it stauns tae reason. It's lik money. The likes a some'dy that hisnae goat much is gonnae look efter whit e's goat. Well! Ther yar then! It's the same wi families. Folk that's only goat wan or two weans ur gonnae take kerr ae them. But thae cathlicks wi eight or nine weans, or merr, they're no gonnae gie a bugger, ur they?'

'They eat babies an aw!' said Peter, mocking.

'You kin laugh,' said Billy. 'But ah'm tellin ye, that's how they huv such big families in the furst place. It disnae happen here mindye, but see in some a thae poor countries wher ye've goat famine an that, they widnae think twice aboot eatin a baby or two. Usetae happen aw the time in the aulden days. Likes a the middle ages, y'know.'

Peter didn't argue. It might well be true and anyway it didn't really matter.

'Whit d'ye make a that cunt this mornin then?' asked Robert. 'Cryin us aw fascists!'

'Ach ah've goat a cousin lik that,' said Peter. 'Wan a they students y'know. Wurraw fascists except him like. E wis layin intae me the other day aboot the Ludge, sayin it was "neo-fascist" and "para-military" an shite lik that. E says the Juveniles is lik the Hitler Youth an Ian Paisley's another fuckin Hitler. Ah don't know wher they get hauf thur ideas fae, neither ah dae. E used tae be a nice wee fulla tae. But is heid's away since e went tae that Uni. Tell'n ye, if is heid gets any bigger, e'll need a fuckin onion bag fur it!'

'Sounds lik mah nephew,' said Billy. 'Tryin tae tell me that King Billy an the pope wur oan the same side at the Boyne! Talks a lotta shite so e dis. Ah jist cannae understaun them ataw. Ah mean, if wurraw supposed tae be fascists, whit wis the war supposed tae be aboot?'

(Those old newsreels again. Nuremberg rally. Speeches. Drums. The liberation of Paris. VE Day.)

'Ach fuck them all!' said Peter. 'Smah round, intit?' He made his way to the bar. 'Three haufs'n three pints a heavy, Jim!' He made two journeys, one for the whisky, one for the beer, and when he sat down again Robert was telling a joke.

'Huv ye heard that wan aboot the proddy that wis dyin? Well e's lyin ther oan is death bed an e turns roon an asks fur a priest. Well, is family thoaght e wis gawn aff is heid, cause e'd always been a right blue-nose. But they thoaght they better humour im like, in case e kicked it. So anywey the priest comes.'

'Impossible!' said Peter.

Billy shooshed, but Robert was carrying on anyway.

'An the fulla says tae the priest, "Ah want tae turn father". So the priest's as happy as a fuckin lord, an e goes through the ceremony right ther, an converts um intae a cathlick. Then e gies um the last rites, y'know, an efter it e says tae the fulla, "Well my son, ah'm glad ye've seen the light, but tell me, what finally decided ye?" An e lifts imself up, aw shaky an that, an wi is dyin breath e turns tae the priest an says, "This'll be another durty cathlick oot the road!"'

'Very good!' said Billy, laughing. 'Very good!'

'Ah heard a cathlick tellin it,' said Peter, 'only the wey he tellt it, it wis a cathlick that wis dyin an e sent fur a minister!'

'Typical!' said Robert.

'Ah'll away fur a pee,' said Peter.

While he was gone, Billy asked Robert if he'd seen any of Peter's cartoons.

'Ah huv not,' said Robert.

'Great, so they ur. E's a bitty an artist like. Anywey, e goat this headline oot the paper – y'know how the pope's no been well – an this headline says something aboot im gettin up, an Peter's done this drawin a the pope humpin this big blonde. Ye wanty see it!'

Peter came back.

'Ah've jist been tellin Robert aboot that drawin a yours, wi the pope.'

'Ah think ah've goat it wae me,' said Peter. He rummaged through his wallet and brought out a piece of paper. Gummed on to the top was the headline POPE GETS UP FOR FIRST TIME, and underneath Peter had drawn the pope with an utterly improbable woman.

He passed it round the table.

'Terrific!' said Robert. 'Fuckin terrific!'

Peter put it back in his wallet.

The talk of Peter's artistic talent reminded Billy, yet again, of the ruined Plasticine model. He quickly slopped down some more beer.

He set down his glass and held it in place as the room swayed away from him then rocked back to rest. He was looking at the glass and it was suddenly so clearly there, so sharply in focus. All the light of the room seemed gathered in it. Its colour glowed. The gold of the beer. Light catching the glass and the glistening wet mesh of froth round the rim. He was aware of his glass and his thick red hand clutching it. The one still point in the room. And in that moment he knew, and he laughed and said, 'Ah'm pished!'

The group over at the bar were singing 'Follow Follow' and Billy shouted 'Hullaw!' and the three of them joined in.

'For there's not a team
Like the Glasgow Rangers
No not one
No not one.

An there's not a hair
On a baldy-heided nun.
No not one!
There never shall be one!'

The barman made the regulation noises of protest, fully aware that they would have no effect.

'C'mon now gents, a wee bit order therr!'

'Away an fuck ya hun!'

The accordion band drummer produced his sticks and somebody shouted 'Give us The Sash!' The barman gave up even trying as the drummer battered out the rhythm on the bartop, and the drunken voices rose, joyful, and on past closing time they sang.

'Sure it's old but it is beautiful
And its colours they are fine
It was worn at Derry, Aughrim,
Inneskillin and the Boyne,
My father wore it as a youth
In the bygone days of yore
And it's on the twelfth I love to wear
The Sash My Father Wore.'

Billy was vaguely aware of Robert going for a carry-out and Peter staggering out into the street. He swayed back and aimed for the door, lurching through a corridor of light and noise, getting faster as he went, thinking he would fall at every step. Out of the chaos odd snatches of song and conversation passed somewhere near.

'C'mon now sir, clear the bar . . . '

'An ah didnae even know the cunt . . . '

'RIGHT gents!'

'So ah shouts oot tae um Make a space Make a space . . . '

'Ah'm gonnae honk . . . '

No not one.

Into the street and the sudden rush of cold air. Yellow haloes round the streetlamps. The road was wet but the rain had stopped. He leaned back against the cold wall and screwing up his eyes to focus, he looked up at the sky and the stars. All he knew about astronomy was what he had learned from an article in the *Mail* or the *Post* called 'All about the Heavens', or 'The Universe in a Nutshell', or something like that. Millions of stars like the sun making up the galaxy and millions of galaxies making up the universe and maybe millions of universes.

Robert came out of the pub clutching his carryout under his arm. Peter emerged from a closemouth where he'd just been sick.

'Yawright son?'

'Aye Robert, ah'll be awright noo ah've goat it up.'

Robert handed him a quarter bottle of whisky.

'Huv a wee snifter.'

'Hanks Robert.' He sipped some and shuddered, screwing up his face. Then he shook hands lingeringly with each of them, telling them they were the greatest.

'Ah fancy some chips!' said Robert.

'Me tae,' said Billy.

'Ah've took a helluva notion masel,' said Peter, and the three of them swayed off towards the chip shop, passing the bottle between them as they went.

At the next corner, Billy stopped to drain the last drops, head tilted back to catch the dregs. Tenements looming. The night sky. Dark. Galaxies. He looked at Robert and asked him, earnestly, if he'd ever smelt fall.

'Smelt whit?'

Recovering from a coughing spasm, he tried again, this time enunciating his words very carefully.

'Robert.'

'Aye.'

'Whit ah meant tae say wis, have ye ever felt small?'

Robert looked thoughtful for a moment, before replying, emphatically, 'Naw!' Grabbing Billy's lapel, he continued, 'An you're the biggest cunt ah know, so ah don't see whit YOU'RE worried aboot!'

'An neither dae ah!' said Billy, laughing. 'It's fuckin hilarious!'

And in all the stupid universe there was not a man like himself, not a city like Glasgow, not a team like the Rangers, not a hair on a nun, not a time like the present, not a care in the world.

Telling it, he shouted.

'God Bless King Billy!'

'EE-ZAY!'

And he hurled his bottle, arching, into the air, into the terrible darkness of it all.

Brilliant

Shuggie's gaffer Tosh had been in a hurry to get home, so the whole painting squad had knocked off a few minutes early and by the time the factory hooter went, Shuggie was already in the toilet having a smoke, looking up, aimless, at the walls and doors of the cubicle where he sat. Somebody had spoken to Tosh about re-painting them, trying to brighten it up. It must have been years since it had been done, whitewash engrained with grime, patterns eroded by the damp, and over it all the slogans, messages, drawings. Years of them, names and dates, football scores, headless, limblesss, naked women, giant cocks, gang-symbols, initials, invitations, challenges, claims; all jostled together, crowded each other out, layer over faded layer.

He liked to come across ones he'd written himself.

EVEN THEM WHO RULE SUPREME

SHITE IT FROM THE CRAZY GOVAN TEAM

He was pleased with that. It was good. The Govan Team was his gang. Across the top of the door he'd written SHUGGIE OK.

The whine of the hooter died away and he heard scuffling footsteps, then Eddie's voice. 'Izzat you at it again? Makes ye deef so it dis.'

'Away ye go ya fuckin arse-bandit!' shouted Shuggie.

'Right!' said Eddie. 'Here it comes. Wanker's doom!'

He jumped up and threw an oily rag over the top of the door, down into the cubicle, just missing Shuggie's face and landing in his lap. Shuggie lobbed the rag back over the top, but as it hit the floor Eddie was already on his way out. Shuggie heard him laugh, the door banging shut behind him.

There was no paper in the toilet, so Shuggie took the folded newspaper from his jacket pocket and tore off a piece from the front page. The banner headline said BELFAST BOMB TERROR. Three dead. On the back of it was a picture of a girl in a bikini. Curvacious 23-year-old Lynn Waters. Hobbies ski-ing, dancing, reading. Would like to go to America.

He wiped himself and flushed Lynn Waters away with the three Irish dead. He had a look to see what was on television. Nothing much. Then he remembered the advert. He found the page and read it over again. JOIN THE PROFESSIONALS. A soldier with a machine-gun. Smaller pictures of the same soldier, playing football, jumping down from a tank, wandering through an Arab bazaar.

He tore round the advert, folded it carefully and put it away in his pocket. Then he stuffed the rest of the newspaper down behind the cistern. At the side of the wash-hand basin was a tin of stain-remover, thick and black. He scooped some out and did his best to clean the paint from his hands, before heading home.

Thursday was his mother's night out so he had to get his own tea. She'd be off with her friend to the pictures or along to the bingo at Cessnock. Shuggie's father had died four years ago, knocked down by a lorry. Shuggie had been twelve then. It seemed a short time, but already his father's memory was fading. Sometimes he couldn't remember his face.

(At other times he could see him clearly. His father sparring with him and his big brother Davie. His father giving them money. His father, drunk, singing 'Moonlight Bay'.)

Davie had served his time as a welder and gone to Australia, so now only Shuggie and his mother were left in the house.

On his way home he stopped in at the chip shop. It had only just opened, so he had to wait a bit for the chips to be ready. The woman before him in the queue was about thirty. Her hair was dyed blonde, lacquered and piled high on her head. He could smell her scent, even in the thick atmosphere of vinegar and smoking fat. Behind him, two small boys about ten, a girl a year or so older. The boys were grappling, the girl ignoring them. An older man came in, nodded to the woman.

'How's Maisie!' he said.

'How's John!' she replied.

She stretched and yawned, shook her head and smiled at the man. Above the deep-fryer was a long mirror, tarnished and blotched here and there. At either end were old faded adverts for Tizer (The Appetizer) and sparkling Vimto. Shuggie stared at the woman's reflection, but she was looking away, somewhere else. He shifted his gaze along to the top of Louie's shiny bald head, reflected. Louie was banging and shaking a basket of chips, lifting them clear of the bubbling fat. He shouted across at the boys to stop their fighting or he'd put them out. They stopped for the moment, sniggered, began prodding and digging each other quietly. The blonde woman bought some chips.

'See ye Louie,' she said. 'Cheerio John.'

'Cheerio.'

Shuggie bought a fish supper and a penny pickled onion. He hurried home the last few blocks, the greasy brown packet a patch of warmth, clutched against his side.

As soon as he got home he lit the gas fire in the kitchen and switched on the radio, letting music blare through the house, fill the empty space. Then when he'd gobbled his tea he kicked off his boots and slumped down into one of the armchairs. He sat there for a bit, stretched out, limp, staring into the fire. Then he remembered the advert in the pocket of his overalls. He looked at it again. If he joined the army he would maybe see a bit of the world. He had never been any further than a bus-run to

Morecambe at September weekend. In the army he could learn a trade. That might keep his mother happy. Sometimes she moaned at him. If his brother could get a decent job, why couldn't he, instead of just labouring like his father.

Shuggie's father had been a labourer in the yards most of his life. For years he had worked in Harland's. Shuggie passed the site every day on his way home from work. The yard had closed down now and the buildings were gone. Just a wire fence and a flat expanse of concrete, here and there weeds growing, bits of rusted metal.

After a while he got up and put on a kettle of water, to wash himself at the sink. He looked out across the back court. Demolition had already begun on the tenements facing. There were no lights, the shape was ragged where walls had been knocked away, where bits had crumbled and caved in.

Soon the demolition would reach round here and Shuggie and his mother would be rehoused. He didn't like the idea of being put out to one of the schemes. Castlemilk. Nitshill. There was nothing to do. They were too far away from anywhere.

He looked down below to where a scabby-looking mongrel was snuffling and rummaging in the midden, poking among the tin cans and ashes. He remembered something he'd read in the paper about one of the schemes, Easterhouse or Drumchapel, where packs of wild dogs were supposed to be roaming the streets, fighting and chasing each other and even attacking people. The paper had blamed people who bought the dogs as pups. Then later, when they couldn't look after them, they turned them out. And now they were banding together, in packs.

The kettle was boiling. Before he washed, he dug out a blunt stub of pencil from his pocket and filled in his name and address on the army application form.

When Shuggie had washed and changed into his suit, he headed down to the corner where Eddie was already waiting, pacing

97

back and forward, hunched, hands in his jacket pockets, looking about him, spitting through his teeth. Shuggie feigned a swipe at him and Eddie ducked, swung with his boot, just missing Shuggie. Then they both made as if to butt each other, and laughed.

'Good joab fur you ah'm in a good mood pal,' said Shuggie.

'Ach don't annoy me son!' said Eddie.

'Wherr ur we gawn the night?' said Shuggie.

'Don't know,' said Eddie. 'Mibbe wait'n see if any a the boays come doon. Ah fancy a wee bit bevvy 'n then up tae the dancin.'

'Nothin oan the pictures?'

'Naa, fuck aw,' said Eddie. 'Wan a they musicals or some pish lik that.'

'Whit aboot that horror picture?' said Shuggie.

'That's no oan till Sunday.'

The corner was where they always met, outside an old dairy that had closed down a few years before. Here too they had carved their names, sprayed their slogans, on the barred doors and boarded windows.

'See that wan wee Rab done,' said Shuggie, nodding towards the wall. 'Fuckin great but, intit.' Rab had sprayed an enormous symbol, made up of the letters RGT – Real Govan Team, the letters overlaid, the R and T contained, within the great curve of the G. It was five feet across, bright red glowing paint, big sweeping strokes, and here and there, long trickled lines where the paint had dripped and run.

'Looks lik blood!' said Eddie.

'Ah wis thinkin it wis lik the Rangers badge,' said Shuggie. 'Ye know that RFC.'

'Rangers Football Club,' said Eddie.

'Rangers Fuck Celtic,' said Shuggie.

'If ye staun right back,' said Eddie, 'it looks lik Chinese writin.'

'Mao Tse-tung!' said Shuggie.

'Hoo Flung Dung!' said Eddie.

'Hey look at whit's comin!' said Shuggie. On the other side of the road Betty and Helen were passing by, arms linked, heels clicking in step. They had identical hairstyles, earrings, coats. Betty was slightly taller, thin, her features were sharp. Helen was smaller, more rounded, dark.

'How's it gawn!' shouted Eddie.

'No bad,' shouted Betty. She whispered something to Helen and they laughed.

'Gawn tae the dancin the night?' shouted Eddie.

'Ye askin?'

'Meet ye inside?'

'Gan ya big chancer!'

They walked on.

'See ye efter?' shouted Eddie.

'No if ah see you furst!' shouted Betty. Helen laughed again and looked back at them over her shoulder.

'Whit wid ye dae tae that yin?' asked Eddie.

'Ur wee pal's awright tae,' said Shuggie.

'Get right in therr Shug!' said Eddie.

If they stood at the corner long enough, just about everybody they knew would pass by, sooner or later. The girls had just gone out of sight when Aleck came round the corner. Aleck had been a friend of Shuggie's when they were at primary school but he'd gone on to a high school in town and Shuggie had gone to the local junior secondary and left at fifteen.

Aleck was wearing his school uniform. Over his shoulder he had a haversack full of books and under his arm he carried a flute in a long black case. He nodded towards Shuggie as he passed. 'How's Shug!' he said. Shuggie nodded. 'This you jist gettin hame fae school?' he asked.

'Ah steyed late fur band practice,' said Aleck. 'Then ah hid somethin tae dae in toon.'

He couldn't bring himself to use the word Orchestra to Shuggie. Band came more easily to the tongue.

'Izzat yer flute?' said Shuggie.

'Aye,' said Aleck.

'Kin ye give us The Sash yet?' said Shuggie.

'Oh aye,' said Aleck. 'Follow Follow as well.' He laughed, self-conscious.

'Ah seen ye up the dancin the other week,' said Shuggie. 'D'ye go up therr a loat?'

'Ach naw,' said Aleck. 'That wis ma furst time.'

'Wis that boays fae yur school that wur wae ye?'

'Aye,' said Aleck.

'Ye gawn up the night?' said Shuggie.

'Naw,' said Aleck.

'Huv tae stey in an dae yer homework?' said Shuggie. Eddie sniggered. For answer Aleck laughed again, the same embarrassed laugh, as he moved on.

'See ye,' he said.

'Aye,' said Shuggie.

'Whit ye talkin tae that poofin wee cunt fur?' said Eddie.

'Wee brainboax,' said Shuggie. 'Ach, e's awright.'

'Fucksake but!' said Eddie. 'E'll still be at school when e's whit . . . eighteen. Ah mean imagine that! Some wee shite ae a teacher giein ye the belt fur talkin! "Come out here Clarence and I'll warm your fingers. You naughty boy!"'

Shuggie laughed. 'Ach well,' he said. 'E'll come oot wi a good joab an that. Nae fuckin overtime fur him.'

He remembered the advert in the paper.

'Ah wis thinkin aboot joinin the army,' he said.

'Wur ye!' said Eddie.

'Aye,' he said.

'Might be awright,' said Eddie.

'Get me away fae here fur a while anywey,' said Shuggie. 'An ye kin learn a trade anaw. See a bit ae the world.'

'Mibbe ye'd get sent ower tae Ireland,' said Eddie, laughing. 'Get intae some a they cathlick bastards!'

'Ah mind a thinkin that when ah wis wee,' said Shuggie. 'Imagine the proddies and the cathlicks really fightin. Jist lik the aulden days. King Billy an aw that. Ah mind wan time ah wis it the ne'erday match wi wee Aleck an we seen these papes kickin fuck oot a Rangers supporter an ah says tae Aleck wintit be great if thur wis a real war wi thum ower in Ireland an the Orange Ludge went ower tae fight an we hid another battle at the Boyne.'

'Whit did he say?' said Eddie.

'He didnae fancy it,' said Shuggie.

'Ach!' said Eddie.

'Always wis a crapper when it came doon tae fightin,' said Shuggie.

Eddie began singing, prancing back and forward, stabbing his arms into the air as if he was brandishing a scarf.

> 'If the pope says no
> We will have another go
> On the banks of the Boyne
> In the morning.'

'Here's Pudge and Bugsy,' said Shuggie.

'Pudge is a cathlick,' said Eddie. 'Ye wanty get in some bayonet practice oan um!'

Bugsy and Pudge were the names they'd always been called. Most of their friends had forgotten their real names, or never knew them. Pudge was stocky and squat. As a child he'd been fat. Pudgy. Bugsy had always had nits when he was small. Bugs. (From time to time the school clinic would shave his head, leaving just a tuft of hair at the front, his head stubbly, dabbed with gentian violet, bright purple antiseptic.) He'd always been in fights, and usually he'd won. (Once, when he was about nine, he'd shoved another boy off the top of a midden and the boy had broken his leg. The headmaster had given him eight of the belt and called in the police, and Bugs had been sent to a probation officer.) At first Bugsy had hated the name. But later he'd thought it sounded like the name of an American gangster. Bugsy. Bugs. So he'd kept the name, made it his own. Nicknames were good to paint on the walls. Mental Bugsy. Bugsy Rules.

Eddie grabbed Pudge. 'Right Bugsy,' he said. 'You get is other erm. Shuggie's gonnae start killin cathlicks, startin wi this papish cunt.'

They pinioned him to the wall, laughing.

'Aw c'mon,' said Pudge. 'Leave us alane!'

'Fenian dog!' said Shuggie, and half-serious he began poking Pudge, slapping him and pummelling his belly, as he struggled and yelled and tried to break clear. Then Shuggie brought out his steel comb with the long pointed handle and pretended to stab him and finish him off.

They let Pudge go and he shrugged them off. 'Shower a mental bastards,' he said, annoyed at them all.

'Ach c'mon Pudge,' said Eddie, punching his shoulder, consoling. Pudge elbowed him aside and stuck out a boot at Shuggie, and he felt better for that, even although they were still laughing.

After a while, Pudge's young brother Frankie came sauntering past, a ball under one arm, comics under the other.

'C'mon son,' said Pudge. 'Gie's a kick ae yer baw.'

'You get!' said Frankie, still mad at him because they'd fought at tea-time.

'Aw!' said Pudge. 'The wee boay's in the huff!' He let Frankie go past, then pounced on him from behind, grabbing him round the neck. Bugsy punched the ball out from under his arm and ran clear with it. Frankie squirmed free, dropping his comics on to the pavement, and tried to tackle Bugsy who tapped the ball across to Pudge. Together they managed to keep the ball moving, always just out of Frankie's reach. Shuggie had picked up the comics and was flicking through them. *Creepy Worlds.*

FBI. Superman. Sergeant Rock. He leafed over the pages of *Creepy Worlds*, but it was one he'd read before. He stopped at the page of adverts. Guitar Tuition. Hypnotism Made Easy. He'd often thought of learning the guitar, but the few times he'd tried he'd given up, annoyed and frustrated, unable to get it right. He wondered if hypnotism really was easy. He could think of uses for that. He showed it to Eddie.

'Fancy bein a hypnotist?' he said.

Eddie laughed and waved his hands in front of his face. In a faraway quavering voice he wailed, 'You will come wi me intae the back close an drop your knickers.' Then in his own voice he said, 'Aye, that wid be fuckin gemmie.' He looked at the page again and pointed at a half-page spread on body-building. 'Imagine bein built lik that!' he said.

'Fuckin Tarzan,' said Shuggie.

The other adverts were ones they'd seen since they were small, each advert in a box with a drawing and the price in American money. Itching Powder. Black-face soap. Stink bombs. And something called a Seebackoscope, for looking behind you.

Bugsy and Pudge had tired of taunting Frankie so they'd given him back his ball. He came over and snatched his comics from Shuggie, and as he ran off he shouted back at Pudge. 'Ah'm tellin ma mammy 'n you. An you'll fuckin get it!'

Pudge just laughed and turned to the others. 'Wherr is it the night then?' he said.

'Dancin,' said Eddie.

'Gawn fur a kerry-oot furst?' said Bugsy, lighting up a cigarette-end he'd found in his pocket.

'Aw aye,' said Shuggie.

'Gie's a fag Bugs,' said Eddie.

'This is aw ah've goat,' said Bugsy.

'Gie's a drag, well,' said Eddie.

'Aw c'mon fur fucksake!' said Bugsy. 'It's jist a wee dout. Lookit the size ae it!'

'That's awright,' said Eddie. 'Ah'll remember that.' Then he saw Dan on the other side of the road and waved across to him. Dan was a bit older than them, nineteen or twenty. He too had been one of their gang, their team, but now he was married and he'd quietened down.

'Been daein overtime?' said Eddie.

'At's right,' said Dan.

'Seen wee Rab?' said Eddie.

'Saw um doon the pub aboot hauf an hoor ago,' said Dan. 'Mibbe still therr.'

'Right,' said Eddie. 'See ye.'

'See yis,' said Dan.

'Bet e's daein overtime oan that wee wife a his!' said Pudge.

'Must be tremendous,' said Shuggie. 'Comin hame tae that every night. Nice wee single-end. Jist the two ae ye. Dead cosy.'

'Fuckin nice,' said Bugsy.

They were silent for a moment, imagining it. Shuggie felt a sudden emptiness, a lack. Then Eddie leered and said, 'Plenty a nooky!' He turned to Shuggie and said, 'Never you mind, Shug. Wance you're in the army you'll be gettin bags ae it!'

'You joinin the army?' said Pudge.

'Mibbe,' said Shuggie.

Bugsy coughed, almost choking as he sucked the last gasping drag from his cigarette-butt.

'Serves ye right ya mingey bastard!' said Eddie. 'Hope it chokes ye!'

'Ah jist minded a Dan the other week,' said Pudge, 'readin oot that book.'

'Aw aye,' said Eddie. 'That wis great. You wurnae therr Shuggie. Dan brought oot this book, the *Kama Sutra*, aw aboot different weys a gettin yer nooky. Some laugh!'

'Ah've heard aboot that,' said Shuggie. 'Ther's another wan tae. *The Perfumed Garden* ur somethin.'

'Thur supposed tae uv made a picture ae the *Kama Sutra* wan,' said Pudge.

'Need tae see that when it comes,' said Bugsy.

'Anywey,' said Eddie, 'ur we gawn doon the road the noo?'

'Aye, comin?' said Shuggie.

'Naw,' said Eddie, 'ah'm jist breathin heavy!'

On the way they passed the pub, so Eddie and Shuggie looked in to see if Rab was still there. He roared at them across the bar and made his way towards them.

'Wur jist gawn up the dancin,' said Eddie. 'Bugsy and Pudge ur ootside.'

'Great!' said Rab. 'Ah'll be we yi in a minnit.'

He finished his pint and followed them out.

Further on they bought a carry-out from a licensed grocer's – a few cans of beer, some wine, a bottle of cider. They went into a back close to drink it, swigging back the beer, passing round the cider and the wine.

'Ah seen ye yesterday Shug,' said Rab. 'Oan the back ae a lorry ye wur.'

'Aw aye,' said Shuggie. 'Wan ae the drivers gave us aw a run doon the road.'

'It's great that, ' said Eddie, 'when ye get a hurl oan a lorry. We sometimes go doon in wan tae dae a joab in toon. Fuckin tremendous!' (To be up there, gliding through traffic, looking around you, laughing, cursing, shouting at girls, straddling the edge of the lorry, balanced, holding yourself on with one hand; to feel like part of an invading army; like the feeling when you were on the supporters' bus and everyone stopped to look as you passed, scarves and banners streaming from the windows as the whole bus shook to your singing and stamping, together.)

'Dead gallus, intit,' said Rab.

'Pure fuckin brilliant,' said Shuggie.

And that was it. That was the way of it. Gallus. Pure Brilliant. That was the way for it to feel. In spite of everything, to be rollicking, alive. To be shouting, We are the PEOPLE, We are the REAL Team. To show them all. To let them know.

They threw their empty bottles and cans into the back court and went on their way.

They jumped off the bus at the traffic-lights because that was nearer to the dance-hall than the next bus-stop.

Before going in they had to file into a small anteroom where they were searched for weapons by one of the bouncers. Shuggie and Bugsy had to hand over their steel combs, Eddie his belt with the heavy metal buckle. 'Aw wait a minnit,' said Eddie, handing it over. 'Ma troosers'll faw doon!'

'Wull jist huv tae pit ye oot then,' said the bouncer.

'Never mind that,' said Rab. 'Good joab they never seen aw the chibs in yer poacket. Ye think theyda seen a cuppla knifes an a bayonet and a hatchet an a tommygun!'

'Fly man,' said the bouncer, not so much as a flicker on the hard, set face.

Rab went on, 'But ah don't know how e could've missed that fuckin hydrogen bomb up yer jook!'

'On yer way!' said the bouncer.

Once they were in the hall, Shuggie felt good. The drink had hit him now, and the music was loud and familiar. Something rose in him, a joyful recognition; it rose and moved to the steady thumping rhythm. The song they were playing was an old one, but one that everybody still loved. Shuggie was singing along.

> This old heart a mine
> Been broke a thousand times . . .

The dance-floor itself was circular, and round the perimeter were tables and seats. Above was a balcony, overlooking the floor. Eddie had to shout to make himself heard above the noise.

He was saying he wanted to go up on to the balcony. Shuggie nodded and they all shoved their way up the stairs.

They leaned over the balcony, looking down at the packed floor below. The small stage where the group played was brightly lit in contrast to the rest of the hall. Revolving coloured lights threw shifting patterns of red and green on to a circle at the centre of the floor and on to the dancers who passed across. Just at the edge of this area Shuggie saw a group of girls dancing together, and as they danced, they moved round towards the centre of the floor and the circle of their dancing intersected the circle of coloured light. Then Shuggie spotted among them the two girls, Betty and Helen. He nudged Eddie and pointed them out. Rab had already decided he felt like dancing so they all moved back downstairs together. They made their way round to a table where they'd seen a few other boys from their team.

'Wull no ask thum jist yet,' said Eddie, looking over to where the girls were still dancing. 'Wull wait a wee while.'

Something about the songs always got to Shuggie. He had a head full of them. He only had to hear the opening bar and he'd be filling in the backing, playing every instrument, adding every voice. Sweet soul music. It lit something in him. It was something he wanted to spill out. He wanted to flail his arms and sing and laugh, sharing it. But he just stood, watching, bobbing his head, tapping his foot, looking now at the girls, dancing, now at the group, pounding out the music.

> Now it's the same . . . old song
> But with a different meaning
> Since you been gone . . .

Maybe he could learn the drums, he thought, instead of the guitar.

As he looked back to the floor he saw that two boys had broken the circle and were dancing with Betty and Helen.

'Fuck it,' he said, to Eddie.

'Disnae matter,' said Eddie. 'Wull get thum efter.'

But the girls stayed up with the two boys for the next dance, and the next, then they went and sat with them at one of the side tables.

'They look lik fuckin schoolboays,' said Shuggie. He was feeling restless and annoyed. Eddie seemed happy enough just to sit there, and that just irritated Shuggie all the more. Rab was dancing with a big redhaired girl called Rita. Bugsy and Pudge were leaning against a pillar. Shuggie noticed a small blonde girl standing by herself. He pushed over towards her and asked her to dance.

'Ah'm arready wae some'dy,' she said.

He turned away. He saw two girls dancing together. He stepped in between them.

'D'ye wanty dance wae me?' he asked one of them, his back to the other.

'Naw,' she said, shaking her head.

'We don't wanty get split up,' said her friend.

He went back to the table, scowling at Eddie.

'Never mind Shug,' said Eddie. 'Thur no worth it. Fuck them all!'

Across the hall Shuggie saw Betty and Helen going into the ladies' toilet. The two boys were hovering around, waiting for them.

'Ah'm gawn tae the lavvy,' he said, heading for the other side of the hall.

'Me tae,' said Eddie, following.

Shuggie saw the two boys as he came up to them. He singled out the one that had been dancing with Helen, and deliberately brushed against him as he passed.

'Watch who yer shovin son!' said Shuggie, pushing the boy again.

'Wait a minnit!' said the boy.

'Think yer a fuckin hard man?' said Shuggie, and he butted the boy in the face and brought his knee up into his groin. The boy's friend stepped forward but Eddie stuck in his boot, stopping him.

'We're the Govan Team pal, so don't fuckin mess!' said Eddie.

A few girls had screamed and there was a commotion round about as people backed away. Three bouncers were heading across, to see what the trouble was.

'C'mon,' said Eddie. 'Nae point in takin oan them as well. The boays ur aw away acroass the other side.'

Shuggie turned to the boy he'd hit and said, 'You're claimed ootside!' as Eddie dragged him on to the dancefloor where they split up and made their separate ways back to the others.

Betty and Helen came out of the toilet and looked around them, bewildered.

They had left a bit early and they stood across the road from the dance-hall, waiting; Shuggie and Eddie, Rab, Bugsy and Pudge, and two others, Jackie and Stu. Opposite the big red neon sign that said DANCING flashed on and off, on and off, lighting up the pavement.

Through the doorway the crowds were beginning to spill out. Shuggie's eyes were fixed, watching for the two boys. 'Shouldnae be long noo,' he said.

'This should be good,' said Eddie. 'Didye see that wee guy's face when ah says we wur the Govan Team! Jist aboot shat is sel! That wis the best laugh. Fuckin tremendous!'

Shuggie laughed and reached into his pocket, feeling the steel comb with the long pointed handle.

'Mental!' he said.

'Brilliant!' said Rab.

The Rain Dance

With improvised maraccas – a shake of small stones in a tin can; with tambourine, cymbal and drum – assembly of biscuit-tins and lids; with a bell, a rattle and a party squeaker left over from Christmas; with streamers, with a rose, with a paper hat, Kathleen was paraded through the lamplit streets of the scheme. Her maids and ladies-in-waiting were girls from the same office, Agnes and Jean linking arms with her, the rest of the clattering procession straggled out behind.

Faces appeared briefly at windows as they passed, drawn for a moment from the television before fading back into its blue light, jerking shadows on the ceiling. Curtains were opened on living-room windows, screens that the procession moved across and was gone. Curtains were closed.

Some there were that leaned out and waved, or stood watching from closemouth and pavement, some smiling and glad, others tightlipped and knowing.

'Tommy Brady's lassie.'

'Gettin married at Martha Street themorra.'

'Married oantae a Proddie tae.'

Passing silent judgement on this double heresy. Not only marrying a Protestant, but marrying at Martha Street Registry Office. And for a Catholic girl, that was no wedding at all.

But the girls were untroubled as they sang into the night. The

bells are ringin for me and my gal. The clamour and racket of the
bridal dance.

> 'Everybody is knowin
> To a weddin they're goin
> An for weeks they've been sewin
> Every Susie and Sal.'

Breaking off into shouts and laughing whenever man or boy
should stray across their path. Then they would gather round the
victim, willing or not, sometimes lurching across to the opposite
pavement, or even stopping cars in the middle of the road. And
Kathleen would be jostled towards the captive, offered for the
ceremonial kiss, a final flirtation, benediction, farewell.

There was a young boy of about fourteen who blushed and
was clumsy and missed her mouth.

There was an old silverhaired man, out for a walk with his
dog. He smiled and kissed her forehead and said, 'God bless ye
lass.' Then he added, tugging the lead, 'An whit aboot Rab?' So
she bent and kissed the dog's wet nose.

There was a boy with the smell of drink on him, who had
known Kathleen at school. The girls clapped and stamped and
cheered as he gave her a long deep kiss, probing with his tongue.

'Drunken bugger!' said Kathleen, laughing and prising him
clear at last.

'It's a bite late fur that, son,' said Agnes.

'That's the wey it goes,' he said.

They moved on, their voices raised again.

> 'And she sang and she sang
> And she sang so sweet
> His name is Brian
> Ah hope ye will agree.'

(A song from their childhood. A memory of long summer
evenings. Her friends in a circle moving round her in step,

chanting the magic name, the name of the boyfriend, the name that would release her, to take her place again in the circle of linked hands. Songs and games. Just a few summers. Chalk-marks on the pavement.)

They rounded a corner, past a stretch of open ground. The noise and the singing came echoing back from a gable end. Their pace grew slower. It began to rain.

Brian had to get a bus to Hillhead so Tommy saw him to the bus-stop in Hope Street. Tommy had to get a bus to Pollok.

'Ah'll see ye doontae the bus-stoap,' said Brian.

Supporting each other, they made their erratic way down past Central Station towards Midland Street. By the time they got there it had started to rain and they were glad of the shelter of the railway bridge above them.

'Ah'm tell'n ye Brian,' Tommy was saying, 'Canada . . . at's wherr yis should go. See wance yer time's oot at the college . . . land a opportunity . . . See Peter . . . ye huvnae met Peter . . . Peter's ma son . . . Kathleen's big brurra . . . ah'll show ye a fotie . . .'

'At's awright Tommy,' said Brian, 'ye showed me it arready. Jist pit yer wallet back in yer poacket before ye drap it.'

'Aye . . . aw aye. Yirra good boay Brian. Tell'n ye . . . See you an Kathleen . . .' He broke off as a train rumbled overhead.

'Mon ah'll see ye up tae the bus-stoap,' he went on.

'Naw, look . . .' said Brian, 'wu've arready been up therr; ah mean, don't think ah don't appreciate it . . .'

'Sawright,' said Tommy.

'Anywey,' said Brian, 'it's wet. Nae point in the two ae us gettin soakin. Look . . . here's yer bus comin. Ah kin jist dive roon tae St Enoch's an get a subway.'

They both got on the bus, Brian guiding Tommy into a seat.

'Ah'll see ye themorra then,' said Brian. 'That's if ye've sobered up!'

'You don't need tae worry aboot me,' said Tommy, slowly nodding his head, spreading his fingers like an opening fan. 'Nae bother!'

'Right yar,' said Brian. 'Martha Street themorra.'

'Themorra,' said Tommy, poking the air with an emphatic finger.

Then somehow Brian was outside on the pavement, knocking on the window. Tommy wiped the steamed-up glass and through the clear patch saw Brian's face, focused, mouthing words he couldn't hear. Then he was gone and the window misted over again as the bus moved out into the main stream of traffic and across Jamaica Bridge.

Kathleen had gone to bed but Mary her mother still sat, leaning on the windowsill, seeing nothing but the rain streaming down the glass. The window had clouded a bit from her breath and she drew a face on it with her finger. Like a child's drawing, the mouth turned down and doleful. Half past eleven. Tommy shouldn't be long now. She had made a pot of tea and poured herself a cup. Thinking maybe, that the smell of the tea would bring him home. Funny how you half-believed things like that. No sooner would the tea be ready than somebody's head would be round the door. Tommy or Kathleen or Peter. Three years now Peter had been gone. And now it was Kathleen. One more day. The house would be strange without her. Just herself and Tommy. And Kathleen and Brian would begin it all again. Mary liked Brian well enough but she was troubled about the wedding. She remembered the bit in the missal about not marrying outside the church. And that meant both ways. It meant marrying a Catholic and it meant a proper church wedding. So she was worried for Kathleen. Father Boyle had put the fear in her about the wedding not being blessed. Not that Kathleen cared, or Tommy either. Little enough he cared about anything, especially the church. Sundays he usually spent recovering from Saturday nights and only rarely could she drag him along to Mass.

And now he was somewhere out there, roaming and daft and drunk. Him and Brian both. But he couldn't be much longer now, allowing for the last lingering pint and the chipshop queue and the time it took him to get a bus . . .

She looked out at the same old street, wet by the same old rain. She saw him turn the corner, unsteadily, and veer across towards the close, and she was relieved and annoyed all at once at the sight of him.

She stood up from the window. The cup of tea she had poured herself was cold and untouched.

Tommy woke, stiff and cold, huddled on the living-room couch. That was where he had slumped, a deep drunk sleep ago, his head drooping forward, his jaw sagging open. The shifting room had closed over him and Mary had taken off his shoes, covered him with his coat and left him be. Now he moved from a dream of creatures like cats or owls surrounding him, waking to a dream of ashes in his mouth, sickness dry in his throat. In the first grey light of the day the room resolved itself into vague familiar shapes, shapes from another dream. There was the table, television, display-cabinet, gas-fire. He gave them names and remembered them as real. He remembered who he was and where. He tried to get up but he was too weak to move. A sick dull throb had replaced his head and the room tilted and threatened to swamp him again. He turned over with difficulty, almost falling off the couch, then pulled his coat tighter about him and went back to sleep.

When he woke again his body was one long ache. He managed to open his eyes long enough to see Mary looming over him, like a mourner at a wake.

'So it's come back tae the land a the livin his it? C'mon, get up!' She clumped into the kitchen.

He screwed up his face and groaned. The light was too bright and harsh. Mary was banging about in the kitchen. He could hear outside the noises of the morning, voices, traffic, children on their way to school. Then he heard Kathleen ask the time and he remembered what day it was and why he was not at work. The wedding. Christ! Still, it wasn't till the afternoon and another half-hour wouldn't . . .

'Oh Jesus, ma guts!' He creaked to his feet and wobbled towards the door. As he fumbled with the doorknob it came away in his hand and the knob on the other side thudded on to the hall floor.

'Oh ya bastard!' He glowered accusation at the crucifix on the wall.

When he had replaced the handle and opened the door, Mary stuck her head out of the kitchen and bawled.

'An ye kin fix that door before we go oot!'

'Ach!'

A little later, purged, he braved the kitchen. Mary was scraping the cinders from bits of charred toast. She shoved them in front of him, banging down the plate, rattled the cups and saucers and poured him some tea.

He sipped at it, fingering the blackened, brittle toast. He pushed the plate aside and started to retreat.

'Ah canny face the burnt offerin hen.'

'Ye need somethin in yer stomach.'

'Aye, maybe efter. Ah'm no feelin too good.'

'Aye, well hell mend ye, that's aw ah kin say.'

'Noo don't start! Ye gave me enough shirrikin last night. Bloody dog's abuse.'

'And no bloody wonder!' she said. 'God forgive me.' (Slipped in like punctuation as she put down a plate so she could cross herself.)

'Ach be reasonable Mary. Ah mean it wis the boay's last night a freedom before e pits is heid in the auld noose.' He yanked an imaginary rope above his head and jerked his neck to the side. But that brought back the nausea, so he sat down before going on.

'We hid tae gie um a wee bit send aff, ye know whit ah mean.'

'Ah know whit ye mean awright, an ah know wherr ah'd send the perry yiz! Noo get ootma road. An will ye go an . . . DO somethin ABOUT yerself!'

He went back into the living-room and fumbled in his coat pocket for his cigarettes. His hand met the grisly remains of a fish supper and a copy of the *War Cry*, absolute proof of how he'd spent the night before. He wondered vaguely if the *War Cry* was ever sold anywhere else but in pubs. He remembered the girl that had sold him it, black cape and bonnet and bright moon face. Into battle with her *War Cry* for the Salvation Army. He didn't know anything about what they believed, just that they were another kind of Protestant, but something in him had always warmed to them for the way they went at it, with their brass bands and their banners. Some of them still had the fire and the joy of it, and that was how it should be. He tried to imagine old Father stoneface Boyle rattling a tambourine or beating a drum. He looked again at the *War Cry* and suddenly saw the words for what they were. A war cry was what an Indian would make, or a Dervish, or a Zulu. He had a sudden picture of the whole Sally Army birling and yelling and charging through Pollok. He looked at the main article on the front page. It was a report of a conference in London with a photo of delegates looking serious and purposeful.

'Ach!' he said. He wrapped the paper round the cold soggy chip-bag and threw it in the bin.

He sat down on the couch again and closed his eyes. He was still feeling crumpled and raw. Kathleen poked her head round the door and asked if he'd like another cup of tea.

'Aw thanks hen,' he said, 'Ah'd love wan. Ah've git a tongue in me lik a spam fritter.'

She brought through his tea and a cup for herself and sat down beside him.

'Aye, well,' he said. 'The day's the day.'

'Aye,' she said. They smiled at each other, reassuring.

'Did Brian get hame awright last night?' she asked.

'Och e wis fine!' said Tommy. 'As a matter a fact he wis lookin efter me. We didnae really huv that much.'

'Aye, tell me another wan!' said Kathleen.

'Naw ah'm no kiddin,' said Tommy. 'Some a they pals a his wur merr bevvied than the two ae us pit thegether. Ah mean we knew we hud tae keep wursels right.'

'Away ye go!' she said.

'You're as bad as yer mammy,' he said, shaking his head. 'How wis she when ye wur in the kitchen?'

'Och she's still playin the martyr.'

'Aboot me?' said Tommy.

'Jist aboot the whole thing,' said Kathleen, 'because it's no a church weddin an aw that. Ah suppose you jist made ur a wee bit worse, comin in steamin. But ah think it's maistly that auld priest that's been gettin oantae ur again, pittin ideas intae ur heid.'

'Interferin auld bugger,' said Tommy.

'Never mind,' said Kathleen, 'wance she sees the actual weddin she'll be fine.'

'Suppose so,' said Tommy.

'Anywey,' said Kathleen, 'ah'm away tae huv a bath, so ah'll see ye efter. Oh, could ye take the cups intae the kitchen?'

'OK hen, ah'll see ye in a wee while.'

He took the cups through and rinsed them out. Mary was sweeping the floor.

'Ah think ah'll go oot fur a wee walk an get the paper,' he said. 'Maybe the fresh air'll clear ma heid a bit.'

'Fine,' said Mary. 'It'll get ye oot fae under ma feet as well.'

'Look hen,' he said, 'Ah'm sorry aboot last night. But ye know how it is. It's jist wan a these things.'

'Aye, well . . .' she said. 'Jist . . . away ye go an gie's peace!'

On his way out he called through to her, 'D'ye want anythin when ah'm oot?'

'Naw,' she said. 'Thanks aw the same.'

And he heard the tone of truce in her voice and was glad. He stepped from the close and felt the wind cold in the shadow of the building. He crossed the road into the sunlight, too bright for his eyes still and it made him feel grubby and sticky, but he welcomed its warmth, enough to ease the chill from his bones.

Brian could see most of the park spread out below, the green hillside stretching down to the fountain and the pond, beyond that, a glimmer, the Kelvin, and further, across Kelvin Way, the Art Gallery, the University tower. Further still he could see the shipyards of Partick and Govan, the cranes, giraffe-necks, jutting, grey. Govan was on the other side of the river and somewhere behind that was Pollok. There was nothing to distinguish it, no way he could recognize it from here. But that was where Kathleen was. He wondered what she was doing, what she was thinking. Probably the same as him, the same inconsequential stream of nothing in particular. Tangle of branches. Flight of ducks. Hunger. A bit of an old song. Let us haste to Kelvingrove bonnie lassie o, through the . . . something . . . let us rove bonnie lassie o. He'd learned that at primary school but only recently had he remembered it and connected it with the park. Every day now for almost two years he'd passed through the park on his way to the university. The park was his calendar. Here he could read the traces, the changes, the slow shift of the seasons. The daft dance of it. In a few more hours he would be married. A few more months he would be a father. Tick tock. On it went. A few more steps in the dance.

He looked up at the statue of the horseman, silhouetted at the top of the hill, and remembered the wedding of Richie and Meg. The papers had called it a mockery and gone on about long hair and bright clothes. None of the parents had come because it was at Martha Street. But somehow none of it had mattered. They'd all come here to the park afterward for a ceremony of their own, running mad and laughing across the grass. They'd climbed to the top of the hill, about thirty of them, and they'd linked hands and danced in a huge circle, round and round the statue of the horseman. And as they'd danced they'd chanted, and tried to levitate the statue, and with it the park and the rest of Glasgow, and raise it into orbit forever.

Richie and Meg were in London now. He'd heard they were living apart.

The grass was still wet from last night's rain. Everything felt fresh and new. It was almost spring now. Nothing definite yet, no riot of leaves on the trees, no blaze of daffodils and tulips, just a feeling of everything hesitant, about to be, of opening, unfolding, a slow stirring to life.

A dog went panting and scampering up the hill, stopped and chased its tail, lay down and rolled and wriggled in the grass. Brian laughed.

'Daftie!' he said, out loud. He made his way towards the gate. On his way home he stopped in at the Indian grocer's, to buy some milk and rolls. He liked the shop, and Mr Rhama who owned it. It had a warmth and a brightness about it, open till all hours, an improbable clutter of boxes and bags, of bundles and packets and tins, piled, haphazard, to the ceiling, and always the smell of spices or cooking from the back shop.

Before him in the queue, two tiny Indian boys with broad Glasgow accents dithered over the penny tray – candy balls or bubble-gum, jelly beans or caramels. Brian reached down and helped himself to a pint of milk from the blue plastic crate perched by a wall of tins – hamburgers and mangoes, creamed rice and Scotch broth, corned beef and pineapple and curried beans. Above the crate hung a sacred heart calendar, Jesus gazing up at the legend PL Trading Co. – Cash And Carry –

Maryhill Road. Next to it was a poster for a showing of Indian films.

'Anything else please?' Mr Rhama grinned aross the counter at him, between a basket of tomatoes and a tray of meat pies.

'Jist four rolls,' said Brian. 'That's all.'

The rolls were in a breadboard balanced across an orangebox. Mr Rhama eased his way between bags of coal and a pile of newspapers, put four in a paper bag and passed them over the counter.

'Today's the big day, yes?' he said. Brian had told him about the wedding.

'It is that,' said Brian.

'Ah well,' said Mr Rhama, 'now you have to stop messing about. You have to settle down and bring up family.'

'Suppose so,' said Brian.

'No suppose,' said Mr Rhama, laughing. 'It's really true. No more messing about. But never you mind. I tell you, married is best.'

At the far end of the counter, his wife moved among packing-cases and sacks, the swish of a blue sari, the glint of a gold-embroidered hem, a jewel in her nostril, a glitter of rings.

Brian wondered about their wedding, how long ago it had been, in Glasgow or in India, what the ceremony had been like. He remembered the West Indians he'd seen in London, just a glimpse as he'd passed, a splatter of bright colours, bopping and jigging out of the church into the street. He was about to ask Mr Rhama about Indian weddings, about his own, but a fresh delivery of milk arrived, the vanboy lugging crates in the door, and Mr Rhama had to see to it. No matter. If he remembered he would ask him the next time he was in the shop.

'Good luck!' said Mr Rhama.

'Thanks,' said Brian.

On his way out the door he turned as Mr Rhama called out to him.

'Hey! Next time you come here you be a married man!'

Kathleen lay, soaking in the warmth and comfort of the bath, nothing in her head but just drifting, lazy, not wanting to stir from it, ever. Steam rose and hung in the air, misted over the windows and the mirror, condensed and trickled down the tiles.

Through the wall she could hear her mother in the kitchen, familiar noises, far away, her mother, she supposed, still troubled and thinking about old Father Boyle, filling her head with purgatory and hellfire. She remembered how he'd seemed to her as a child, arms raised, intoning the Mass, glorious in his vestments, exalted and terrible like God himself, the voice of judgement in the deep musty dark of the confessional. Father forgive me for I have sinned. I have committed a sin of impurity. Yes my child. I have kissed a boy on the lips. And is that all? Yes Father. Yes Father. She leaned against the sides of the bath, buoyed up so slightly by the water, stretching, bobbing in the warm stream, and she thought of the life that moved deep inside her, the tiny life that was growing, becoming, the child that would be hers and Brian's. And at twelve she'd wanted to be a nun. It had seemed so beautiful. The bride of Christ. Jesus the lover, the bridegroom, gentle Jesus. Father forgive me for I have conceived out of wedlock. How many acts of contrition and Hailmarys for that? Impurity and dirt. Wash it all away. She laughed and lathered herself with the soap. Sandalwood. Brian had bought it for her in the Indian shop. Fragrance. Like the incense he burned in his room. Hail Mary full of grace. Mother Mary working in the kitchen, on the other side of the thin wall. And once Kathleen had been no more than a stirring inside her, had been one with her, curled and safe in the warmth of her womb. She slid back down into the water again, lapped in the warmth surrounding. She brought her knees up to her chest then stretched again, looking down at her body, pale through the soapy water, the curve of breast and belly breaking the surface, the black seaweed tangle of hair, flattened out by the water, felt below it the soft depth of hole, open, the dark emptiness her being centred around. Blessed art thou among women. Blessed is the fruit of thy womb.

The taxis were waiting, purring at the close.

'Huv ye seen ma black tie?' said Tommy.

'It's a weddin wur goin tae,' said Mary, 'no a bloomin funeral!'

'Ye coulda fooled me,' said Tommy, turning, stiffnecked because his collar was up in readiness for the missing tie.

'Whit's that supposed tae mean?' she asked.

'Your face, that's whit,' he said. 'Kin ye no gie's a wee smile hen. Ah mean it is YOUR daughter's weddin tae!'

'Aye, well,' she said. She brought out a blue tie from the wardrobe. 'Here,' she said, throwing it to him. 'This'll dae ye.'

In the next room Agnes and Jean, who had led Kathleen the night before with such devoted rattling of cans, were again fussing over her, making sure that no talisman was forgotten.

'Right,' said Agnes. 'That's the flowers an the horseshoe. Noo make sure ye've got the lot. Somethin old, somethin new, somethin borrowed, somethin blue.'

'This cameo's old,' said Kathleen. 'Used tae be ma granny's.'

'An yer shoes are new,' said Jean.

'Ah huvnae anythin borrowed,' said Kathleen. 'Ye'll huv tae len me somethin.'

'Take this hanky,' said Agnes.

'Where'll ah put it?' said Kathleen. 'Ah'm no takin a bag.'

'Therr's a rude answer tae that wan!' said Jean.

'Jist shove it up yer jook,' said Agnes.

Kathleen wrapped the hanky round the stems of her flowers.

'An mind an gie me it back sometime,' said Agnes, 'otherwise it's no borrowed!'

'Yer dress is blue,' said Jean, 'so that's everythin.'

'Expect yer nosy wee neighbours'll huv somethin tae say aboot that,' said Agnes. She looked down her nose, disapproving. 'And not even a white wedding.'

'Ach they'd huv somethin tae say anywey,' said Kathleen.

'C'mon!' shouted Tommy from the hall. 'The taxis ur waitin!'

At the closemouth, a few peering faces, a handful of confetti, a huddle of children waiting, eager, for the scramble of loose change. Bundling into the taxis, Kathleen and Tommy in the first, Mary, Agnes and Jean in the second.

'Huv you got change fur the scramble?'

'Godalmighty, did ah pit oot that gas?'

'Mind yer flowers in the door!'

A cheer. A flurry of waving hands. Tommy bestowing a shower of coins from the window, jolted back into his seat as the taxis moved off. Agnes turned in her seat for a last look at the scramble before they rounded the corner.

'God, wid ye look at them!' she said, laughing. 'Lik flies roon a toly!'

'Ah remember readin,' said Jean, 'that scrambles go right back tae the aulden days, when the didnae keep records an that. An it wis so's the weans an everyb'dy wid remember the weddin. Then if they ever needed witnesses, they'd aw mind a the money gettin scrambled.'

Jimmy and Ann, like most of the other children, had just been passing, on their way back to school. They were triumphant as they fought their way out of the tangled, scrambling pack, jostling and grappling in the roadway.

'Much d'ye get?' asked Jimmy.

'Tanner!' said Ann. 'An you?'

'Eightpence!' said Jimmy, counting it out into his palm.

'Race ye doontae the café!' said Ann, and they both pelted off down the road. By the time they reached the café near their school, and elbowed their way into the semblance of a queue, the taxis were moving along Paisley Road, towards the town.

Tommy smiled across at Kathleen.

'Ur ye still feelin rough?' she asked.

'Ach, no too bad,' he said.

'Never mind,' she said. 'No doubt a coupla wee halfs'll set ye right.'

'Hair a the dog,' he said.

'Ah thought that would set yer wee eyes twinklin!' she said. 'But we've got the small matter ae a weddin tae get over wi first!'

It was over so quickly, embarrassed introductions, Brian's mother Helen to Tommy and Mary, grins and hello to the friends that had come, crowding, awkward, on the pavement, trying to keep out of the wedding-group photos of the couple that had just come out; confusion over which door to go in, then somebody showing them the way; hustle along a corridor, a few minutes' wait, hushed, in the hall; a door opening, another wedding-group bustling past; another door opening and the registrar ushering them in.

In a low, bored drone he intoned the preliminaries, about how the ceremony was no less serious and sanctified though it wasn't in a church, and about general impediments to marriage.

Tommy thought he was going to laugh, then suddenly for no reason, when he saw them standing there, he wanted to cry. He looked at Mary and he saw the confusion in her eyes.

Kathleen too had to stifle a laugh, changing it to a cough and turning her face from the registrar. Brian was staring at the pattern on the carpet, as if he could read there the meaning of it all, the meaning they all knew at that moment. Not the lifeless ceremony, the cardboard stage-set, the dead script, the empty sham. Not that, but something at the heart of it, something real. In spite of it all, they knew, and that was what moved them, to laugh or to cry.

The exchange of vows. Signatures on the line. Out along the corridor, past the next group waiting to go in, out into the street and it was done.

'We've done it now!' said Brian.

'So we huv!' said Kathleen, and he kissed her and they laughed.

Outside, waiting, were the friends that hadn't gone in. Somebody showered more confetti as they gave themselves up to the backslaps and handshakes and hugs. Ian and Kenny had cars. They were two of Brian's friends from university and Ian was the best man. They took as many as they could crowd in. The rest followed in taxis as they headed back to Pollok, to what had been Kathleen's house, for the reception.

In the boys' playground, Jimmy was finishing the sweets he'd bought with the money from the scramble. He screwed up the bright coloured wrapper and kicked it high over the railings.

In the girls' playground, Ann was pushed, giggling, to the centre of the circle. Her friends linked hands and moved round her in step and as they moved they sang.

> 'And she sang and she sang
> And she sang so sweet
> His name is Jimmy
> Ah hope ye will agree.'

And when she at last agreed, somebody else was pushed into the centre and the dance began again.

Instead of buying a cake, they'd got Mary to bake an enormous dumpling. Tommy carried it carefully into the living-room and solemnly laid it on the table. With exaggerated ceremony, Brian took the knife and flourished it in the air.

'Feels lik a Burns Supper!' he said. 'Great chieftain o the puddin race! Or is it Wee sleekit courin tim'rous beastie?'

'C'mon you an stop yer nonsense!' said Kathleen, laughing.

'See that!' said Tommy. 'She's got ye under the thumb already!'

Brian guided Kathleen's hand and everybody cheered as they carved the first slice. Kathleen went on slicing it and Agnes helped her to dish it out. Mary and Jean carried plates from the kitchen, piled with bread and bun, biscuits and cake, while Brian and Tommy brought through the carry-out, bag after bulging bag. When all the glasses were filled, Ian got up to make his speech and read the telegrams.

'Three telegrams,' he said. 'The first one's from Peter in Canada. It says ALL THE BEST TO MY WEE SISTER AND HER LAD.'

'Aw the nice!' said Mrs Robertson from downstairs. 'Luvly boay Peter,' she said to Mary. 'Luvly boay!' She smiled into the distance.

'The next one,' said Ian, 'is from Uncle Danny and Auntie May.'

'Ma brother in Ireland,' explained Mary to Brian's mother.

'Sure it's from the ould country,' said Tommy.

'It says,' said Ian, raising his voice, 'GOOD LUCK GOD BLESS AND MAY ALL YOUR TROUBLES BE LITTLE ONES.'

That one brought a laugh.

'Nudge nudge!' said Jean.

'The last one,' said Ian, 'is from Gerry in London. It says NORMAL IS REALLY NICE.'

Again everybody laughed.

'Whit wis that aboot?' said Tommy to Kathleen.

'Och it's jist Brian's pals up tae thur nonsense again.'

'An whit's the matter wi a wee bit nonsense?' said Brian, tickling her.

'Aye bit whit dis it mean?' said Tommy.

'The whole universe is a wee bit nonsense!' said Brian.

'A wee bit order therr!' said Ian, who wanted to propose a toast.

'Aye, wheesht the perry ye!' said Kathleen.

'Ah've got no intention of wastin time makin a speech,' said Ian.

'Hear hear!' said Brian.

'So ah'll just say good luck and happiness and long life to you both.'

He picked up his glass. 'The bride and groom!'

All the glasses were drained and set down empty on the table.

'C'mon now people,' said Tommy. 'Get wired in therr!'

'Eat up,' said Mary. 'Yer at yer auntie's!'

Several refills later, Brian turned to Kathleen.

'Tommy's peed already,' he said.

'Yer no doin too bad yerself!' she said.

'Ach well,' he said, squeezing her, 'it's no every week ye get married.'

'See Kenny an Ian are gettin quite pally wi Agnes an Jean,' he said, nodding to where the four of them sat squashed on the couch.

'Ah'm watchin ye!' he shouted over. He crossed to where his mother was talking to Mary.

'Gettin on OK mammy?' he asked.

'Ah'm jist fine,' she said. 'Me and Mary are havin a right old natter.'

'Don't believe a word she tells ye about me,' he said to Mary. 'Honest, ah'm innocent!'

'Who's gonnae give us a song then?' asked Tommy, raising his arms and calling for order.

Mrs Robertson let herself be coaxed on to the floor and began the singsong with 'You're The Only Good Thing', then she dragged her husband, protesting, to his feet and he sang 'Green Grow The Rashes O', and 'Of A' The Airts'.

'It's nice tae hear an auld Scotch song,' said Mary.

'She better be quiet,' whispered Ian, 'or e'll be givin us "Scots Wha Hae".'

Mary was next with 'Honky Tonk Angels', then Tommy with 'Take Me Back To The Black Hills', and the afternoon grew late and the bottles and cans were emptied, and everybody sang the songs they always sang. 'Nobody's Child', 'There Goes My Heart', 'Please Release Me', 'The Blue Of The Night', 'You're Free To Go', 'Among My Souvenirs'. They forgot themselves, they wallowed, grew happily maudlin as they sang. And through it all Tommy kept calling for order, 'C'mon now there, one singer one song,' and joining in all the choruses himself.

'How is it,' said Kenny, 'the whole a Glasgow likes Country an Western?'

'Everyb'dy likes tae get a wee bit sentimental when they get bevvied,' said Ian. 'It's a wee escape.'

'Aye,' said Kenny, 'but whit ah mean is, whit is it aboot Glasgow? Ah mean, how come Country an Western?'

Tommy swayed over to where they sat.

'How aboot youse young yins?' he said. 'How aboot givin us some ae yer modern stuff? The auld rock an twist an aw that jazz!' He gyrated his hips and snapped his fingers in attempted imitation of the dance style of ten years ago.

'Naw,' said Ian, 'we'd need a backin group.'

'Ach!' said Tommy, dismissing them, 'yer aw the same. Canny dae anythin withoot electricity!' He supported himself, leaning heavily on the back of a chair, and announced that he was going to sing one more song.

'For ma wee lassie,' he said, and began singing.

> 'I'll take you home again Kathleen
> To where your heart will feel no pain . . .'

When he'd finished she went to him and gave him a hug.

'Wherr's Brian?' he asked. 'Ah wanty talk tae um.'

'E's away doon tae Mrs Robertson's tae phone a taxi,' she said. 'E'll be back in a minute.'

When Brian reappeared, Tommy took him by the arm and looked at him earnestly.

'Brian . . .' he said. 'Ah jist wanty tell ye yer a great kid!'

'You too Tommy,' said Brian. They shook hands on it.

'See you an Kathleen . . .' said Tommy, 'Canada . . .'

He took out his wallet and once again showed Brian the photo of Peter and his family.

'Ah told ye aboot wur hoalidays therr in the summer, din't ah? Peter peyed wur ferrs. Daein well so e is. Terrific it wis, nae kiddin . . .' He stopped and raised his hand to cover his mouth. The room was going up and up and up, like a television when the vertical hold goes. He belched out an explanation and lurched towards the bathroom, leaving Brian holding the snapshot. A young couple with a baby between them, sitting in front of a Christmas tree. Bright colours, like a photo in a magazine.

'The taxi's here,' said Kathleen, tugging his arm.

'Ah'll jist give this back tae Tommy,' he said, holding up the photo. 'Ah think it's too precious tae leave lyin here.'

They found Tommy in his own room, rummaging in the cupboard.

'Ye feelin better noo?' said Brian.

'Me?' said Tommy. 'Ah'm champion! C'mere an sit doon a minnit. Ah wanty show ye somethin.'

'We canny wait, daddy,' said Kathleen. 'We're jist gawn.'

'Here's yer fotie,' said Brian. 'Mind ye don't lose it.'

Tommy shook Brian's hand. 'Aw the best,' he said

'Same tae yersel,' said Brian.

'Cheerio daddy,' said Kathleen, hugging him again.

They shouted a quick farewell into the living-room and hurried to the door. Mrs Robertson was in the hall, and before they fled, Kathleen stopped and said 'Could ye gie ma mammy a wee warnin. Tell er ma daddy's lookin fur is souvenirs, and that prob'ly means e'll be givin is party piece any minute.'

'Right yar hen,' said Mrs Robertson, opening the door for them. 'Good luck tae ye.'

Outside on the landing stood Father Boyle, his hand raised to knock the door. Kathleen and Brian almost banged into him as they rushed out. They all stood for a moment, embarrassed, looking at each other.

Then Brian grabbed her hand.

'Cheerio Father!' she called back to the priest as they clattered down the stairs.

'Ur ye comin in Father?' said Mrs Robertson.

'Well, I . . .'

'Mary!' she shouted. The priest stepped into the hall and she closed the door behind him.

Tommy still sat in his room, looking down at the floor. That was it. She was gone. He looked again at the snapshot he was still holding in his hand, then turned his attention to the cupboard and the cardboard box full of souvenirs from Canada, a heap of mementoes he'd brought back from their holiday. A pair of moccasin slippers, a chipped plaster ash-tray shaped like a maple-leaf, a miniature Canadian flag, a doll dressed like a mountie, a stick-on plastic badge and all the other wondrous, useless things he'd gathered. Digging under a jumble of post-cards and guide-books and leaflets, coins and maps and assorted tickets, he unearthed what he was looking for. It was an Indian head-dress, made up of red and white feathers, fitted on to a cardboard headband and bordered at the front with brown fur.

'Yes, said Father Boyle, 'I wanted a wee word with you and Thomas, but it looks as if I've chosen an awkward moment. Maybe tomorrow . . .'

'Yes Father,' said Mary. 'Well you see . . .'

'Oh Mary,' said Mrs Robertson. 'Ah nearly forgot. Kathleen says tae tell ye Tommy's lookin fur is souvenirs.'

'Aw naw,' said Mary. 'No another performance! If ye'd excuse me a minute Father, ah'll jist . . .'

'Ah ya bastard!' Tommy was struggling with the door and the handle had come away. The door thudded twice under his boot then there was a final crash as it swung open and he came stumbling into the room. 'Wahoo!' he shouted, brandishing the doorknob. The head-dress was perched on his head, tilted forward so that the fur covered his brow.

'I think I'll just be going,' said Father Boyle, but Tommy came over and grabbed him by the arm.

'Hello therr Father Boyle,' he said. 'Wull ye huv a wee half tae drink ma daughter's health?'

'I really must be going,' said the priest.

'Ach c'mon,' said Tommy. 'Melt yer auld stone face fur wance in yer life!'

'Godalmighty!' said Mary, looking in despair at the ceiling.

'Wish ah had a camera,' said Kenny. 'This is jist too much.'

'Auld Father Gilligan widnae uv said naw,' said Tommy. 'He liked is wee dram wi the best ae thum. Fine man e wis tae. Red nose an aw! Jesus, d'ye mind the time e hid the weans up dancin a paddy ba oan the altar, the time the bishop came! Ye shoulda seen aw the frozen faces tut-tuttin away. By Christ they wurnae long in gettin rid ae um efter that.

'But ah'll tell you,' he went on, waving the doorknob at Father Boyle, ''e wis twice the man you'll ever be, God rest um.'

The priest was making his way towards the door, Mary behind him, apologizing.

'Perhaps some other time,' he was saying, 'when Tommy's sober.'

'An anyb'dy that says ma wee lassie's no right's a no user!' shouted Tommy after him. 'An that goes fur yer church an aw!'

'C'mon Tommy!' said Ian, laughing. 'Do yer Medicine Man! Give us a Rain Dance!'

Tommy straightened his head-dress and stamped a rhythm

with his foot, shaking the doorknob like a rattle above his head, howling and patting his pursed lips with his palm.

'Gawn yersel!' said Kenny, as some of the others shouted encouragement and took up the rhythm, beating it out on the furniture or clapping their hands.

'Ah don't believe it,' said Ian, as Tommy twisted and shook, waving his arms in the air, getting faster and faster till he finally collapsed, exhausted, face down on to the couch, and his head-dress dropped to the floor, a few of the feathers crooked and bashed.

Tommy was still lying there, huddled, dead to it all, long after everyone had gone home. Only Mary still sat, thinking she should tidy up the debris left from the party, but feeling engulfed by it, and unable to move.

'The tea'll be ready in a minute,' said Kathleen. 'Ah'm jist lettin it mask.'

'Great,' said Brian, who was busy filling the paraffin stove.

She took a joss-stick from the packet and lit it, blowing out the flame and watching it smoulder and glow. She placed it in the brass holder on the mantelpiece, watched the smoke curl and rise past the wooden image of Siva that Brian had bought at the Barrows, Siva with his four arms, his fire and his drum, dancing in a circle of flame.

She went to the window and looked out. It had begun to rain again and it was just beginning to get dark. A few people were passing on their way home from work. She could hear, faintly, the stream of traffic from Great Western Road. Through a gap between two gable ends opposite she could see the shapes of trees in the park, branches dark against the sky. The streetlamps went on then. She could see five or six, reaching to the end of the street. She thought of them going on all over Glasgow, a linked network of lights, strung across the city, and everywhere people coming home.

She could smell the incense now, the fragrance of sandalwood permeating the room, and with it the warm smell of paraffin burning. The tea was brewing. The stove was lit.

Looking down below, outside the close, where they'd stepped from the taxi, she could still make out a few tiny specks of colour, bright flakes of confetti, scattered on the pavement, wet by the rain.

The Palace

The first touch of his feet on the cold floor as he swung out of bed
had set him coughing, fumbling for his matches and the last of
his cigarettes.

At last it was Friday again, his day for signing on at the
labour exchange. This week he had managed well. The last of
his money had gone the night before, into the meter for the
fire and light in his room. He had made it through another
week, and sometimes he felt that was miracle enough to be
grateful for.

The face that looked back at him from the mirror as he shaved
was old and tired. Even he could see that now. He suddenly
remembered a habit of his that had always annoyed his wife.
Any time he'd be making plans or arrangements, even for the
following day, he would say 'If God spares me.' These days he
probably said it more often than ever and meant it more
seriously. At times it was a wonder to him that he survived from
one week to the next. He had been out of work now since the
summer, almost eight months. Somewhere in him he still felt
ashamed to be signing on and taking money, but there was no
other way. Jobs were scarce, he had no special skill, and now he
was getting old. So on it went, week after week. God had spared
him. Sometimes he wondered why.

But today was different. Today he would have some money
and the world would be brighter. It was like pay-day. Even

134

though he had no job, nothing to fill his days, the weekend still felt special.

He smiled at the mirror as he scraped away with the razor. When his face was like that, covered with lather, his lips showing through, he always thought it looked like the white mask of a clown. He remembered thinking the same thing as a child, watching his father shave.

(The slow steady scrape of the open razor on his father's cheek, the razor that looked like a toy, clutched in that big powerful hand that could wield the blacksmith's hammer with such ease. The way the blade took the soap from his face in clean straight strokes. Like making a path in the snow with the edge of a slate. His father contorting his face as he peered into the mirror, the easier to shave the awkward contours; suddenly aware that he was watching and turning towards him, the clown's mask screwed up, grotesque. His father, chuckling to himself. 'Aye well,' he'd said, 'ye'll be shavin yersel soon enough.')

Soon enough.

It was strange that he could remember something like that so clearly. Sometimes things that had happened thirty or forty years ago were just as clear, just as real to him as anything going on now. He was always remembering; things were forever repeating themselves; forever reminding him of something else. Sometimes he had the strangest of feelings he couldn't explain, that he had always been living through the same day. He had grown up, married, become a father. His wife had died, his son had moved away. It all seemed like a dream. Something in him was dreaming it; something had watched it all going on and was watching still. He had gone through these changes, he was growing old, but he was still the same person he had always been.

With a click the light went out and the fire died. The money in the meter had run out.

'Ach!' he said, setting down his razor. He pulled open the curtains. Outside it was still dark. One or two lights were on across the road. A man was passing on his way to work, or perhaps coming home from nightshift. Overnight there had been a light fall of snow and it lay on the street, on the roofs of parked cars, adding its silence to the early morning still.

He carried on shaving, in the dark, then he finished dressing, put on his coat and scarf for warmth, and sat down to wait. Nobody else in the house would be up for another half-hour or so.

Some of his neighbours he had never even seen. Sometimes he wondered about all the different people who had lived here. He liked to imagine the way it must have been in Victorian times. That was what the street always brought to mind; the terrace houses, the faded elegance. He could imagine the great dark rooms, the old solid furniture, heavy velvet drapes. He could almost smell the polish, hear the discreet chime of a clock, the faint sound of a piano from an upstairs room. The facade was unchanged, the only signs of passing time the crumbling paintwork, the concrete slabs where a garden had been, the rows of names on every door, some typewritten, some carefully inked, others roughly scribbled, and each name with its own bell. It wasn't the same as having his own place, but in some ways he liked it as well as anywhere he'd ever lived. The area still had a sedateness and tranquillity that pleased him. He could walk down to Great Western Road and along to the Botanic Gardens, or in the other direction, to Kelvingrove. It was a strange irony, now that he was poorer than he had been in years, to be living here in the West End. It was true that he could probably find somewhere cheaper, in Maryhill perhaps, or back in Govan, but he justified it to himself that the saving would be slight. Living here seemed less of a defeat than moving back to the tenements. He could never bring himself to go back to Govan now. He had never been too fond of it, but now it was worse. It was not even

136

the place he remembered. Half of it had been pulled down. The life had gone out of it.

Living here he knew was only a transition. The names on the outside door were always changing. But then sometimes, looking back, he felt his whole life had been a transition. All the years he'd spent in Govan, thinking some day there would be something better. And yet in the years since he'd moved from there, things in many ways had got worse. There had been the move out to the Nitshill scheme. The house had been decent enough. It had even had a small garden. He remembered the first summer out there, evenings painting the garden fence, planning what he would grow. But gradually the bleakness had taken hold of him. The place had no heart. By the time he left, his garden was overgrown, the fence daubed with gang-slogans.

Since then he had lived in a succession of furnished rooms. He had been made redundant and laid off work. And still, through it, the same feeling had persisted, keeping him going, the feeling that it would all pass. Once he was over this spot of bother. Once this year was out. If only he could get through this week. If he could just survive today . . .

Increasingly lately his memories had been of his childhood, isolated bits and scraps, vivid in their clarity, with no apparent shape or meaning. He had grown up in Kinning Park. That was where he had lived until he had married and moved down the road to Govan. From one room-and-kitchen to another. But occasionally he remembered even further back than that, back to his earliest childhood, to Campbeltown where he was born. He had only lived there until he was five or six. Then the shipyard had closed down and they'd moved to Glasgow so that his father could find work.

Often he had thought of going back there, to Campbeltown. It would be a good place to retire to, to live out his old age. But retire from what? Unskilled and unemployed. He saw the humour of it and he smiled. But there was a sadness in it. The thought of ending his days in this dingy furnished room.

The rooms had been divided so that they could be let out to more people, so his was really only half a room, oblong instead of square, half a bay-window at one end. The circular cornice-work on the ceiling, round what had once been the central light-fitting, was cut in two by the partition so only half of it was in his room, the other half next door. For some reason that had annoyed him. He wanted to look up and see it whole. He thought it reminded him of something, but he didn't know what.

Next door an alarm rang itself out and he heard his neighbours stirring. The partition was thin and he could hear their every movement. The man was about thirty, the girl a little younger. They both worked on the buses. That was all he knew about them, though at night, if they were in, he could hear their talk, their laughing, their quarrels, sometimes even their lovemaking.

Soon their radio would go on. He would be glad of that, raucous though it was. It didn't matter what the music was. The noise was enough. It was some small comfort in itself. He stretched himself and shivered. It was growing lighter. He could make out more clearly the objects in the room. A chair. A table. A wardrobe. A bed. There was no space for more.

Through the thin wall he heard the sound of a kettle being filled, then a click and the blare of the radio; jingles, the disc jockey's babble; the raised voices of his neighbours above it.

SO THERE I WAS UP IN THE OLD BBC CANTEEN WITH ME CUPPA TAR I MEAN CHAR HA HA HA

'Whit's that yer sayin?'

AN SHE JUST WALKS RIGHT PAST AND OUT THE DOOR WITH IT BEFORE I CAN SAY JACK ROBINSON SO I THOUGHT T'MESELF AH WELL THERE YOU GO THAT'S LIFE

'Ther's eggs . . . an beans.'

TOO RIGHT Y'KNOW ANYWAY

'Sausages.'

SO AT TWENNY FOUR PAST THE HOUR OF EIGHT WHAT'S IT GONNA BE FOR THE NEXT

'Ye kin say whit ye like, ah mean ye kin see aw kinds, long wans an short wans an fat wans an skinny wans but ye never see the wan yer lookin fur.'

MORE MUSIC MORE MUSIC MORE MUSIC

'When it comes right doon tae it, whit uv ye goat? Nothin!'

HA HA HA HA HA

'Many eggs ur ye wantin?'

SO LET'S GO WITH A GOLDEN OLDIE A BLAST FROM THE PAST A RAVE FROM THE GRAVE

LET ME TAKE YOU DOWN
COS AH'M GOING TO
STRAWBERRY FIELDS
NOTHING IS REAL

Soon it would be light enough and he would read and re-read last night's paper until it was time to go.

As always, he arrived at the labour exchange about ten minutes early, and he joined the queue of waiting men. The woman behind the counter avoided looking at them. She moved the indexed box of cards an inch to the left, removed the plastic cap of her ball-point pen, adjusted her spectacles on her nose, drummed with her fingers, looked at her watch. Nobody was allowed to sign so much as a minute before the allotted time. The man before him in the queue turned to him and shook his head.

'Ah don't know!' said the man.

'Thur no in a hurry anyway,' he replied.

The woman had a brittle, jerky manner, a permanent disdainful expression on her face, as if a particularly unpleasant smell was being wafted towards her by the draught that blew in through the swing-doors.

He rubbed his hands together, trying to generate a little warmth.

'Cauld aw the same, intit,' he said.

'Freezin,' said the man. 'It's gettin worse aw the time.'

'Yer right therr,' he said. 'Perishin.'

By this time, after all the months of signing on, some of the faces in the queue were familiar to him. But it didn't go much deeper than that. A nod. A gruff word. A shared complaint against this brusque attitude or that bland face behind the desk with its barricade of filing-cards. And yet there was something else they shared, something unspoken that went beyond resentment, and at the back of it was a laugh. The man he was talking to had once summed it up. 'Ah well,' he said. 'If ye canny beat them an ye canny join them, ye might as well fuckin use them!'

The man was a short and stocky-built, redfaced with a harsh rusty bark of a voice that always sounded as if he needed to cough. He always wore a donkey-jacket and old baggy denims, his cap pulled down over his brow.

In the next queue an old man was trying to stop a puppy from yelping.

'Look at that poor bugger!' said the man in the donkey-jacket. 'Disnae look as if e could feed is sel, never mind a bloody dug.'

He looked across at the old man, trying to calm the puppy which he had on the end of a length of string. Another bit of string was tied round the waist of his long shabby coat. He looked as if that might be all that was holding him together. But in the band of his old bashed hat was a feather, and in his breast pocket a paper napkin, folded like a hanky, and in his buttonhole a plastic rose.

He didn't look at the man too long. Something in that precarious dignity was too much for him to take. Perhaps it was too close to his own. For a moment he felt saddened again. There was not much room for dignity in this place, with its boxes and forms, its numbers and its cards and its queues. They could call it what they liked. Unemployment benefit. Social Security pay-ment. But the echoes of the Means Test were still there. The fact that Social Security was called *SS* spoke for itself.

Once, when he was about twenty and out of work, the man from the Means Test had come to the house, about eight o'clock in the morning, hoping to catch him in bed so that his money could be cut because he wasn't out looking for work. He'd been out in the toilet on the landing and he'd stayed there, listening to his mother say he'd been out since six. She had let the man look round the house, to make sure, and at that he had grudgingly gone. He had heard stories of people having their money cut because they had a decent bit of meat in the house. ('If ye kin afford that,' they'd been told, 'ye must be aw right.')

At least it wasn't as bad as that now, though sometimes he thought the attitudes hadn't changed much.

The queue at last moved up. He handed over his card, signed, and queued again to collect his money.

On his way out, he held open the door for the old man with the dog.

'Thank you sir,' said the old man, smiling. 'A gentleman.'

Outside he bought some cigarettes and the morning paper, then headed into town to walk around and fill in the day.

He needed a solid pair of shoes and a heavy pullover, so he made his way down to Paddy's Market to see what he could find.

Just across the road from Paddy's was a low building where smoke seeped from every crack, every gap. Painted on the wall was a sign that always made him smile. It said NO NEED FOR ALARM. FISH BEING CURED. And here, under the dank arches, beneath the railway bridge, the smell of fish was everywhere. It hung in the air. It seemed to ooze and trickle from the damp glistening walls.

Crossing over, he could hear a jig being played on a tin whistle, as bulging bundles were dumped on to the pavement from the back of a horse-drawn cart. Into the market itself, along Shipbank Lane, he picked his way past the heaps of old clothes spread out on the ground, stopping now and then to investigate any woollens that caught his eye. Here was something soft and green, here something patterned, Fairisle, here what looked like a sleeve. But what he unravelled from the fankled heaps were a woman's cardigan, an old scarf, a jersey frayed away at the cuffs and under the arms.

Sometimes he would walk the whole length of the lane and find nothing, and the place would assail him with its dismal drabness. Then he would notice only the smells and the dirt; nothing but old junk and stinking rags. Even the people would look bedraggled, pathetic, their faces brutalized and harsh.

There were times though, when the place had another quality altogether, when it seemed colourful and alive, when every stall might reveal some treasure and everything pulsed with a warm underlying humour. He remembered coming here as a child with his mother, the atmosphere, the clamour, the feeling of adventure it had held for him then. (Even in the mad scrambled chaos of everyone trying to grab their things and run whenever the police had raided the lane.)

Paddy's was a link for him with those days. The old days, remembered. It belonged to a Glasgow that was almost gone, bulldozed and flattened, gutted out. And while the gutting was perhaps necessary, there was still the feeling that something was lost, something that could be glimpsed here, even in spite of the grey.

He stopped to look at a heavy black coat, but it was stiff and greasy with age. He picked up a pair of shoes, but both the soles were worn through.

'Jist need a perr a rubber soles,' said the woman who was trying to sell them. Her voice was without enthusiasm, without hope. She was about his own age. She sat amongst her sad rags, resigned. He was feeling cold. The day was looking bleak.

But on the wasteground behind the lane he noticed a few young people had lit a fire and were gathered round it. One was playing a mouth-organ, another was tuning up a guitar.

He moved on and pushed his way into one of the indoor markets. Just facing the door was an old stove and he warmed himself in front of it, rubbing the life back into his numbed fingers. Propped up on the stove was a sign reading NO LOITERING AT THE STOVE, and beside it another which said WHERRABOOTS . . . AWRERR, with an arrow pointing across to a stall stacked high with workboots and shoes. A few minutes' rummaging unearthed a pair of brown brogues that were only slightly too big, and that could easily be set right with a cardboard insole or a thicker pair of socks. He bought the shoes and, feeling brighter already, moved further in.

At one corner, the passageway was crowded. He eased past a big brash woman who was trying on a fur coat. Her hair was dyed blue-black, a stiff-lacquered haze round her head. With her was a little girl about six years old who was holding her mother's umbrella and handbag, walking up and down with them, delighted, as if they were her own. A young Indian man had bought a red shirt, patterned with yellow sunburst flowers, and now he was trying on the jacket of a chalkstripe demob-suit (lifted down from its place on a rack beside a velvetcollared teddyboy-jacket, a Beatle-blazer with brass buttons, a leather jerkin and a morning-coat with tails).

A young girl who looked like an art student was holding up a velvet curtain, examining it for stains and flaws. Passing, he could smell the soft scent of her. Thin bangles jingled together with every move of her arm. She was dressed in a long flowing cloak and she might have been unfolding bales of silk in some far Oriental bazaar.

Presiding over the stall were two old women, perched on rickety chairs, their bony hands wrapped round mugs of steaming tea. Like old spey-wives they sat, looking out on all

143

that passed, breaking off their mumbled and endless conversation to haggle over prices or accost any likely customer. Under their scrutiny, he began to look through the tangle of woollens on the table. He told them what he was looking for and one of them dragged out a huge hand-knitted cardigan. Across the vast back of it, blue reindeer ran in ordered lines through an off-white tundra broken by scattered firtrees.

'Rare an warm,' she said.

He said it was too big, and anyway he wanted something a bit plainer. She looked at him as if to say there were plenty of big stores up in Argyle Street for folk that could afford to be fussy, and she sat down again, went back to her mumbling and left him to look for himself. And eventually he found something good – a thick white Aran-knit jumper, just about the right size and all in one piece.

The child had lifted a pair of high-heeled shoes, climbed into them and wobbled forward, scuffling and clacking as she went. Her mother broke off from preening herself in the fur coat to yell across at the child. The Indian had almost decided to buy the demob-suit. The girl had found a hole in the velvet curtain. The women talked on.

'Mind you, she fair suits er new teeth.'

'Wull you do as yer told an put them back.'

'How much for suit please?'

'Ah won't tell you again malady!'

'Course he's no half the man e was.'

'None ae us gettin any younger.'

'Nice bit a velvet dear. That's whit aw the young yins are after.'

'That'll go nice wi yer shirt son. Don't make suits lik that anymerr.'

'Much ye wantin fur the coat?'

'I take it.'

'No thanks, it's not really . . .'

'Will you pit thaym DOON!'

Fumbling in his pocket for change, he paid for the jumper and moved on again, pausing for a last heat at the stove before heading back outside.

Further along the lane he stopped at another stall, a jumble of bric-a-brac and paperback books. What had caught his eye was a stack of old gramophone records, old 78s, many still in their brownpaper sleeves. A record was just the kind of fine and useless thing he felt inclined to buy. Although he had pawned his record-player, he had kept up the payments, hoping some day to redeem it. Meanwhile he could add to his collection and look forward to music and better times. The labels of the old records were beautiful – intricate, graceful designs, golds against reds and blues, lovely melodic names, like Regal Zonophone, Beltona.

There were a few records he would have liked to buy, but the one he finally chose was John McCormack singing 'There is a Flower that Bloometh'. The man at the stall gave him an old carrier-bag and he put the shoes in the bottom, the pullover on top and eased the record down the side.

He was almost at the end of the lane, so he turned and headed back. There were more people gathered now round the fire on the wasteground. The man with the tin whistle had joined them and was playing 'Amazing Grace'.

And suddenly it was all unreal, like a scene from a film, with that thin frail sound as the background music; and everything moved to it, moved without knowing; moved in that place and that time.

Turning away, he went from the lane, carrying his treasures with the greatest of care.

At the corner of Stockwell Street, buffeted by the cold wind from the river, he hesitated, wondering which way to go. The pubs would be open now, and he felt like a drink to warm him. But instead he decided he should put some food in his belly. So he walked along the riverside, two blocks, to Community House. There the food was good and cheap, and he liked the atmosphere. It was big and spacious, half way between being a café and a canteen, with something more besides, something peaceful that maybe came from having a chapel in the back. Along one wall was a mural showing what looked like Glasgow in the thirties, people queuing at a soup-kitchen, a background of tenements and shipyards. He didn't know much about the Community, just that it was connected with the island of Iona.

He bought a bacon roll and a bowl of soup and sat at a table near the window. At this time of day there were not many people in the place – some drivers and conductors from the red-bus terminus across the road, a few old folk here and there, marooned at their tables, lingering over cups of tea.

The soup brought the life back to him and he savoured each bite of the bacon roll, wiping his soup-bowl with the last of it. Then he settled down to read the paper, with a cup of tea and a cigarette.

An old woman, who'd been sitting over in the corner, began to make her way towards the door, stopping at some of the tables to give out gospel tracts. 'God bless ye sir,' she said as she handed him one. He thanked her and read it over. On the front it said COME BACK TO GOD. COME HOME. Inside was an obscure story about a drunkard who had lost his job and his house and sunk from one disgrace to another, stealing, beating up his wife and children. Somehow it ended with them all on their knees at a gospel-meeting, being welcomed into the church. Then there was a text from St John's Gospel – 'In my Father's house there are many mansions . . .' That was part of the text that had been read out at his wife's funeral. So long ago it sometimes seemed, but the words had stayed with him. They were beautiful, moving words and they said so much more than the stupid TRUE LIFE STORY, that had no reality at all. He put the tract in his pocket and went on reading his paper over a second cup of tea.

When he left, revived, he didn't feel like going home just yet. So he wandered about the city centre, peering in shop windows at things he'd never buy, cut by the freezing wind, till it finally began to snow again and he stood in a queue for a bus back to the West End. But instead of going home, he got off the bus at the Botanic Gardens. He would go for refuge to the Kibble Palace.

In the Palace it was always summer. Outside there might be snow, sleet, ice; but in here it was warm the whole year round.

The whole structure was of glass, two main domes connected by a short passageway. At the entrance was a plan, showing the overall shape, with a key to the names of the statues and the grouping of the plants. It explained that these were arranged 'according to their habitats'. So the area under the large dome was divided into North and South America, Australia, New Zealand and Temperate Asia. He smiled at that. It was pleasing to think that his leisurely dawdle round the Gardens would take him through four continents.

Passing inside he felt the warmth, the gentle humidity of the atmosphere; condensation, wetness of leaves. He breathed it in. The smell of it was green. He walked round the pond and along the passageway, through South Africa to Australia. It was a whole different world from the cold and grey outside. Sounds seemed accentuated, the crunch of his footsteps on the red ash of the path, the steady drip and spray of water from hosepipes and sprinklers, the song and chatter of tiny birds. The green was ease to the eye, creepers and tree ferns reaching up on either side, dark luxuriant growth; it breathed a rich fragrance, vegetation, the damp of the earth. In imagination he could be deep in some tropical rainforest.

In the Temperate Asia section he passed two Indian women, one old one young, sitting on one of the benches. And it was as if a joke was being played on him; as if they had been placed there to be part of this reality; Temperate Asia at the heart of a drab Glasgow day.

Further along was an empty bench and he sat himself down, glad of the rest. He set down his precious bag beside him, peering inside to see that nothing had mysteriously disappeared. Reassured, he leaned back and closed his eyes.

Perhaps he had actually dozed a little, or was just afloat between waking and sleep. He couldn't be sure. But the voice startled him.

'Ah'm sayin d'ye mind if ah sit here sir?'

Looking up, he recognized the old man he'd seen that morning at the labour exchange, with the string round his coat and the feather in his hat.

'Not at all,' he said, fully awake now. 'Not at all.'

'Sorry for disturbin ye,' said the man. 'Ah didn't realize ye were sleepin.'

'That's awright,' he said. 'Ah jist shut ma eyes fur a minnit.'

'Oh aye,' said the man. 'It's a nice place tae come for a wee rest. Ah come here quite a lot maself in this weather. Here or else down tae the library. Ah think this is better aw the same. The library's no bad mind ye, but the atmosphere's . . . well, some a they auld tramps, they smell a bit, y'know.'

Pot calling the kettle black, he thought to himself, looking at the old man, but all he said was 'Oh aye, in here's nice an fresh.'

'Beautiful,' said the man. 'Mind you,' he went on, 'the thing aboot the library is ye can get a good read as well. Eh, would that be the day's paper in yer pocket? Could ah get a wee look at it?'

'Aye, sure,' he said, handing it to him. 'Ye kin jist keep it. Ah've finished readin it.'

'That's very kind ae ye. Mind you, sometimes ah don't know why ah bother. Papers can be awfy depressin things tae read. Still, there's always the jokes.'

He realized something in him was wary of the old man, drew

back from him. But behind that was something more. A sympathy perhaps, complicated by that discomfort he'd felt in looking at the old man that morning, and seeing in his shabby dignity something of himself. In his wariness was a lifetime of attitudes to old dossers. The hand on your arm as you passed a closemouth; the reek of wine on the breath, the stink of old clothes that had been slept in for weeks or months or years; and always the hustle for money.

But over these last few years his attitudes had been eroded, eaten away by his own worsening luck. He had seen how easy it was to slide. And this old man had just slid that bit further. And yet he was very far from being a wreck. He had that quality, that tattered dignity, the paper napkin in his pocket, the plastic rose in his lapel. His very eccentricity was a kind of affirmation. There was life in his eyes, in his voice.

He remembered the pup the man had had with him at the dole. To be looking after a dog, he must have a place to stay. So he wasn't even a tramp, just an old man down on his luck.

The old man was chuckling at the cartoons in the paper. But as he scanned the pages, he shook his head. 'Ah don't know,' he said. 'Nothin but disasters an tragedies an God knows what. Ye'd think nothin good ever happened. Ye know, it puts me in mind a some auld minister ah heard on the wireless years ago. He started is talk bi sayin Good News is No News.'

'That's very good, that is.'

'Ah thought so maself,' said the old man. 'An it's true as well.' He folded the paper and put it away in a carrier-bag he'd left under the bench.

'Same as mine,' he said, pointing to his own bag.

'Snap!' said the old man, laughing. 'Been doin a bit of shopping then?'

'Aye,' he said. 'Ah've jist been down tae Paddy's Market.'

'Paddy's!' said the man. 'God, ah havnae been down there for years. Many's a good bargain ah've got in Paddy's. Tell ye no a bad place as well, jist down the road – that Oxfam shop in Byres Road. Ah went in this mornin tae get a pair a gloves an ah found these.' He held up his hands to display a pair of bright red woollen mittens.

'Jist the job.'

'Ah'll show ye what else ah got.' Carefully he took from the bag an old print in a wooden frame. Faded and brown, it was a drawing of St Francis surrounded by birds, hovering about him, pecking the dust at his feet.

'Ah thought it wis really nice,' said the old man. 'An ah wis kiddin maself on that it wis a bit like me. Ah mean, ah've seen me comin in here tae feed the birds, say if ah've got some old bread. No that ah let a lot a bread get stale wi the price it is. But the drawin puts me in mind a that. That's whit it feels like when yer feedin them.'

Then, chuckling, he added, 'An e's even got a bit a string round is coat lik me! Course yer always thinkin somethin lik that aren't ye? Like ah'll be standin there feedin the birds an jist feelin fine, an then it's lik ah'm watchin maself, y'know. Ther's this voice sayin "Here's me bein St Francis."'

'Ah know whit ye mean,' he said. 'Watchin yerself.'

'In fact sometimes,' said the man, 'ah think yer never done playin at somethin or other. Still, ye could do worse than bein St Francis! Thing is but, next minute yer bein somethin else, yer snivellin away or yer narkin at somethin.'

'That's jist it,' he said.

'Ach well!' The old man put the print carefully back in his bag, shoving it down beside a package wrapped in newspaper. 'This is jist a bone for soup,' he explained, 'an some scraps for the dog.'

'The puppy,' he said. 'Ah've seen um with ye at the burroo. Nice wee fella.'

'The burroo!' said the old man. 'That's it. Ah knew ah'd seen yer face before. Signin on this mornin. It's a small world, eh! A small world.' He smiled, thinking to himself, then went on, 'Now there's a thing. D'ye ever say somethin an then ye hear the words different? Like they mean somethin else? Like ah'm jist after sayin it's a small world an ah looked up an remembered ah wis thinkin this place here wis a small world. The Palace ah mean. A wee world in itself. The different continents an that.'

'Ah wis thinkin that as well,' he said. 'Whole world tae choose fae. Go where ye like.'

'There yar then,' said the man, grinning and nodding his head. 'Ah see yer a Temperate Asia man yerself!'

'Oh definitely,' he said. 'Never go anywer else!' and they laughed. He was beginning to like the old man. There was something of a twinkle in his eye and he was a good talker. His voice too was easy on the ear. In the rhythm of it was a lilt that hadn't quite been overlaid by Glasgow. It still had a lightness to it that was Highland perhaps, or Irish. He was muttering now about getting home soon to feed the dog. 'How d'ye no bring um out wi ye?' he asked.

'Och,' said the old man, 'ye canny bring um in here. Ther's this notice at the door. Big capital letters, it says NO SMOKING NO DOGS NO PERAMBULATORS.' He said it in a clipped, mimicking voice. 'Awful posh eh! Ah don't know. See these folk wi ther notices. No bloody perambulators!'

He told the man about the notices he'd seen at Paddy's, and they laughed again.

'Oh that's comical that is,' said the man. 'No need for alarm. Fish being cured. It's lik somethin out the Marx Brothers!'

'Makes me think a some doctor tryin tae cure this sick fish on a slab, an it's slappin aboot an makin a rammy!'

'An whit wis the other wan?' said the man.

'Wherraboots . . . Awrerr.'

'Oh aye. That's very clever. D'ye see aw the different meanins in it? Wherraboots means "Whereabouts" or "Where's the boots". An Awrerr means "Over there" or else "All rare".

Really really clever. Must be a bit ae a genius made it up. Jist shows ye aw the same. Words are queer things. Folk should be careful how they use them.'

For a moment the old man was silent again, inside himself, thinking. Then he said, 'Ach aye. They should use words tae cheer ye up. No need for alarm. Imagine puttin that on big posters! Here, never you mind me sir. Ah'm jist ravin away! Tell me, did ye get anythin nice down in Paddy's?'

He told him about the pullover and the shoes, then showed him the old record.

'Is that no beautiful,' said the man. 'There is a flower that bloometh. Oh, that should definitely go on posters. Put it along wi the other wan. No need for alarm. How about that for the front page ae a newspaper! Great big headlines. THERE IS A FLOWER THAT BLOOMETH. NO NEED FOR ALARM!'

Handing back the record he said, 'That'll be a collector's piece that. John McCormack. Lovely song. Flower that bloometh. Thing is, if everyb'dy could jist stop for a minute an appreciate the flower that bloometh than ther *would* be no need for alarm. No need for all that bloody nonsense ye read about in the papers. Here, ah'm away again! Ye should jist shut me up.'

Reaching into his bag, the old man brought out a half-bottle of wine and offered him a drink. He was momentarily thrown by it. The man was once again a dosser, an old winey, and he seemed to sense the reaction, adding 'Oh no offence sir, no offence,' and explaining that he just bought a bottle now and again, to have with a meal, or to share when he was 'in good company.'

The whole thing seemed suddenly ridiculous, as if they were connoisseurs of the finest food and drink. It was like the way they had spoken of the grand tour they could make in their circuit of the Palace. Relaxing, he grinned and told the old man how daft he thought it all was.

'A couple of swells,' said the man, quoting an old song, and he raised his little finger as he took a swig from the bottle.

There was something not quite real in all this; to be idly passing the time of day with this strange old man. He had put the bottle away and was twinkling back at him like a grizzled old leprechaun.

'Would ah be right in thinkin you're fae Ireland?' he asked.

'Fancy you noticin that,' said the man. 'Ah thought ah'd jist about lost ma accent. Ah havnae been back there for donkeys' years. The auld country's in a terrible state these days, eh? Ah've lived in a few places since ah left mind ye. But somehow ah've finished up here. Are ye a Glasgow man yerself?'

'Well,' he said, 'ah've lived here most a ma life, but ah wis actually born in Campbeltown.'

'Is that no incredible,' said the man. 'D'ye know ah lived there for five year.'

'Away!'

'Small world right enough, eh!'

'We left when ah wis jist wee like, but ah used tae go back for ma holidays when ah wis auld enough tae go campin an that.'

'Oh aye, it's a great wee place Campbeltown. Course it'll be changed nowadays. Jist lik everywher else. Prob'ly full a cafés an chip shops an bingo. They'll likely av made the saint's cave intae a museum wi a turnstile. An they'll be sellin genuine relics. Actual chuckies wi real birdshit on them!'

'Ah'd forgot all about that cave. Imagine you knowin about it! Whit wis the saint called again?'

'Kieran.'

'That's it. St Kieran.'

(A hollow, green with seaweed, in the rocks battered by the waves; an ancient design carved on a flat slab of stone; call of gulls; the sound of the sea.)

'Ye know e's supposed tae uv carved that stone imself.'

'Oh ah don't doubt it,' said the man. 'A circle wisn't it, wi a kinda Celtic cross in it.'

'Amazin tae think ae it still lyin ther.'

'Unless some'dy's sold it tae an American!'

'They must a been tough these auld fellas aw the same, livin in a cave lik that. Tellin ye, we don't know we're livin.'

'Oh that's true,' said the old man. 'Makes a single-end in Partick look lik a palace! Makes ye appreciate yer wee comforts.' Bringing out his bottle again, he swigged some more wine. 'Here's tae Campbeltown! Sure ye don't want a wee slug?'

'Naw, naw,' he said. 'Ah'm fine thanks.'

'Tell me,' said the man, 'd'ye ever mind a gettin fish off the boats?'

'Ah do,' he said. 'Ah mind a goin down wi ma mother early in the mornin, when it wis still dark.'

(Boats bobbing in the harbour, everything bigger than life. Bulking shapes, the men unloading their catches on to the quay, shimmering silver harvest, glinting in the moon's pale light. Bustle as crates and barrels were filled to the brim and to overflowing, always a few fish for the baskets of the waiting women. The town taking shape in the first grey light. The creak of the fish-frail his mother carried home.)

'That's incredible,' he said. 'Ah kin remember that really clear. Ah kin jist aboot smell the fish!'

'Amazin thing the memory,' said the man. 'It's all in here y'know,' tapping his head. 'Everythin.'

'Ah've often thought that,' he said. 'Ah'm always rememberin things, even fae when ah wis wee. An whit's funny is, a lot a the time it's jist daft things that come back tae ye. Things that don't matter.'

'Ah!' said the man. 'That's wher yer wrong, see, cos it ALL matters. Every wee thing. If you remember somethin, ye kin be sure it's important. Ther'll be some meanin behind it somewher. Course, at the same time, none ae it matters a damn!'

Laughing, he offered him the bottle again, and this time he took a sip, shuddering as the taste of the wine hit him.

'Good stuff that,' said the man. 'None ae yer rubbish. Listen, while we're doin a wee bit reminiscin about Campbeltown, did ye ever go tae Davaar Island?'

'Walked across tae it at low tide!' he said.

'An see the paintin in the cave?'

'Ah did that,' he said.

(Jesus, his hands raised in benediction, painted on the wall of the cave, where the sunlight, shafting in through an opening, lit up a halo round the head.)

'Ah don't mind tellin ye,' said the man, 'the first time ah saw that it fair took ma breath away. Ah wisnae expectin it like. The sun must av jist come out fae behind a cloud, an there it was, aw lit up.'

Now they were passing the bottle between them, like old cronies, as they talked. His liking for the old man was growing. There was a strangeness in a lot of what he said, but there seemed to be a depth to it, a wisdom he could recognize and almost grasp, and a feeling that mirth was never far away.

The old man drained the last drops of wine and, stuffing the bottle back in his bag, said, 'There ye go, another dead man!' then, looking about him, 'Ye have tae watch the parkies don't catch ye drinkin or they'll put ye out on yer ear.'

'Kin they do that?' he asked.

'Oh well,' said the man, 'it's mibbe no up on the notice, ah mean it disnae actually say NO BEVVYING! But ah think they might take a wee bit exception. An that wid be us. Out in the cauld.'

'That wid be a shame,' he said. 'It's nice in here.'

'Warm.'

'Like a big greenhouse.'

'A greenpalace!'

'That's it,' he said. 'Like somethin out a story. The Winter Gardens. Somethin fae another age.'

'Magic,' said the man. 'D'ye ever look at the statues? Very nice they are. But ah'll tell ye somethin that bothers me. They've all got fine names lik Eve and Ruth an Sisters of Bethany, but what ah want tae know is what's King Robert of Sicily doin in among them? That's the fella jist at the right as ye come in the door. Ah mean who is e anyway? Ah what's e doin sittin in the bare buff wi a monkey in is lap?'

'Takes all sorts,' he said.

'An then ther's Cain at the other side,' said the man. 'Poor bugger. Funny thing as well, ah don't know if ye've noticed, but right next tae um ther's this door that leads in tae another bit ae the garden, a wee side bit, and ther's a big barrier across it. Now isn't that jist like the thing? Auld Cain sittin ther wi is face trippin um, an all thae beautiful flowers jist across the way, an a big CLOSED sign keepin um out!'

'That's it, isn't it.'

'An doesn't the bit that's locked always look the best?'

'The grass is always greener.'

'Ah mean, that jist has tae be the finest part ae the Palace. Ah've peeked in there many a time when nobody wis lookin. Poor auld Cain.'

'Hisnae got a look in,' he said. 'Here, ther's somethin ah wis gonnae show ye. Ah wis in Community House the day an a wee wifie gave me this.' The gospel tract had been crumpled in his pocket. He smoothed it out and showed it to the old man. 'Ther's another headline for ye!'

'COME BACK TO GOD,' read the old man. 'COME HOME. Ye could do worse.' Reading over the story, he went on, 'Community House ye got this? It's a queer sorta thing for them.'

'Aw naw,' he said. 'The wee wifie didnae belong there. She wis jist in fur a cuppa tea, lik me.'

'Ah wis wonderin!' said the man. 'Still, ah suppose these folk mean well enough. If they'd jist stop grabbin ye bi the collar!'

'Right enough,' he said.

'But tell me,' said the man, 'did ye ever go tae Iona itself?'

'Ah did not,' he said, 'but ah've heard a lot about it.'

'God,' said the old man. 'Whit a place that is.' Again he was far away, and his voice was more quiet as he went on, feeling for words. 'It's no like . . . how kin ah explain it? It's nothin ah could describe tae ye, y'know. Ah mean ah could tell ye all about the place, the abbey an the ruins an the sea an . . . everythin! But even if ah could describe every last wee thing on that island, ah still wouldnae be able tae say it. It's jist a feelin. Ther's jist this incredible peace, an it's as if nothin's ever changed. Ye kinda half expect tae see Columba imself. Ah mean it's like . . . e's still there! As sure as God, it's magic. Ah'm no even explainin whit ah mean. But the time ah wis ther . . . it wis only for a week mind ye, but ah've never forgot it . . . anyway when ah went ah wis in a bad state, cos ah'd jist lost ma wife ye see. But as soon as ah got there ah felt this peace ah'm tellin ye about. An then ther wis one evenin . . . ah'd been out for a walk an ah wis comin back down tae the abbey. An ah stopped, an looked about me, an it wis jist gettin dark, an ther wis jist the stillness, an this fine fine rain soakin intae me, but it didnae matter, an nothin else mattered, an ther wis jist this feelin a being out maself . . . an it wis like ah wasn't even feelin it, there wis jist the feelin itself . . . an it wis like ther wis no time, an ah wis part a everythin that had ever been . . . an ah KNEW!'

The old man's eyes were bright with the remembrance, and his wrinkled face, for a moment, looked ancient, as if he had looked deep into the mystery of things and found at the heart of it a smile.

The crunch of footsteps on the path brought them back to where they were, as a young couple passed by, arm in arm.

'Ach well,' said the old man. 'It's gettin late. Ah better get home an feed that dog before e chews the house down! It's been nice talkin tae ye sir. Maybe see ye next week at the burroo.'

'Should do,' he said.

'Cheerio then,' said the old man, picking up his bag to go. 'An remember, No Need For Alarm!'

'Right!' he said, waving, and the old man was gone.

He sat for a while, trying to gather himself. His head was fuddled from the wine. The afternoon had drifted away in talk with the old man, whose words had seemed to have a crazy kind of sanity to them. He had enjoyed the company and didn't feel much like going back to his half-room. But eventually he stirred himself to get up and head out.

Further along, the two Indian women were still sitting. He suddenly thought how far they must be from the bright land that was their home.

In the passageway, he heard footsteps behind him and a park-keeper came striding past and across to the statue of Cain. Perched in the statue's lap was the old man's empty wine-bottle. The keeper snatched it and threw it into a litter-basket, turning and glowering round about. For a moment he thought he was about to be accused. Perhaps the keeper had smelled the wine on his breath as he passed. He prepared an imaginary dialogue in which he replied to the keeper, with dignity, 'I ask you sir, do I look like an old wine-mopper?'

But in fact the keeper just barged right past him, as if he didn't exist, muttering something to himself.

He couldn't keep a smile from his face at the thought of the old man leaving the bottle in Cain's lap. He could almost imagine him, his arm round the stone shoulder, telling Cain to cheer up and see the flower that bloometh, reassuring him there was no need for alarm.

Standing at the pond, he looked down into the water, watching the fish swim slowly round, the shapes they traced, gliding, darting, the rhythm of their movement a perfect flow. Reflected in the water was the glass domed roof, a circle of sky at the bottom of the pond, the frame of the dome a radial pattern, broken by the rippling fish, the rocks, the trailing plants.

He thought of the cornice-work, cut in half, in his room, and the emptiness he felt from it; and remembering, going back, he saw the whole design, on the ceiling of their room in Govan.

(Lying with his wife on their wedding-night, first night in their own home. Because it was wartime, furniture was scarce and they hadn't a proper bed, just a mattress in the middle of the floor. The air-raid sirens had been whining, but they were staying where they were. The week before, a shelter had been hit in Clydebank. Here at least they could have a little time together. By the side of the makeshift bed they had lit a small candle, the blackout curtains tightly closed, and in its flickering light he had lain awake half the night, staring up at that pattern on the ceiling, hearing the bombs drop somewhere else, safe in her arms, lost in her soft warmth.)

Looking up at the dome, he could see the snow was falling thick. Near the top it was even beginning to settle. The quality of the light was a sad yellow-grey. Leaning forward he could see his own reflection in the pond, breaking up, dissolving as the fish rippled across.

Another memory was coming to the surface, a memory from further back.

(He was back in the house in Campbeltown; he was only four or five years old. He could see the design on the carpet where he had played. The carpet had been old and frayed but the patterns had still been clear. Out of the shapes, he had made a whole world, of flowers and faces, stars and leaves, all merging into each other, fishes and birds, a stain that looked like a boat. He remembered the smell of the room, the familiar enclosing warmth of the house around him. He would lie there, curled, in that circle on the carpet. It was his place, his territory. Within it he was safe. He remembered the feeling; centred, contained, whole; listening to the heavy comforting tick of the clock on the mantelpiece, the sounds his mother made, working about the house. Every evening at the same time she would look up at the clock, and tell him his father would be on his way. And he would jump up and run outside to watch for him. And there he would be coming slowly up the steep cobbled street. And his father would wave, and he would go pounding down the hill, running to meet him in a surge of simple joy, and his father would lift him on to his shoulder and carry him home.)

The keeper he had seen a little earlier passed by again.

'Closin in a few minutes, sir,' he said.

As he headed out into the snow, his head felt clearer, though the taste of the wine was still sour in his mouth.

Greensleeves

The ice-cream van it was with its harsh metallic jangle. She could only just recognize the tune for what it had once been. Not that coarse parody, stilted and mechanical, a tin brashness, a gaudiness of noise. But somewhere in it, all but lost, was an echo of something old. Still to be heard through all that distortion. The faintest of memories of times long past. She heard and she remembered. The tune was called Greensleeves.

She must have learned it first at school. So many years. Half a century and more. But further back than that it went, all sadness and grace, all minstrels and knights and ladies in high towers, imprisoned.

And this was a tower high enough. Twenty-two storeys of concrete and glass. Boxes on boxes, and hers right at the top. Half way to heaven as the young man next door would say. People on the lift were always saying things like that. Whoever was nearest the door would press the buttons for everyone, repeating the numbers like a bingo-caller. Legs eleven they would say, or Lucky for some, thirteen. Like a language all of its own. For her floor it would be Top of the House, or All the twos, or sometimes Two little ducks. That was the one she liked best, though she thought a two was more like a swan. Two little swans. Swans were like the tune again, the way it used to be. Played on a flute, bending and gliding. Curve of the swan's neck, dipping to meet its own reflection. Ripples on an old pond. Swansong.

At first she'd been terrified of the lifts, the rickety way they clanked and jarred from floor to floor. But gradually she'd become used to it although sometimes the fear came back, especially if she was alone. The lift would creak and shudder its way up and up and she would feel the emptiness below her, increasing as she got further from the ground, suspended, supportless, a sheer black drop into nothing at all.

But the lifts were about the only place she ever saw her neighbours. It was like passing through a strange town and just catching glimpses of the people who lived there. Descending or rising through layer after layer, and every layer a few more lives she would never know. Sometimes people were friendly, but there were times too when nobody would utter a word, all lost in themselves. Strange the atmosphere when nobody spoke, every one staring straight ahead or looking down at their feet, anything rather than catch another's eye. Sometimes it was just surliness, like the young man from the seventeenth floor with his neat suit and his newspaper and his rolled umbrella. He never seemed to talk to anybody. Others she thought were just shy, like the little apprentice from the ninth. More often though, the people who didn't talk just seemed too tired or preoccupied to make the effort, coming home deadened and tense after a day's work. Then at other times it was all bustle, people babbling away, children chattering and crowding on with footballs or scooters or bikes. Sometimes it was nice at weekends, people coming home in the evening, glad for the moment to be free. She liked it then, everybody was happier, more relaxed, more ready to talk and joke and laugh. But the lift would gradually empty towards the top and by the time it reached her floor she was usually alone again. Sometimes at the weekends though it became a bit chaotic, and the lifts were always breaking down because too many people would crowd on at once. And there was always sure to be somebody loud and drunk. At times it could be really disgusting, with people being sick or even using the lifts as toilets. And then the poor caretaker would have to clean up the mess. Only the other day the big Highlander from the fourteenth had caught somebody at that.

A young boy it had been.

'Staunin therr bold as ye like,' he'd said, 'pishin in the coarner! So ah took um bi the scruff a the neck an rubbed is bloody nose in it! Told um if they acted lik wee dugs they'd get treated like them. Dirty wee tikes!'

She'd thought that was a bit cruel and maybe a bit coarse as well, but she couldn't help laughing with the others. The Highlander was an ex-policeman. A fine big man she thought. She could imagine how angry he must have been at the boy. The lifts were always marked with their slogans, strange symbols, their own names, the names of their gangs. The Highlander called them cave-paintings, said the boys were animals. The slogans, scraped and painted, were spreading to other parts of the building. Even downstairs, right outside the caretaker's office, where the sign said No Ball Games No Loitering, the walls had been daubed and sprayed. But at least it wasn't as bad yet as other blocks she'd heard about. According to the papers and the television, some of them were already on the way to being slums. She'd even heard people on the bus talking about these blocks here as if they were slums. Two women it had been, sitting just behind her.

'And I mean,' one had said, 'you should see some of the children, running about wild. Like wee savages. And as for some of the language!'

'Mind you,' the other had said, 'you can't really expect anything else. They're all just shifted out from Partick and Govan, and all these dirty old tenements are just falling to bits. It's not as if they've ever known anything better.'

She thought of her own home over in Ibrox. Near enough to Govan, but nowhere near to being slums. A decent red sandstone block, clean and solid and old, with tiles in the close and polished wooden banister-rails and stained-glass windows on every landing. The one on her landing had the head and shoulders of a young knight or squire, panels of twining flowers on either side, yellow, red and green, and up above patterns of red and blue squares. The whole close was always quiet, and the daylight that filtered through the windows was tinted and softened by the coloured glass. The back court itself, when seen through windows like these, was a bright painted garden, a landscape tinted and framed.

That was how she liked to remember it. Like another age. The stillness of a summer afternoon. It had been a fine building. Even the storm of a few years back hadn't damaged it at all. But the area was due for redevelopment, so down it had to come to make way for a supermarket or a wider road or another block of flats.

One afternoon, a month or two after she'd moved, she'd been back in Ibrox to go to a jumble-sale. When she'd passed by they were pulling the building down, grey rain drizzling on the wasteground where half a street had been. She'd stood and watched as the workmen heaped spars of wood on a bonfire and bulldozers and lorries cleared away the rubble. The ground had shaken, a terrible rumble and crash as another wall crumbled and fell in a cloud of choking yellow dust. The dust cleared and the building stood, laid open like a doll's house, and there where the second storey had been was one wall of her home, old layers of wallpaper peeling, tattered edges flapping in the wind. And where the fireplace had been was the back of a blackened hearth and a broken chimney and a line of soot left by every fire she'd ever burned. And the whole ruin flickered and wavered in the haze of the workmen's bonfire, crackling and hissing and spitting in the rain.

A fire was something she missed here, the glow of it in the evening, the stories she could read into the dance of the flames. Now she had the television to look at and the under-floor heating to keep her warm. It was good though on winter mornings, not to have to rake out ashes and footer with paper and sticks and fumble with matches when her fingers were so numb and cold. But she did like a fire to sit by. Still, the heating was good for her plants. She had four, in pots along the windowsill – geranium, some ivy, morning-glory and a small spiky cactus – and all of them were thriving. In the geranium pot there were even some weeds flourishing, tiny blue flowers and a thick tangle of leaves. She hadn't had the heart to cut them, she'd just let them grow like the others. She thought the seeds must have come drifting in through the window, and by some miracle had settled on this few inches of soil, and that was reason enough to let them live.

She stirred herself to get up and go into the kitchen. She filled a small milk-jug from the tap and, carrying it through, watered each plant in turn and stood looking at them, content, the shapes of flower, stem and leaf, just so, against the evening sky. Somehow she always thought it added something to the landscape, to see it framed by such graceful shapes, to see them silhouetted against it. And the view from these windows was one thing she was grateful for, some consolation for all the rest. She would never tire of looking at it, the houses so far below stretching away on all sides. And there were the hills of Renfrewshire, away to the left across the river, and there to the right the hills of Dumbarton and Kilpatrick. And from here you could still see it was a valley, the river winding down through it, now hidden behind buildings, now glinting and flowing through shipyards or open ground, past tenements and factories, on through patches of green, traces of how it had been before, when all of it was farmland, or wild, like the hills.

Sometimes she was amazed at how much there was to see, how much there was going on all at once. She would be looking down at the blue train clattering out towards Balloch, she would follow it out till her eye was caught by faraway streams of traffic, then a gull would flap and glide up past the window, up into the open sky, the sky she could look at forever. All day long she could watch it flowing, watch the weather turn and change, lose herself in the colours and shapes. Now the clouds would come bulking and threatening up the valley, bringing the rain up steadily from the west, now the sun would light on a patch of hillside away across the river, now the clouds would drift on and the whole sky would clear.

The sun had gone now, down behind the hills, and all the street lamps were lit. By the light of the lamps nearest, a few small boys were still playing football, directly below in the playing area, a fenced-in rectangle of red ash. They weren't allowed to play on the grass but they didn't usually pay much heed and the caretaker was forever chasing them. They were always up to something. If it wasn't trampling the grass it was barging about the drying-area upstairs, or running and yelling in the entrance-hall, or playing in the lifts. One of their favourite tricks was to press all the buttons so that the next one to use the lift would stop at every floor. That was one that seemed to annoy everybody, and the boys were always in danger of being thumped for it.

A sudden rap at the letterbox made her jump. She wasn't used to having unexpected visitors and she was flustered, wondering who it could be, as she hurried to answer it. It was the young man from next door.

'Hello,' he said, smiling. 'Ah wis wonderin if ye had any change fur the telly.'

'Oh, yes,' she said. 'Ah'll just away an have a look.'

She came back fishing out coins from her purse.

'Here you are,' she said. 'A two-shilling bit. Ah've actually got two but ah'll be keeping one for maself.'

'One's jist fine,' he said. 'Thanks a lot. Here yar then, ten pence.'

'Of course,' she said. 'Ah don't think ah'll ever get used to this new pence business.'

'Aye, it's a lot a old nonsense,' he said.

'Is there something good on the television the night?' she asked.

'Ah don't really know,' he said. 'We shove it oan at teatime an that's it oan fur the night.'

'Och well,' she said, 'it's good company.'

'It is that,' he said. 'Well, thanks again.'

'Not at all,' she said. 'Cheerio!'

'Cheerio!'

From the newspaper she saw that there was a quiz programme just finishing. Then she had a choice between a programme on current affairs, a comedy show and an old film. She decided to watch the film. She had seen it years before, but that didn't matter. She could barely remember it. It was called *Grand Hotel*. She liked the old films best. She hadn't been to the pictures in years.

She put her coin in the slot at the back of the television set. At least it would be enough to last till the end of the film. The night before, the money in the box had lasted right up to the beginning of *Late Call*. The young minister had started very earnestly. 'Tonight,' he'd said, 'I want to talk specially to those of you out there who are old, or lonely, or sick.' Then the money had run out. The minister had disappeared with a ping, shrunk to a white dot, nothingness, the screen suddenly black. That had given her a funny feeling. She'd thought of the minister in a studio somewhere, smiling at a camera, mouthing into a microphone, not knowing that she could no longer see or hear him. Those of you out there.

When she switched on the set, the quiz programme was coming to an end. The quiz-master was grinning. 'And so, from all of us here to all of you out there, Good luck, Goodnight, God bless and See you next week. Bye!' Then the theme music started and the credits rolled up. Glitter of prizes. Treasure. Applause from the studio audience. See you next week. All of you out there. That was what the minister had said. Out there. God bless.

The advertisements came on then. The first was for packets of powdered soup, an old-fashioned iron pot bubbling away over a blazing log fire, a scrubbed wooden table, a heap of fresh vegetables. Rain on the window, a hungry family, steam rising from the pot. 'Country Fresh,' said a deep, rich voice.

The next was for soap powder, though she always confused it with one for life insurance and another for margarine. It showed a young family, all dressed in white, leaping and running across fields in slow motion. There were shots of the sun, caught in the trees, gleaming modern buildings, an aeroplane, a white bird. The music was clean and bouncy and bright. A voice was saying 'Tomorrow's world . . . Today!'

She was startled by another rap at the door. This time she was even more confused. Two visitors in one evening. The place was never usually so busy.

It was a man selling locks.

'Ah fit it fur ye as well,' he said. 'That's included in the price.'

'Well, there's nothing really wrong with the lock ah've got,' she said.

'Ah but this is a special mortise-lock,' he said. 'It turns four times. They don't make them any merr burglar-proof than these Missis.'

'Well, I don't really think . . .' she said.

'Please yerself Missis,' he said. 'But ah hope ye don't mind me askin ye, d'ye live here yerself?'

'Well, yes . . .' she said.

'Aye well,' he said. 'Ye only huv tae read the papers these days tae see the kind a things that's happenin aw the time. D'ye know whit ah mean?'

'That's true,' she said. 'Maybe ah'll think about it. But ah don't know if ah can really afford it anyway.'

'That's nae bother,' he said. 'Ye kin pey it up every week.'

'Well,' she said. 'Ah'll see.'

'Fair enough Missis,' he said. 'Ah'm roon here every month. Ah'll maybe catch ye in again sometime.'

'Right,' she said. 'Cheerio.'

'See ye,' he said.

She closed the door and heard him rapping her neighbour's letterbox.

The film had just started and she settled down to watch it, and as she watched she began to remember it. Not clearly, it was too long ago for that, only a vague stirring as the story unfolded, the hotel and all the people in it, never really knowing each other, all their lives so separate but intertwined. And there was Greta Garbo, all sad and lovely and wanting to be alone, and the thief she was to fall in love with. She remembered that. She remembered they wanted to run away together and she remembered that somehow he was to die. And there was the man with the strawberry birthmark. He just sat and watched it go on all around him, and all he ever said was 'Grand Hotel. People come. People go. Nothing ever happens.'

At the advertisement break, she got up to put on the kettle for some tea. Then she heard the tune again, Greensleeves, clangouring through the night air, and she remembered she wanted to buy some milk from the van. In the evenings it came round every hour. She was glad of that; there were no shops open nearby; no Handy Stores or Indian grocers here.

She put on her coat against the chill and hurried out to the lift. When she pressed the button, the light didn't go on. She pressed again and again but it was no use. Only the click of the button and a dead, heavy clanking, echoing up from far below. Both lifts must have broken down. She pressed her face up close to the small window, peering into the shaft. She could hear people on the other floors banging the doors in annoyance and raising their voices. The cables just hung, swaying slightly in the gloom.

Sadly, she turned away. Even if she could have managed to get down the stairs in time to catch the van, she would never manage to get up again. Twenty-two flights was too much for her to cope with. Luckily she had never had to try. The lifts had always been fixed in time. But tonight it was getting late. The workmen might not come till morning, and she couldn't take the chance. She was stuck here. Trapped. Twenty-two floors. All the twos. Two little ducks. Halfway to Heaven. Top of the house.

She stopped and looked out the landing window. The boys had all gone and the playing area was empty. Directly opposite was the next block, lit up against the dark. She remembered then how she'd seen it once, early on a winter morning. It had been so dark and foggy that she couldn't make out the outline of the building, only the blackness and the lights. At first it had looked as if the lights were just suspended there, hanging in the air. Then she'd seen it as if the whole sky was one vast black wall, with these few lights set in it. That had given her the same empty, bottomless feeling she sometimes got on the lift.

She had left her door open and she could hear the television set blaring. The soap powder advert was on again. She recognized the music. Tomorrow's world . . . Today. The light in the corridor was bright and cold.

From outside she heard again the din of the tune from the van, moving on to the next block. She was never quite sure of the first words of the song, whether it was Alas my Love or Alas my Lord. Alas my Love you do me wrong, to cast me off so discourteously.

The film would be starting again. She would go in and watch it till the end.

She closed the door and turned the key, locking herself in for the night.

THREE

Changes

Epiphany

The movement was always one of returning, back to the source.

I could remember it all, back to that one sweet flow, the mothering warmth that gave suck, gave succour, held me, enfolded, safe from all harm.

And back before that.

Afloat in the fluid that nourished, sustained me, as curled round my lifeline I grew. All was my mother then, heart that beat through me, pulse of the universe, was one, was whole.

And back before that.

I was two become one. The upstream surge and thrust of seed, seeking home.

And back before that.

There was one and it was light.

And always there was pain. Pain at the loss of that bliss. Pain of birth, pushed out, cut off, cast adrift. Pain of withdrawal from the sweetness of the breast. Pain of separation. Pain of the fall.

And all that was left was a longing and an ache and a deep sleep of forgetting . . .

I was in a dull bedsitting-room in London; huddled in front of the only source of heat, a two-bar electric fire with one bar broken. And why was I in London? Escaping the desolation of another Glasgow New Year. As if it really mattered where I was.

At the other side of the room sat Doug, my friend, cross-legged on the floor. We had shared Doug's supply of his precious sacramental drug, two yellow capsules called Sunshine, a couple of pounds' worth of eternity, bought in the pub at the corner. We had sat up far into the night, come face to face with our inner heaven and hell, glimpsed at something beyond both. And now there was the faint lingering sadness of comedown. Early morning. London. Back into time and space.

The clock had stopped just after midnight and we hadn't bothered to rewind it. Time had seemed like something of a joke. But now once again it was asserting itself, inexorable. Asleep in the corner was Doug's wife Jenny. She had long since gone to bed, and in a few hours more she would have to be up again for work. Doug crossed to the bed and stood for a long time looking down at her, reaching out once to stroke her hair back from her face.

I had kept a sheet of paper by me, thinking I might feel like writing. Across the top I had scribbled WHAT WAS YOUR FACE BEFORE YOU WERE BORN? Underneath I had drawn circles and spirals and a shape like a baby in a womb. (Once, on another trip, Doug had gone scrambling around searching for pen and paper to write down an important message he had received. The message had come, he said, from the furthest reaches of the universe, and was a statement of the ultimate truth, of the aim and purpose of all creation. He had managed to write it down then seal it in an envelope and hide it somewhere safe. Much later he had opened it and read what he had written. The message read HELLO THERE.)

Faraway in another room, further up the house, somebody was playing the Beatles.

> Get back. Get back
> Get back to where you once belonged

'Other folk still up,' said Doug. 'Ravin the night away. Hey, is that the name ae a song?' He sang.

'Everybody's ravin . . . ravin
Ravin the night away.'

'Twistin,' I said.

'Eh?'

'The song. It wis Twistin the night away. Sam Cooke used tae sing it.'

'That's it!' said Doug, delighted. 'See you an yer old songs. You should get on one a these quiz programmes. Double Yer Money an that. Win yerself a fortune.'

'I have measured out my life with old songs,' I said, draping myself across a chair, the back of one limp hand to my forehead. 'Ah the dear dead days beyond recall!'

I had been raving to Doug about the Universe being one vast musical, a cosmic extravaganza, starring Fred Astaire as Shiva and Ginger Rogers as Kali, tap-dancing to the music of the spheres.

Jenny stirred in her sleep and we both fell quiet, Doug shooshing with a finger to his mouth. When he was quite sure we hadn't wakened her, he went to the window and looked out into the street.

'Soon be light,' he said.

'Fancy goin out?' I asked. 'See if we can get some milk an rolls or somethin, for breakfast?'

'Aw that wid be beautiful,' said Doug. 'Have it ready for Jenny when she wakes up.'

Outside it was cold and wet as we scuffled along through grey dismal streets, past crumbling terrace buildings, past heaps of rubbish gathered during a dustmen's strike – stacks of black plastic bags, spilling out cartons and bottles, a discarded Christmas tree, a mattress, a broken guitar – past a slogan daubed on the wall, WE TEACH ALL HEARTS TO BREAK. And in spite of the rain and my heavy boots and the fact that I couldn't

really tap-dance, I went bounding into a forties' musical routine,
singing

> 'I feel a song comin on
> An ah'm tellin ya
> It's a victorious
> Happy an glorious
> NOO song.'

And I raved on to Doug about these songs being celebrations,
invocations, hymns to God in his manifest forms. As if there
were deeper meanings behind the words; as if this scabby old
world went on praising, in spite of itself; as if these love songs
were devotional.

'But we can only hear it as an echo,' I said, 'because that's all it
is to us.'

'That's because we're in the Kali Yuga,' said Doug. 'That's
what this time-cycle's called in Indian mythology. The dark age.
Millions a years.'

'An here we are stoatin along in Notting Hill!'

'In the dark.'

'On a freezin wet mornin.'

'Working out karma.'

And I laughed, for that was Doug's answer to everything.
From toothache to global war, he lumped it all together as part
of the endless cosmic cycle of cause and effect, the fitness of
things, a profound order underlying the seeming madness of it
all.

'We'll get there in the end,' he said.

'There we are,' I said, pointing across to where a milk
lorry had come clanking round the corner. 'The goal is in
sight!'

The driver sold us a pint and directed us to a bakery where we
went round to the back door and bought a loaf from the day's
first batch.

'God,' said Doug, breathing in the warm fragrance of the fresh bread. 'Sometimes life can be awful good!'

Jenny was already up when we got back to the flat, and the clock had been set right.

'So there you are,' she said.

'Are we?' I asked.

'Where?' said Doug, looking over his shoulder.

'C'mon,' said Jenny. 'Ah'm too tired for all yer nonsense.'

'Ah, you might think it's nonsense,' said Doug, 'but it's actually very profound.'

'Profound ma bum,' said Jenny.

'I see we're in the presence of a master,' I said.

'Oh Great Mother,' said Doug, and we bowed low to her wisdom.

'Will ye both give it a chuck!' she said, laughing. 'Where have ye been?'

'Aah!' said Doug. 'If only words could tell!'

'Ah know ye've been out yer heads,' she said, impatient again, 'but where were ye just now?'

'Out tae the shops,' said Doug.

'On a cosmic quest for the Holy Grail,' I said.

'An here it is,' said Doug. 'The bread of life and the milk of human kindness!'

I placed them on the table. 'A loaf an a pint a pasteurized!'

She took them and made food for us, toast and tea, muesli from a big sack. We ate together, grateful for the simple sharing.

Our talk, as ever, went back, always back. Our time together had been a picking up of threads. Loose ends.

I had hoped to visit other old friends from Glasgow, a couple, Ritchie and Mag. But Doug told me they had long since split up and Ritchie had gone to Ireland.

(A few years had gone now since we'd first come down to London together. Doug and Jenny, Ritchie and Mag, Mary and

Me. All young and daft, arrogant innocents, lost in a dream of who we thought we were.

'Remember that time?'

So long ago it seemed. Drift of incense in the summer air. Singing that with our love we could change the world. Stoned-happy laughter in the bright sunlit park. Lazing at our ease through the long summer days. With the first chill of autumn I had come back to Glasgow with Mary. The others had stayed on.)

Each visit now seemed to find us all further apart, our lives more fragmented.

'You and Mary should come down here for good,' said Jenny.

'We'd have to get back together first,' I said.

'Oh,' she said. 'I didn't realize.'

'Did ye ever see that Groucho Marx thing?' said Doug. 'Somebody says "Do you mind if I join you?" and he says "I didn't realize I was coming apart!"'

'Ye never do,' I said. 'Tell me, when did Ritchie an Mag finally split up?'

'Must be about a year ago,' said Doug.

'That figures,' I said. 'Last time ah saw Ritchie was just before that. E was stayin in Earl's Court an Mag was away down tae Brighton for a coupla days. E was talkin about goin to Ireland even then.'

(Relating was hard that time. Ritchie's talk now was of Revolution and the People's War. I showed him a Zen book I had been reading and he was scornful of it. 'Here in one volume,' he read, 'are gathered the experiences of Zen.' Measuring the thickness of the book between finger and thumb he said, 'Pretty thin experiences!' and tossed the book back at me. Our talking faded out after that. The silences grew and deepened between us. We sat, listening to the rumble of the traffic outside, till at last I said I should go. That was as well, he said, for he had friends coming round, to talk. They arrived as I was leaving, a young

Irish couple. Ritchie didn't introduce them and they gave no more than a nod in my direction. Parting, there was even more of an awkwardness. 'Have a good time in Ireland,' I said. 'If you go.' He smiled at that, a sad, cynical smile, across a great distance. Whatever his business in Ireland might be, good times were no part of it. It was only out in the street, when the cold air hit me, that I realized how oppressive it had been to be with him. Late afternoon, the traffic growing heavier. Lights coming on, people hurrying home. Another world.)

Remembering all this now, I told it to Doug.

'God help Ritchie,' he said, 'if e's away wi that pair. They're really heavy man. Naw really. Ah'm no kiddin. They're intae the whole bit. Bombs an everythin.'

'Bombs?' I said. 'In Ireland? But Ritchie was never intae that rubbish, the auld Catholic Protestant thing.'

'An neither are they,' said Doug. 'They're jist usin it. Stirrin it up. Mixin it. They jist want tae smash the lot. Blow it tae fuck an start again. Ye know the kinda space yer head can get intae!'

'Jesus!'

'It's crazy, isn't it?' said Jenny. 'The different roads we wind up takin.'

'Karma!' said Doug.

'An what about Mag?' I asked. 'Where's *her* karma takin her?'

'God,' said Jenny. 'Ye might ask!'

'Ye were tellin me she got busted,' I said.

'That's puttin it mildly!' said Doug. 'She's been dealin for a while, y'know. An these guys she was in wi, they were real heavies, man, like the fuckin Mafia or somethin. Anyway, she was round at their place when it got done. An wee smart-arse Mag, she musta been zonked out her skull, she says "Oh ah'll take the stuff, they'll no touch me!" Honest tae God man, there was tons ae it. Every fuckin illegal drug known tae man, an prob'ly a few more besides! An Mag stuffs them intae er shoulder bag and tries tae walk out the door!'

'An where is she now?'

'She's down in Brighton,' said Doug. 'Somebody got er out on bail and she's waitin for the trial tae come up.'

'One of the guys in the flat had a gun,' said Jenny.

'The guys that got busted with her?'

'Right,' said Doug. 'They're jist gangsters, man. Gangsters.'

He fell quiet again, before going on. 'Ah went tae see er in jail, at the visitin hours. It wis a bit depressin. Made me kinda sad. I mean it wis a horrible place. An there wis wee Mag behind this barrier that ye had tae talk through. She wis sorta giggly, but there wis somethin kinda manic about it. She wis tellin me er teeth were all rottin because she'd been takin that much speed, an one ae er teeth had broken on a chop or somethin she'd been eatin in the prison canteen. Then she started goin on about this velvet dress she'd seen down the Portobello Road, an she'd been gonnae buy it but it wouldnae be there when she got out an thinkin about it wis makin er miserable. By the time ah left ah wis glad tae get away. Out intae the air.'

'Like me when ah left Ritchie,' I said.

'An it's funny,' said Doug, 'how yer mind goes back. Ah got this image in ma head of Mag when we first met er bein that sorta prim she wis embarrassed at eatin an apple in the street! She wis all stiff an awkward y'know, lookin about er, an she could hardly eat the thing.'

'That's her education that did that,' said Jenny. 'She had it drummed into her it wasn't nice.'

'Ah was thinkin back as well,' I said, 'rememberin when we were all at the Uni. There was some demonstration goin on, an Ritchie started jumpin about wi a wee plastic machine gun! D'ye remember?'

'That's right,' said Doug. 'An there were a coupla young polis gettin really worried till they saw it wis jist a wee toy!'

'They were still thinkin about bustin him though. But everybody was laughin an it just passed over.'

'Like everything,' said Doug.

'Eh?' said Jenny.

'Like everything,' said Doug. 'It jist passes over.'

'That you bein profound again?' said Jenny.

'You've been warned about that already!' I said.

'Here, listen,' said Jenny. 'I'll have to be goin soon, to work. Tell me, are you goin back to Glasgow today?'

'Maybe,' I said. 'Ah'm not sure. It makes no difference either way. Ah'm supposed to start back at work tomorrow, but ah don't really care.'

Almost a year now I'd been working in a hospital, an auxiliary in a psychiatric ward. As always, a few days of freedom had made me feel sick at the thought of going back. Sick of sickness.

Doug suggested I should cast an oracle.

'Toss a coin?' I said.

'If ye like,' said Doug. 'Or do it wi a wee bit more ceremony. Consult the *I-Ching*. Ah've been workin out how tae use it.' He searched along a shelf, picked out a heavy paperback book and passed it to me. *I-Ching. The Book of Changes*.

'There's actually special wee Chinese coins ye can get for castin the oracles,' he said. 'But ah'm sure any coins'll do.'

'Ah thought ye used yarrow stalks.'

'That's the right way,' said Doug. 'The way they used tae do it.'

'Sounds beautiful,' I said. 'Casting the yarrow stalks.' The very sound of the words had a texture, a grain. The picture they conjured was concrete and vivid. An old man, eyes crinkled with an ancient knowledge, his movements deft and unhurried, fingers nimble as he gathered the stalks and cast them in the dust. Reading there the meaning, the underlying order at the heart of chaos. (Like the meaning he could read into the shifting of clouds, the chance patterns weathered on a stone wall.)

'Have you any change love?' asked Doug. 'We need three coins the same.'

'Should be some on the mantelpiece,' said Jenny.

'We used that this mornin,' said Doug, 'for the breakfast.'

'All ah've got's a coupla pound notes,' I said. 'That's ma lot.'

'Why don't ye just open the book at random,' said Jenny. 'See where it takes ye.'

'Should be OK,' said Doug. 'As long as ye do it wi a wee bit reverence. It's the attitude that counts.'

Taking the book, I concentrated, and let if fall open.

'Hexagram 24,' I read. *'Returning.'*

'What does it say?' asked Jenny.

'Decision,' I read. *'Returning. Freedom and progress lie ahead. The superior man can come and go without being opposed, friends come to see him and after seven days return with no error having been made. Movement in any direction will be of advantage.'*

'Amazing,' said Doug.

'So, d'ye think ah'm set for an auspicious return to Glasgow?'

'Could be,' said Doug. 'Was that what ye were plannin anyway?'

'Ah think so.'

'This is the thing,' said Doug. 'Ye can really read anythin intae it. An ah suppose tae do it properly ye have tae spend a lot more time on it. An if ye use the coins, ye get what's called moving lines that can give ye a completely different thing. Another hexagram altogether.'

'You just want him to stay in London, don't ye?' said Jenny, and we laughed.

'There's a beautiful bit further down the page,' I said, reading from the commentary. *'Do we not see the moving intelligence of Heaven and Earth? Change is the law of nature and society; when decay has reached its climax a recovery must take place. Brightness will increase day by day and month by month.'*

Closing the book, I handed it back to Doug. 'Ah'd better get ma things together,' I said. 'Might as well try to get out on the road early.'

'Don't forget your book,' said Jenny.

The book was a new one I had bought, a volume of translations from Japanese haiku, by R. H. Blyth.

'Should ah consult this as well?' I asked. 'Just to be on the safe side?'

'Why not?' said Doug.

I opened the book. 'Jesus!'

'What dis it say?' asked Doug.

I read –

> 'This is the bell that never rang
> This is the fish that never swam
> This is the tree that never grew
> This is the bird that never flew.'

'That's incredible,' said Doug.

'There it is,' I said, showing him the page. 'Jingle on Glasgow city arms.'

'What's it doing in a haiku book?' asked Jenny.

'That's what ah'm tryin to figure out!' I said, reading on. 'He seems to be using it to try and describe a state of mind. Emptiness. Being-in-non-being.'

'Quite a coincidence anyway,' she said.

'No such thing as coincidence!' said Doug.

I put the book down the side of my rucksack.

'Here,' said Doug, 'Ah've been meanin to give you this.' He handed me a little booklet called 'The Four Noble Truths'. I had been reading it earlier, but now I turned the pages with a new interest and a greater care.

Jenny was making up a pack for me, bread and cheese, a couple of apples.

'Ah really will have to hurry now,' she said. 'The tube's that crowded at this time.'

Looking up at the clock on the mantelpiece, she suddenly remembered it was Epiphany, the twelfth day of Christmas.

'Time to take down the cards an things,' she said.

Doug got up and cleared them away. And just in that moment, I seemed to feel all the beautiful sadness of our little lives, the fullness and the transitoriness of it all.

Epiphany. Taking down the Christmas cards. The bare mantelpiece.

Getting back

Another lorry went growling past. I watched the red tail-lights dwindle into the night, along the approach road and on to the motorway.

(The driver had laughed and given me the V-sign in answer to the silent supplication of my outstretched thumb. The communication had been perfect and wordless. Raised thumb. Two fingers. Laughter.)

There was a game I had played as a child and a song that went with it.

> One finger one thumb one arm one leg
> One nod of the head keep moving
> We'll all be merry and bright

As it passed through my head now I was grateful for the crazy optimism of it. It even threw light back on my brief exchange with the lorry-driver. My raised thumb had been a greeting. Thumbs up. The driver's response had meant V-for-Victory. Two human beings, adrift in the Void, had hailed each other with gestures of affirmation. One nod of the head/keep moving/We'll all be merry and bright. It was one way of looking at things.

'Any chance ae a lift Jimmy?'

'Get it up ye!'

It must be about two in the morning now. That would make it sixteen hours since I'd hitched out of London. And here I was, stuck, stranded, on the road leading out from Carlisle, ninety-odd miles still from Glasgow. But at least I was approaching home territory. The blue and white signboard, lit up, read GLASGOW AND THE NORTH. And across it, as if to confirm the welcome, ran spidery spray-painted lettering, proclaiming, in gold, RANGERS OK. MENTAL HARRY. BIG JAKE IS PURE MAD.

Sometimes I thought I must be pure mad myself.

I huddled, trying to hug some warmth back into my bones. But there was no warm centre to wrap around. The cold had penetrated the very pith and marrow of me, a numbness and an aching misery.

My old suede jacket was in a terminal stage of disintegration. It had no buttons, no lining, practically no seams. A seamless garment. (Unseamly was what Doug had called it.) It was scarred too with the scuffs and stains of the five years or so I had worn it, even some bloodstains (my own), dark spatters from a punched nose two years back (caught on my way home by a few young team-boys, but glad at the time to escape a bloodier battering).

Mental. Pure mad.

Last night's raving seemed empty now. Up all night setting the universe in order. All I wanted now was to curl up warm and sleep.

I stamped my numbed feet, a steady thump on the frozen ground, and the rhythm became a dance as I rubbed my hands together and chanted my little song. One finger one thumb one arm one leg. And in the repetition, the words became a mantra. One nod of the head keep moving. And I began to improvise on it, wailing, bending the words to some tune of my own, till it sounded more like a pibroch or an Indian raga. We'll all be merry and bright. And I lost myself in it till the next set of

185

headlights caught me in their glare and my thumb went out and yet another car went swishing past, on out of sight.

So many times I had hitched back and forth along this road. And so many times along the way I had been stuck at some junction like this one, wondering what was so great about London to make me want to go there, and what was so great about Glasgow to make me want to come back.

I remembered us all, heading off for London, Doug with a big sign on his bag reading BIG ROCK CANDY MOUNTAIN OR BUST. And here we were, four years on. Going nowhere.

The traffic along the motorway was steady, though not a heavy flow, and there was more of it going south than coming north. That always seemed to be the way of it. Along my approach road nothing came. I paced back and forward, kicked a stone, heard it skite against the pole supporting the signboard.

Empty sound. Stone against metal. Empty night. Waiting at the side of the empty road, kicking a stone in the emptiness.

And yet in the very heart of this emptiness came a fullness, a closeness to all things. The familiarity of everything. Friendly, the night sky. A faint humour in my old rucksack slumped on the grass verge. There, just so. The moment itself, in all its bareness and clarity.

And there suddenly seemed something comic in my being there at all, at the side of this road in the middle of the night, and I felt a genuine amazement at this incredible random process that was taking me home. Here I had been dropped, to make my next connection with somebody right now driving through the night to some purpose of his own. So many people on so many journeys, and I linking them in a journey of my own. And sooner or later I would get back. I knew that. But for now there was this cold, this endless cold in waves passing over me. Shoulders hunched body tight clenched. Croaking out the chant again. One finger one thumb one arm one leg. Stamp pace kick the ground. Keep moving. The song gave way to another.

> You put your left hand in
> You take your left hand out
> You put your left hand in
> And you shake it all about

Just one more daft song, floating up from nowhere. I had a head full of them, old songs, back to 1910. There were times when I felt I had been programmed by some manipulative intelligence. Ritchie would tell me it was the capitalist system feeding on me. Doug would say it was my own crazy ego, keeping me trapped in the endless round of attachment, illusion, desire.

> You do the hokey kokey
> And you turn around
> That's what it's all about

(An image from a couple of weeks back, the last shift I had worked at the hospital. I was working nights so at the start of my shift I caught the end of the patients' Christmas party. And there they were in the games room, dancing in a big circle. Doing the hokey kokey.)

I was trying to push the image away. But it stayed, a discomfort at the pit of my stomach, a sadness I didn't want to face. The song had brought it to the surface.

(Mary had gone that same day, off across Europe for a month or two. She might come back to Glasgow, she might not. I had come to work feeling grey and the place had already made me worse. After the hokey kokey came a call for individual songs. The first up to the microphone was Sammy. Sammy was labelled paranoid psychotic and was also diabetic. Skinny and small, he was always in quarrels and fights. He had a sad little twisted bashed-in face, baffled, like a child's, but never very far from rage.

He stood as if to attention, rigid in front of the microphone, and began to sing. 'They try to tell us we're too young'. Voice toneless and nasal, echoing round the hall.

> They say that love's a word
> A word we've only heard
> And can't begin to know the
> meaning of

It was too much for me to take. I slipped out, along the corridor to the ward, where a few of the patients still were. In the first two beds were two older men, Mr Hendry and Dr Cohen. Mr Hendry never spoke. He never ate. He sat all day, staring at nothing. Dr Cohen was an alcoholic, drying out. They both looked through me, to somewhere else.

I moved on and Andrew called me over. Andrew was young, about 18, and he was diagnosed hypomanic schizophrenic. He was big and heavy and would clump around the ward all day, unable to rest. He told me he was worried about his two friends, Eddie and Kevin, asleep in the adjoining beds. Like Andrew, they had been given shock treatment earlier in the day, electro-convulsive therapy, a kind of clinically-induced epileptic spasm. According to the Charge Nurse, sometimes it helped, sometimes it didn't. They had no way of knowing in advance. All they could do was try it.

'They haven't said a word all day,' said Andrew.

'They'll just be tired,' I said, 'after the ECT. The rest'll do them good. They'll feel better tomorrow.'

'That's right,' said Andrew, looking as if he'd remembered something. 'I had it too, didn't I? I'll feel better tomorrow as well.'

Eddie they said was paranoid, depressive. He was the youngest of a big family and thought they all wanted rid of him. I had seen his mother, and thought he might be right.

Kevin had taken one LSD trip too many. He'd found himself trapped in some grey schizoid world, unable to find his way back. I thought I could see where he was and had tried to talk him through, but I'd only made him afraid. He'd told me he'd been found walking naked along Great Western Road, proclaiming he was God. 'But you are God,' I'd said, and he'd been terrified. 'Don't say that,' he'd told me. 'I don't want to start all that again.'

I had to be more careful what I said.

Andrew showed me something he'd written in his diary. He had taken a line from a song he'd heard on the radio, 'Love is life'. Under that he'd written 'God is love', and under that, as if concluding an equation, 'God is life'. But his eyes glazed over as he was showing it to me. He had lost interest, and he put away the diary and went back to bed. Further along, I stopped to talk to James who was forever telling me tales about his travels. His accent was cultivated and English. His story was that he travelled around and checked himself in to hospitals for free lodging and food. I had no way of knowing if it was true. The Charge Nurse had told me nothing about him, except that I should be wary. 'Watch yer bum,' he'd said. 'He's a ravin poof.'

James had talked to me about the Upanishads, about haiku, about the writings of Sufi masters.

Tonight he had remembered a quotation to tell me, from the opening of a Sufi scripture. The dog barks. The caravan passes.

'There's a haiku for you!' he said.

The dog barks. The caravan passes.)

Another car came out of the dark towards me and my hand went up. The gesture by now was mechanical, almost reflex, and it took a few moments before I realized the car was actually slowing to a stop. Picking up my rucksack, I ran, stumbling towards it. A young couple, only going as far as the next turn-off, a few more miles up the road. But I was grateful to be moving.

The next turn-off was even more bleak than the one I had left. But it made a change. I started all over into trying to keep warm.

In my jacket pocket was the little book that Doug had given me. 'The Four Noble Truths'. I took it out and tried to read it in the light under the signboard. The first truth, it said, was the universality of suffering. Existence is suffering. Samsara.

I realized now that the closer I was moving to Glasgow, the more a fear of it was growing in me.

I fell to thinking about the hospital again.

(The morning after the patients' party, first thing, I was helping out with breakfast, setting the tables, dishing up plate after plate of dull invariable slop and stodge. A dollop of porridge; a slippery fried egg, pale and glazed; a lank streak of anaemic bacon; tea and limp triangles of white bread scraped with margarine.

Everything was as usual. Sammy was stuffing himself with extra slices of bread, in defiance of his diabetic diet, demanding sugar in his tea, swiping leftovers from other plates.

Dr Cohen was complaining that he had been given bacon again, instead of kosher food.

Old Mr Hendry still ate nothing. He looked without seeing at the plate that was offered to him, thin bony fingers plucking at air, skin drawn tight over skull, sunken lifeless eyes, staring out, lost.

Big Andrew was agitated, muttering to himself, unable to sit still. Standing up he bumped the table, making Sammy drop the sugarbowl and spill his tea. Sammy yelled at him.

'Kin you not sit at peace fur hauf a fuckin minnit ya snottery big bastard ye!'

Andrew clenched his fists. 'Slobberin lik a big wean,' said Sammy. 'Pit ye aff yer fuckin breakfast.'

Andrew moved round the table. 'That's it finished,' he said. 'Ah'll kill him.'

Only with difficulty was he held back as Sammy carried on shouting abuse.

James was laughing out loud at their mad antics.

Eddie poked at his food, said he wasn't hungry. He knew there was a plot to poison him bit by bit.

I cleared away the dishes as they all moved out into the corridor to queue for their assorted pills.

The day-nurses had arrived and my shift was coming to an end. That meant the beginning of a few days' holiday, away from the place.

I looked out the window at the courtyard, grateful for the few sparse trees and bushes, somewhere for the eye, and the mind, to rest.

Behind me in the ward, I heard someone call out. Turning, I saw that it was Dr Cohen. The Charge Nurse ran past me. 'Keep them out the toilet,' he said. 'Old Mr Hendry's dead.'

'I found him,' said Andrew. 'He just went in there and sat down and died.'

As I was leaving for home, they wheeled the old man out past me. I wanted to see his face, but he was covered over with a sheet. I wanted to see into his eyes, see into that nothing he had been staring at for so long.

Along the corridor, I heard Andrew still muttering. 'Just sat down and died.'

For most of that day and the following night, I slept, woke, slept again, surfacing from tangled dreams. A recurring image was the dead man passing. But the face I would see as I pulled back the sheet would not be the old man's, but now my dead mother's, now Mary's, now my own.

In the morning when I woke I decided to leave for London.)

The second noble truth, read in the light from the signboard, was that suffering has a cause, and the cause is desire.

No light along the road. Dark night, cold and endless.

On I read to the third truth, that suffering can be conquered, and the fourth, that the way to conquer it is to follow the Buddha-path.

> You put your whole self in
> You take your whole self out
> You put your whole self in
> And you shake it all about

Glimmer of headlights in the distance, the first car since I'd been at this new junction. And again my hand went out. And the car slowed. And the car stopped. And I stumbleran, unbelieving, as the driver opened the door to me and yes he was going to Glasgow and yes he would take me all the way. Down that road. Going home.

The driver was a man about fifty. He told me he was an engineer and he lived and worked in South Africa. He was heading back to Glasgow for the first time in 20 years.

He had taken a detour into Carlisle to visit a cousin. But the cousin had long since moved away. So he'd slept for a couple of hours in the car before heading north again, out along this road where I'd been waiting. We talked and he was obviously glad of the company. He told me about his work, about South Africa. I told him of the changes he would find in Glasgow. He asked me about myself and I told him a bit, about leaving university, drifting between Glasgow and London, working in the hospital.

'You want to get some qualifications under yer belt,' he said. 'Then emigrate son. Make a life for yerself.'

It was warm in the car and his voice kept fading as I dropped into sleep, nodding forward then jolting awake, startled, then remembering where I was. Now we would be passing through hills, now the glare of headlights would dazzle me. Now it had started to snow and the windscreen wipers would swish and click, back and forth.

Then the driver was shaking me awake and we were cruising into Glasgow, past the dark factories, in along London Road.

He was heading for the south side, Pollokshields, so I asked him to drop me in the centre of town.

When we stopped, I thanked him and he shook my hand, repeating his advice. 'Stop footerin about son. Get yerself a decent job and get the hell out of it.'

I thanked him again and waved after him as he drove away.

He had dropped me in Argyle Street, deserted now. Familiar neon above empty pavements. Snow was falling still, gathering here and there, in an odd corner, against a wall.

Here I was. Back.

I headed up towards George Square, where the late-night buses converged every hour. I might be lucky and catch one. I might have an hour to wait. I had forgotten to check the time.

As I walked along Glassford Street, I heard a laugh, a shout. Looking up I saw three boys on the other side of the road. They crossed towards me and I kept on walking, head down. But they stopped a few feet in front of me, blocking the pavement. They were all about seventeen or eighteen. I could smell drink on their breath.

'Got the right time?' I asked, afraid and trying to go out to them.

'Whit ye wantin the time fur?' said the one in the middle.

'Jist want tae know,' I said.

'Cheeky cunt, int he,' said the one on the left.

'Wherr ye gawn?' said the third.

'Hame,' I said.

'Wherr's hame?'

'Up Hillhead,' I said. 'Near the Uni.'

'Ye wan a they students then?'

'Naw.'

'Whit ur ye well?'

'Ah work in a hospital.'

'That'll be handy then, eh!'

I felt as if we were exchanging dialogue, stiff and wooden, in a play. The words were a thin surface only, covering some other unspoken thing. We all knew what was coming next. But for the

193

sake of the play we pretended not to know as the scene moved to its close.

I tried to edge past and they were on me. A shove from behind, a kick aimed at my balls but missing as I dodged back. Then a butt in the face, blood seeping from my nose, a punch to the head and one had me by the neck and down I went in a tangle of legs and the boot went in to my ribs. Seeing, in sharp focus, clear, the dark line of a crack across the wet pavement, a scrumpled newspaper in the road, a spatter of mud on a trouser-cuff, brown stain on blue check pattern. Seeing, in the harsh glare under the streetlight, things just being themselves, in minute and meaningless detail. Iron grating in the gutter. Wire mesh across a shop front. The grain of a worn stone wall.

Something glinted in a hand, a steel comb, its handle sharpened to a point.

'Ah'm gonnae stick the bastard.'

And this was actually happening, real. And somehow I was up and swinging with my rucksack, breaking clear and running, running, faster than I knew how. They gave up chasing me after half a block, too tired or drunk to follow, but they shouted after me till I rounded a corner out of their sight. And still I ran till I reached George Square and slumped down panting on a bench.

When I'd stopped shaking I crossed to the drinking fountain to wash away the blood that still trickled from my nose. But the pressure in the tap was too high and sent a jet of water smashing into my face. The shock of that made me laugh, even as I cursed it. I held back my head till the bleeding stopped, then wiped my face clean and drank deep from the fountain. I was shivering now, probably as much from the fright as the cold.

'Some fuckin welcome back!' I said, out loud, and kicked at my rucksack, half-hearted.

Scattered about the place were a few other late-night stragglers, waiting, like me, for the buses. And we didn't have to wait long. I saw my bus swing its green and yellow bulk into the square, and grateful for that, I hurried across to the stop.

On the side of the bus was the city coat of arms with the bell the bird the fish the tree. I thought of the jingle and of reading it in the haiku book. What was it I had said to Doug? An auspicious return to Glasgow! I dabbed at my nose with a sodden paper hanky.

I sat towards the back of the bus, sideways on the seat, my feet out resting on my pack. I wanted to sleep and sleep forever.

'Been in a bit a bother?' asked the conductor.

'Aye,' I said. 'Got jumped bi three young fellas.'

'Terrible, eh,' he said. 'Bastards int they.'

He took my fare as the bus moved out.

My mouth and throat felt raw, tasted stale. Rummaging in my rucksack, I found what was left of my food-pack. The apples were untouched and gladly I picked one out and bit into it. Clean, it brimmed its juices into my mouth, tasted fresh.

I looked out the window at the empty streets, the city asleep. Glasgow. Home. Mental. Pure mad.

The bell that never rang. The fish that never swam. The tree that never grew. The bird that never flew.

Four hundred miles from my friends, the apples they gave me for the journey.

The same old song

I should have realized it was a dream, for although I was in it, at the same time I was outside, watching it all go on, as if in a film.

I was in the hospital. I knew that though it didn't look the same. My back was to the ward. I was standing at the window looking out. But instead of the hospital courtyard, what I was seeing was a dark, shifting landscape. There was no light anywhere and nothing I could hold in focus; no form, just vague threatening shapes at the edges of my vision. I felt myself being drawn out into it. Darkness leading into deeper dark. The glass of the window was all that kept it from me. I wanted to turn and run, but I knew that if I turned my back it would shatter the glass and engulf me. I tried to call out, but no words would come. My eyes filled with tears and through them I saw the landscape resolve itself into more familiar shapes, less hostile but still desolate. Black had given way to grey. It was more like the hospital courtyard now, but dead, in decay, the colours of bone and ash. All except for one small patch of colour in the foreground.

As I looked it grew clearer and I saw that it was a bush. Its leaves were the faintest green, its single flower a deep intense red. The flower seemed to glow and pulsate. It moved and opened out towards me, passing through the glass as if through air. It touched the centre of my chest, my heart. It was my heart. The rhythm of its pulse was my heartbeat. Its petals unfolded from within me. It had never been outside at all. What I had seen was its reflection in the glass. This was what I had always known, this reality. The flower was my true being.

Looking down at my body, I saw it clothed in the white hospital coat. I saw the plastic badge with my name and NURSING AUXILIARY printed in block letters. There was something comic in the fact that I was labelled. 'This is me,' I said, and laughed, knowing I was so much more, I felt an affectionate warmth towards my little everyday self. I took off my white coat. Underneath I was perfectly naked.

I pressed my head to the glass. I wanted to push through, to the other side. I looked out once more, but instead of the flower I saw the darkness again, filling the space, negating, blotting everything out. And I panicked as the certainty grew in me that the darkness, like the flower, was not out there. I was seeing it reflected in the glass. It was inside. It was here in the room around me.

Turning, I saw three doctors. They laid heavy hands on me.

They covered my nakedness with a patient's bedsmock. They were leading me to the ECT room for treatment by electric shock.

In the room, Doug was waiting. He too had been brought in for treatment.

'Just karma man,' he said, grinning.

Two bodies were wheeled out past us, covered over with sheets. One was Ritchie, the other was Mag, both dead.

'Just karma.'

Behind us, on the other side of a glass wall, Mary and Jenny were trying to reach us, calling us back.

The doctors made me lie on a trolley. They fastened straps across my chest and legs. They made me bite on a bit of rubber. They put the electrodes to my head . . .

Waking, I sat up in bed, the panic still on me from the dream, but glad to wake, even to this. Cold half-light of morning. My head and neck ached, my nose felt swollen, clotted where it had bled.

The dream had left me shaken. It was like one I had had before, a month or two back . . .

(That time too I woke in panic, not knowing where I was. The room was unfamiliar. Above me was a pale square of light. I thought I could hear the sea. Then I remembered we had come away for a few days. We were in Millport. The square above me was a skylight in the sloping ceiling, feathered over with frost. It was cold in the room. I was shivering and could see my breath. Mary was a warm sleepy bundle beside me.

'What's wrong?' she asked, not quite awake. My head was clearer now.

'Thought ah was in the hospital an the doctors had got me.'

'Nobody's goin to get you,' she said, yawning, already drifting back into sleep.

Lying back I looked up wondering at the perfect patterns on the skylight, the fine delicate leaf of frost on the glass. I felt calm now, listening to the wash of the waves on the shore. Mary was asleep, her hair a soft dark tangle on the pillow. To be here beside her was sanctuary and warmth. And this was real. The threatening shadow-world of my dream existed, if at all, out there, in some other universe altogether . . .)

I got up and splashed my face, switched on the fire and crouched in front of it. No sanctuary now, no comforting warmth. Mary had gone, perhaps for good.

Another daft song went singing in my head. Never felt more like singin the blues. Old songs. Old songs. Play it again. One more time.

I thought again of the songs programming me. Once I had imagined a report being made on my progress. I had even written it out, as part of a story I'd never completed . . .

'response of subject to media rape . . . displays considerable deviation from norm . . . difficulty in accepting our version of the way things are . . . insists on levels of reality behind and beyond what we have sought to imprint by back-projection . . . some struggle against entanglement in the dream . . . nevertheless there is one area in which our efforts have been successful . . . subject's susceptibility to manipulative use of pop music . . . effective since onset of puberty . . . obsession with such music masturbatory in character . . . substitute for direct experience . . . provides escape/comfort/refuge . . . exposes subject where most vulnerable . . . womb-longing/sexual guilt . . . Oedipus programme . . . note also subject's association of pop songs and hymns . . . connects religious insight/mystical experience/womb memory/longing for void . . . could perhaps be utilized . . . note particular susceptibility to certain old songs (from 1910 on) . . .'

*

I peered out the window. I had slept late and the morning was almost gone. The overnight snow had been trampled to slush on the pavements.

There had been no letters while I'd been away, not even a postcard from Mary. The only mail had been a reminder from the library to take back two books, *The divided self* and *Metamorphosis*.

That old uncomfortable feeling as I thought again of the hospital. The books were both ones I had read in the ward, through the long bleak hours of the night-shift. And for that the Charge Nurse was forever poking at me. He would ask what I was reading, and dismiss it.

Of the Laing book he'd said. 'That's the guy that thinks we're all mad except the loonies, isn't it?'

'There's a bit more to it than that,' I'd said.

'Well then,' he'd said. 'He thinks it's us that make them the way they are.' I'd said, 'One thing he's sayin is that we all see things too much in terms of "Us" and "Them". What we need's more . . . integration . . . wholeness.'

'Ach!' he'd said to that. 'Words!'

Of the Kafka book he'd been even more terse. 'Another heidbanger,' he'd said. 'Keep readin stuff like that in here son an ye'll finish up as bad as them.'

The place was numbing me. I would distance myself from it while I was actually there. I would cope. Then on my way home I'd feel like crying. Grey and depressed, I'd feel physically sick.

I could talk about wholeness. But what I had to do was find it in myself. The job might be just one more necessary experience. But I knew now I couldn't go back. I was doing no good, to myself or anybody else.

I would phone this afternoon and tell them I was leaving. They would want reasons of course. I'm sorry I can't come back because. Because I am tired. Because Mary has gone. Because my nose has been punched. Because there are no

199

letters. Because the sky is yellow and there is slush on the pavements. Just because.

I decided to take a walk into town and change the library books, pay my fine and redeem myself . . .

On the way I stopped in at the Art Gallery, for no particular reason. I had time to dawdle and I drifted, aimless, peering at suits of armour and model ships, fossilized bones and bits of machine. I had intended going upstairs to sit somewhere quiet, try to lose myself in a painting. But a tiredness came on me and I sat down in the hall of the stuffed animals. Facing me was what had once been a giraffe, front legs splayed out, neck stretching down to the ground. Sad and old and dusty he was, like all the other animals crowded behind glass into this grubby jungle clearing. He was coming apart at the seams, stitched up the front with thick coarse twine, to keep his stuffing in. He straddled a painted stream, reached forward to drink no water. His glass eyes looked at nothing, like old dead Mr Hendry in the hospital. Sad old deadstuff. I got up to go and remembered there were Buddha statues in another room. I sought them out, and suddenly I knew that this was why I had come. This was the no-reason that had brought me here.

The Buddha sat facing me, carved in smooth white stone. Poised and perfect he sat, all grace and ease of bearing, the source and sustainer of the universe. His smile seemed ancient, like something I had known forever, but long long forgotten.

Existence is suffering. Its cause is desire.

And this had been carved by a human hand. Each fold of the garment; the curve of the limbs; the left hand resting, palm upwards in the lap, the right reaching down to touch the earth.

And the smile.

Suffering can be conquered. There is a way.

And whoever had carved it had known that reality, had known that smile from the inside. He had looked at a chunk of marble and seen in it the Buddha. He had chipped away at the stone until this form had emerged. And here it was in Glasgow, smiling at me. Behind the Buddha's head, out through the window, were trees and a lamp-post, a glimpse of buildings against a grey Glasgow sky. Here.

An attendant passed behind me, shoes squeaking on the polished floor. I bowed to the Buddha and made my way out, through the revolving doors, out again into the street . . .

I felt like talking to somebody, so instead of heading for the library, I cut across the park, thinking I would go and visit Tommy. Tommy was a writer. He had lived in London for years, but now he had come back. He was trying to make some kind of life for himself, here, with his wife and his children. He had been through all the things that were drawing me to London. He had come full circle and was back at university, just for survival. Tommy was about the only one in Glasgow I could talk to about spirituality without feeling self-conscious. He had taught me mantras, loaned me books on meditation.

When I rang the doorbell, his little daughter answered.

'Ma daddy's just away out tae the shops,' she said. 'E won't be a minute.'

'Should ah come in an wait?' I said. 'Or just come back after?'

'Just come in,' she said. I stepped inside.

'Come on,' she said, leading me into the kitchen. 'Ma mummy's upstairs in bed. She's got the flu.'

'Ah better be quiet then,' I said. 'Not disturb her.' I sat down to wait.

'It's ma birthday today,' she said.

'What age?'

'Seven,' she said, proud.

'That's big,' I said.

'Ah got shoes an a dolly an a colourin book an paints.'

'That's a lot.'

'It's *quite* a lot,' she said.

'Ah wonder if ah've got anything,' I said, digging into my jacket pocket. I had a packet of sweets I'd bought at the corner, a tube of Smarties, unopened.

'Ta!' she said as I handed them to her, and she flipped off the plastic cap and shook some into her hand.

'Blue yellow red,' she said. 'Red green brown. Take one.'

I took a red one and she swallowed the rest.

In my other pocket, along with a scrumple of paper and a bunch of keys, I had a ten pence piece and a bright green felt-tip pen. I gave her both and she put them in her own pocket, pleased with her haul. She had finished the tube of Smarties, pouring them down her throat.

'Did ye get a birthday cake?' I asked.

'Ma granny's bringin one after,' she said. 'When's your birthday?'

'Couple a weeks ago,' I said.

'Was it! What age are you?'

'Hundred an twenty-two,' I said.

'Ach away!'

'Honest!'

'Ach!'

'Guess what age ah am.'

'Well . . . ma daddy's therty, so you're . . . ah don't know.'

'Guess.'

'Twenty?'

'Nearly.'

'Twenty-one?'

'No.'

'Twenty-two?'

'Oh, yer gettin warm!'

'Twenty-three!'

'Right!'

'Ah'm a good guesser sure ah am.'

'Brilliant.'

'Did you get a cake?' she asked. 'For your birthday?'

'No'

'What did ye get?'

'Socks an a book.'

'C'mon an ah'll make a cake,' she said, jumping up and running to the back door. 'It can be for the two ae us.'

'Where ye goin?' I asked.

'Out the back,' she said. On the way she picked up a bashed tartan tin that had once held a round of fancy shortbread.

The backyard was a muddy square of garden, a little tree against the far wall, a tangled rosebush on a ramshackle frame, some sparse grass in tufts here and there. Scattered around were a bucket and spade, an overturned tricycle, a red plastic ball, burst.

'What kinda cake are ye makin?' I asked.

'A snowcake,' she said.

She was crouching down under the tree where some snow still lay, untrampled. With a bit of broken slate she scraped up snow and grit into the tin. I knelt to watch.

'Looks like it's gonnae be a great cake,' I said. 'We can give some tae yer daddy when e gets in.'

'What did ye come tae see him for?' she asked.

'Jist to talk,' I said.

'What about?'

'Oh, lots a things. London an writin an . . . lots a things.'

'Ah was born in London,' she said, then, for no reason, 'Where's Mary?'

'She's away,' I said.

'Where?'

'Far,' I said. 'Germany or Italy or somewhere.'

'Is she comin back?'

'Don't know. Maybe.'

'There!' she said. 'The cake's ready.'

'Looks delicious,' I said, taking the cake and standing up.
And we laughed . . .

The child was smiling up at me. I held the gift she had given, snowcake melting in a battered tartan tin. We grinned at each other, grinned at the colossal mirth of this suddenly lovely day.

We stood there smiling in the tumbledown garden. Smiling, smiling. Years ago . . .

the same old song sweeter than ever reach out somewhere knowing we can be real love is you love is me walk on so sad about us I need you I can't give you anything again if you know hey little girl save the last dance for me over my shoulder goes one care you ain't nothin but beyond meanwhile I'm thinkin all this world for being an angel but a play on your mind it's time we began to laugh and cry again baby it's you everythin's fine right now it's gonna be alright there is a flower that bloometh you really got blue horizon remember me but it's all right now you do the hokey kokey put your whole self in on a clear day you just you can see forever but love who you are rise and look you feel part of all those endearing young charms believe me if all around you voice is calling our pain love is my sweet lord but I saw the harbour light I don't believe in leaning on a lamp isn't it a pity but it takes so long blues ain't nothin there's a place where I can go thank you slopes of peppermint bay I'm sittin on top of the good ship lollipop I really want to see you where bon bons play on the sunny dear dead days beyond recall thank you thank you it won't be long it's a nice trip the world love's old sweet song bop shewaddy waddy la la la tarara boom dee ay aum aum aum.

Auld Lang Syne

Last day of another year and I sit at the window looking down over Hill Street, out across the city. Glasgow.

Directly opposite, across the road, a row of grey tenements, crazy-tilted chimney pots, a tangle of television aerials. Further along, the red brick block of the cancer hospital. From here, if the lights were lit, I could see right into the houses and into the hospital wards.

Through a gap I can see as far south as the Renfrewshire hills, fading today into grey rainmist. (Out of that mist perhaps came the first straggling settlers to this valley, this green place.) Jutting cranes of the shipyards. Monolithic tower-blocks.

Down in the street, an Indian woman passes in a red raincoat and a gold-embroidered sari; a little boy solemnly drags a huge cardboard box along the pavement, to some secret purpose of his own; a sleek black car goes swishing along towards the synagogue at the end of the road; an ambulance draws up outside the cancer hospital. Beads of rainwater strung along a telegraph wire.

From down the road comes a soft chiming of bells from the church of Saint Aloysius. The chimes are a tape-recording, played through speakers high up in the church tower. This is the bell that never rang.

On the table before me is a book on Celtic art, lying open, pencils and a rubber eraser, a paintbrush and a pot of yellow poster-colour, a sea-smoothed stone, speckled and veined. I have been looking for a design that will fit the shape of the stone, an almost-perfect oval. The one I have chosen is an intricate knot, copied from a page in the Book of Kells. The stone is one I brought back with me from Campbeltown. There I went with my wife in the spring, and we crossed one morning to the far side of Kintyre, the coast facing out to the Atlantic. And there we walked for miles, over fields, along clifftops. We scrambled down slopes of shifting scree, till we stood at the edge of a shallow dip, looking down into the wide sweep of a bay. And the waves came smashing in, thundering along the beach, like nothing we had ever seen or heard before. There was nothing between us and America but this vast being, this great surging ocean.

We picked our way down over the shingle. A single shaggy goat looked down at us, without interest. It was a place where no people should be – dead sheep, dead seagulls, a dead gannet, its feathers clotted with oil. And back a little from the water's edge was the simple grave of some foreign sailor, whose body had been washed up here, far from home. And over the grave was a marker in the shape of a Celtic cross, and the inscription read simply GOD KNOWS. And the ocean rumbled and crashed, endless.

We sat for a time, awed by it, and with nothing much to say.

I had wanted for years to come to Kintyre. In Campbeltown my father was born. There my grandparents lived before coming to Glasgow when the shipyards closed down. Further back than that I know nothing of my family, except that they came over from Ireland, to farm and to fish.

'Imagine bein able to trace right back,' I said. 'All your ancestors, as far as human memory.'

Right back to primitive man. Back through the animals, back through the apes and the reptiles.

'Back into the sea,' she said. 'Back to a tiny wee one-celled creature.'

'And back before that?'

'God knows!'

Before we left, she picked up a stone, to bring back with us to Glasgow from this place. How many years had worn it smooth to this perfect shape for us to find? Wet from the sea it glistened, and its colours were deep and rich.

And here sits that same stone, waiting for me to paint it with an ancient pattern. One line interlacing, looping and turning back on itself, without end.

The patterns my mother made with pipe clay on the stairs and the landing, after she had scrubbed them, down on her knees. Curl and sworl, repeated, a flow like waves.

My first efforts at writing – the same recurring shapes, scrawled with a stub of pencil. Holding it up to my mother. Whit dis it say mammy? Real writing.

I make my first marks on the stone, sketching the design in pencil, tilting the stone to the light from the window to see the lines more clearly, watching the outline slowly take shape.

Rub my eyes, grown tired from the concentration. Lean back and stretch. Look up at the ceiling. Landscapes in the damp patch up there in the corner. Japanese mountains through mist, a waterfall, a tree. When the rain falls heavy it seeps through and drips. The landlady has promised, a man will come from the Corporation, climb on the roof, shift a slate or two. 'That should do the trick,' she says. 'Course it's all storm damage, few years back. Building's never been the same since. Should've been pulled down years ago.'

Years ago.

As a child, writing my name and address on the inside covers of all my books. Elaborately, a very full address.

Top flat right, 115 Brighton Street, Govan, Glasgow, Scotland, Britain, Europe, The Northern Hemisphere, The Earth, The Solar System, The Milky Way, The Universe.

And here I am, years later, back in another Glasgow tenement, another top flat right. Same old universe. Wind rattles the panes. It is cold and I can see my breath. The little electric fire is not enough for such a big room. I should have cleared out the grate and lit a real fire, but I've been lost in the painting of the stone. I can come back to that later, but for now the room needs warmth.

We have coal, in a tea-chest, in a cupboard by the front door. We have old newspapers under the bed. But no sticks. Check out the kitchen that we share with our neighbours, but there's nothing there that could be broken up. Nobody else at home. Our neighbours are two students and an Irish labourer. The students have gone home for Christmas and New Year. Jack, the Irishman, goes home tonight. We will have the place to ourselves; some peace.

Perhaps I can pick up some sticks while I'm out. I should go now. The centre of town will be crowded. It's already getting late.

Outside it is colder than I had realized. Dampness and a wind that stings fingers and face.

The small boy I saw earlier, lugging the cardboard box, has pitched the box on its side, like a tent, on a square of wasteground where a house used to be. Hunkered down inside it, sheltered, he huddles and peers out.

(A New Year's Day, long ago. Going with my father to see Rangers play Celtic at Ibrox Park.

My father worked part-time at the Albion, the greyhound stadium across the road from Ibrox. On match-days they used the Albion car-park and my father worked as an attendant. I went with him, early, and was left in a little office, to wait.

208

My father's friend Bobby switched on an electric fire for me, told me to make myself at home. On the wall was an old framed photograph of Charlie Tully as a young man. Screwed on to the wall, it must have been there for years. As Bobby was leaving, he spat on it, hit Charlie smack in the face. 'Papes!' he said, disgusted. 'Never mind son, we'll murder them the day.' I had a long time to wait. In my pocket I had two little books. A New Testament in modern English I'd been given at Sunday school, and the Rangers' annual handbook. I couldn't settle to reading them. The wind came under the door. Rain beat against the window. The spit moved slowly down the glass on the picture of Charlie Tully.)

At the end of the street, past the last building, the wind whips harder across the empty space. Once the street extended further, down to Saint George's Road. But they cleared away the houses, bulldozed the hillside. And now it is a steeper slope. Grassy green and landscaped, it dips down towards the motorway and what is left of Charing Cross. A concrete footpath leads down, in flat slab steps. A dear green place. Green grassy slopes.

Down there was a pub where I used to go as a student. Long gone. I'd even forgotten its name. But just then I remembered it. The Wee Hoose.

I remembered sitting there, another Hogmanay. There would be a crowd of us, not long up from school, drinking ourselves sick for the New Year. And there was a moment, afterwards, when the pub was closing; and I found myself sitting outside at the edge of the pavement. It was as if I suddenly came on myself, discovered myself sitting there, and it all seemed comical and sad at the same time. There I was, sitting, at the centre of this crazy dream that was my life.

'How did I get here?' I said.

'Jist rolled out the pub an sat down,' said somebody.

'Naw, but here! How did I get here!'

'Ach yer pissed!'

Then there was another voice, in the doorway of the pub, intoning, 'It is closing time now in the gardens of the west . . .'

'That's it,' I said. 'Ah was readin that the other day. Where in God's name was that?'

The same voice came back, sharp and nasal, 'Hurry up please, it's time . . . Good night ladies, good night . . .'

'Who's that quotin all these books?' I said. 'Somebody there knows what ah'm talking about.'

Then it was taken up, an old-time song.

> Good night ladies
> Good night ladies
> Good night ladies
> It's time to say goodnight . . .

Then I was swept off towards a party, somewhere.

> Merrily we roll along
> Roll along
> Roll along

And somehow, later, we were rolling through the Clyde Tunnel. Shouting out old Beatles songs at the tops of our voices, hearing them echo back. Through the tunnel, through the stupid night. Going nowhere. Rolling along.

To walk along these streets is to stir so many memories.

A streetcorner. A shopfront. The texture of a stone wall. The way a girl's hair hangs. The pattern on a dress. Everything brings back moments, trivial in themselves, beautiful and funny and sad. Bits and pieces. Fragments in a dream.

Sometimes I feel I know everything that has ever been, and will one day remember it all. All the fragments will make one great timeless whole. Then these moments remembered, this restless *déjà vu*, seem part of an endless awakening, to something more.

Sometimes it seems the fragments contain the whole; and every moment is eternity, every little thing is infinite. And the moment itself is its own significance, its own meaning.

I turn along Sauchiehall Street, into the crowds, the endless flow. Work is over early today, for most. Now it is all preparation for the Big Night. The whole place is frantically getting ready to relax.

My first stop is a chemist's shop, to buy some ginger essence. It comes in a tiny bottle, a deep rich red, a phial of magic potion.

Out into the street again and the lights are on – streetlights, shoplights, Christmas lights. It's still afternoon, but the dark comes down early these midwinter days. I push on through the tide and come to a stop at the next traffic lights, catching bits and snatches of conversation.

'Honest tae God, it was *that* size . . .'
'So ah says tae her ah says Margaret ah says . . .'
'Course Glasgow's not really Scottish is it . . .'
'An ther he wis . . .'
'More Irish than anything else . . .'
'Fell doon the subway steps an smashed the lot . . .'
'Now Edinburgh. Edinburgh's Scottish . . .'
'Depends what you mean by Scottish . . .'
'A wee carry-out bag . . .'
'But surely . . .'
'All over the place . . .'
'Gonnae be some night the night . . .'
'Watchin it on the telly . . .'
'So ah says c'mere you . . .'
'Anywey . . .'

An old man in a long grey coat, down almost to his ankles, goes shambling and muttering past. 'Nae wonder folk laugh at us,' he says, squinting across to where a man in a kilt is waiting to cross. A cartoon-Scotsman, big-bellied and beefy-red in the face, he stands and waits for the tides of traffic to part. The old man in the long grey coat coughs and spits and shakes his head.

I have met him before, the same old man. There was one day in Hill Street, a big saloon car was easing along slow. It came to a stop, its engine purring, and the driver leaned out and asked the old man the way to the synagogue. I was coming up behind and heard him direct the driver the wrong way, back down into the town centre. I told him the synagogue was at the end of the street, and 'O, aye,' he said, 'yer right enough.' But when the car had gone he turned on me. 'Whit d'ye want tae dae that fur?' he said. 'Wouldnae tell these bastards anythin. Wouldnae give them the time a day.'

There was one other time I met him, walking past Charing Cross, he caught me by the arm.

'D'ye know whit it's all about then?' he asked. 'Lint,' he said, telling me his secret of secrets, repeating it, shouting it into my face.

'Lint! Ur ye deef? Lint! Lint! Fuckin lint!'

Then, 'Ach, whit's the use,' he said. 'Ah don't know.'

Further along comes a young man in orange dhoti, orange anorak, a devotee of Lord Krishna, chiming finger-cymbals and chanting the Hare Krishna mantra, moving through the Hogmanay crowds. A few folk shout at him.

'Gawn yersel son, give us the auld Harry Karry!'

'D'ye know any Country an Western?'

'Harry Harry, Harry Hood . . .'

He catches my eye and I smile but don't stop.

'Hare Krishna,' he says, as I pass.

'Hare Krishna.'

I cut down towards the supermarket, Grandfare, stopping only to peer in at the window of a music ship, at guitar and saxophone, bongo-drums and flute, banjo and autoharp and clarinet, all arranged neatly in display, just so.

The supermarket is like a region of Hell, packed with people stocking up for the coming days. There is a tiredness, in the brightness of the lights, in the ransacked shelves, in the faces of the assistants. And over it all the Tannoy tinkles out tinny music, jingling festive tunes and pop songs, all at the same bland incessant level, muted organ, guitar and drums. Have yourself a merry little Christmas. Welcome to my world. The fool on the hill. I quickly gather up the few things I have come for and join the nearest queue. Whatever queue I join is sure to take the longest, even if it's only half the length. It seems to be a law of the universe, so I surrender myself to it. The woman just before me has two trolleys, filled to overflowing. I prepare myself for a wait of several days.

And it suddenly seems funny, this madness. I imagine us all dancing to that music, linking in a conga-line, weaving through the check-outs.

I make it out eventually, carrying a bulging plastic bag. I have just about come full circle now, am back almost to Hill Street and home.

I stop outside the Chinese shop to look in at the lanterns and ginger-jars, baskets and soup-bowls, toy dragons and kites, boxes and bottles and packets and tins. I stand at the door, smelling spices and teas, and I notice, in the rubbish left out on the pavement, a wooden crate like an orange-box. Remembering I needed some firewood, I pick it out and walk on. The rain has been drizzling on and off all day; now it has started again and gets steadily heavier. Outside the chip shop there is more wood, a broken fish-box. I gather it up, tuck it inside the Chinese crate, and hurry on up the last stretch home; past Saint Aloysius church, past a playground where three boys are kicking a ball about, past a dog being a dog and chasing a cat, past a young Indian girl, past a policeman, past a man struggling up the hill with a crate of beer. I look across to the wasteground where I saw the small boy earlier, crouched inside his cardboard box. The boy has gone now and I stop. Look. The empty box, sagging. Listen. The drip and patter of the rain on wet cardboard.

Home again, the first thing to do is light the fire. Down on my knees, I rake out the grate, scrumple up bits of newspaper, break up the wooden crate for sticks. On the end of the crate are stencilled Chinese characters, and stamped, in red, the words Peoples' Republic of China. It has come a long way to be firewood for us to burn. The fish-box is stamped Aberdeen. I don't need to use it yet, and put it away for another time in the cupboard where we keep the coal.

There is something elemental in it, the ritual placing of paper, sticks and coal, the kindling and coaxing into life. But today it is made difficult by the strong wind that comes beating down the chimney in gusts, damping the fire, filling the room with smoke. I try to create an updraught by fanning and blowing; I open the door; I spread a sheet of newspaper across the wire mesh of the fireguard; and at last it begins to catch, a flicker in one corner, a crackle of sticks, a rush and roar of flame as it draws and flares. I peel back the sheet of paper and the flames settle into a slower, steady dance, a glow that brings the room to life.

There is a picture I remember, with a poem about firewood, in a book on Eastern art. Searching through my books, I find the right one and open it at the page.

The picture is a brush-drawing, *The enlightenment of Eno*, by an artist called Shuai Weng. Eno the Chinese master stands, a bundle over his shoulder; he smiles, attentive, as if listening. A few deft brush-strokes give him life; he emerges from the silence, the white expanse of the page; the lines are fluid and fading, eloquent beyond words.

The verse reads

> The bundle is carried firmly on his shoulder;
> Before him, the way home has no obstructions
> 'Awaken the mind without fixing it anywhere',
> And he knows the house where the firewood burns

I look up to see those Japanese landscapes on the ceiling, and notice the damp patch is spreading, the rainwater starting to seep through. I place a plastic bucket on the floor to catch the drips.

Jack, our neighbour, is home. I've heard him moving about and now he's knocking at the door of our room.

'Hello,' he says. 'Ah'm just gettin ready to go. Thought ah'd say cheerio an wish ye all the best.'

'Same to yerself Jack.' We shake hands on it.

He stands, a bit awkward, not knowing what else to say. He is dressed up for the journey in his good suit, stiff in a shirt and tie.

'What time'll ye be home?' I ask.

'Should make it in time for the bells,' he says. 'The plane gets intae Dublin about ten. Then ah get a bus.'

'That's great. It's really fast.'

'So it is.'

'You'll be glad to see yer wife an kids again.'

'Oh aye, ah will that. It's hard y'know, bein away for so long.'

He has a drink in him and he's talking more than usual, his face pink and gleaming.

'No chance of gettin work nearer home Jack?'

'It's hard,' he says. 'It's hard. Not much doin.'

'It's a long way to have to come.'

*

Up until a month ago we had another Irish neighbour, a younger man, in his twenties, called Terry. One night we were sitting when we heard a roar from his room, a roar that scared us, like a big animal in pain. Then there was a crash and what sounded like an explosion. Then a moaning and crying and the slam of the front door.

Jack was already out in the hall. Terry had rushed past him, out of the house, 'lookin like death,' he said.

It was only later we found out what had happened. Terry had been watching television, ready for a quiet evening, a couple of cans of Guinness to hand. Then the news had come on, with an item about shootings in Belfast. And one of the dead was Terry's young brother. He had roared then, roared at the madness of it all. And the stupid newscaster was already talking about something else, talking about Parliament and smiling as if nothing had happened. And Terry took one of his cans of Guinness and threw it at the smiling face. And the screen and the tube caved in with a bang, the set blew up, showered glass all over the room. And Terry went raging out into the night.

A day or two later he went for good, back home to Ireland with his anger and his grief.

'Ah think when ah come back,' says Jack, 'ah'll be movin on again. Up tae Aberdeen, get a job on the oilrigs.'

'D'you have to do that?'

'Well. Ah could still get plenty work here. They're pullin down that many buildins an puttin up new ones. But Aberdeen's where the money is.'

'Right.'

'Listen,' he says. 'Ah'm away in a minute. But ah was thinkin ye might want the loan a ma telly while ah'm away, seein yis haven't got one.'

'That's very good ae ye Jack.'

'Ach!'

Together we lug the set from his room into ours.

'Lots a good pictures an that on jist now,' he says. 'Reception's nothin great, but it does.'

'Fine.'

'Would that be yer missis comin up the stair?'

'Probably. She's been out visitin her family. Her sister's in the hospital, just after havin a baby.'

'Boy or a girl?'

'A wee girl.'

'Nice.'

The frontdoor bell rings and Jack answers it. 'It's her right enough,' he says.

'Hello Jack,' she says. 'Thanks.' She seems to be tired, glad to be home and to set down the heavy bags she's been carrying.

'Jack's just goin home,' I say, 'and he's givin us his telly while he's away.'

'That's a nice thought Jack,' she says.

'Lots a good pictures on,' says Jack.

He is awkward again for a moment, then he breaks it by looking at the time and saying, 'Here, ah'd better be goin.' He fetches his suitcase and a bundle tied with string, and closes the door of his room behind him. He shakes hands with both of us, formally, wishing us well.

'Right then!' he says.

'Soon be home now,' she says.

'Should make it before the bells,' he says again. The words are coming to have a special sound to him. Like an incantation. Home before the bells.

'OK then.'

'Right.'

'Cheerio.'

'All the best.'

We wave to him from the door, watch him go out of sight round the bend in the stairs.

'Wee soul,' she says, as we come inside again. 'Standing there all dickied up. Your heart goes right out to him.'

'Ye even forget the rest of the year!' I say. 'The times he plays his telly too loud . . . an doesn't put enough money in the gas meter . . . an doesn't clean the bath after him . . . an leaves the big pot full of chip fat . . .'

'I know I know!' she says, laughing. 'But still . . .'

Later, after we've eaten, I put the finishing touches to the painting of the stone; the delicate interweaving of lines, in orange, finely outlined in green. I give it a coat of varnish and it brings out the colours, makes the stone shine, as if still wet from the sea.

Then together we make a start on cleaning up the room. And we talk, about nothing in particular, glad of the space and the peace, glad, for once, to have the house to ourselves.

She tells me about her sister's baby, a poor wee lovely crinkled thing, looking out as if to ask what kind of nightmare was this she'd been born into.

'Any word of them gettin a house yet?'

'Nothing decent,' she says. 'The Corporation keep offering them these dumps away out in the schemes. Really rough. She just doesn't fancy it, stuck in the house all day with the baby, and him out at work.'

'Some bits of the schemes are OK though.'

'Some bits are terrible,' she says. 'Absolute misery.'

There's a bleakness not far away, coming in through our talk, but then suddenly, brightening, she shakes it off.

'Anyway,' she says. 'The baby's lovely!'

Then I start telling her about something I've been trying to write, a long poem about Glasgow, linked together by the heraldic images on the city's coat of arms, the bell, the bird, the fish, the tree.

'Still trying to write it out your system,' she says.

'Right. Ah keep comin across the images too. Ah'm sure it goes back to ma childhood, learnin the jingle.'

> Where's the bell that never rang?
> Where's the fish that never swam?
> Where's the tree that never grew?
> Where's the bird that never flew?

'There really is something magical about it,' she says. 'Mysterious.'

'Like one of those riddles you've got to solve before you can move on towards the Holy Grail, or the Jewel in the Lotus, or whatever.'

'Like Zen koans.'

'Right! The sound of one hand clapping. God! The soundless sound! That's the bell that never rang!'

'Is it?'

'Why not! There's a whole world to be read into it. The symbols are really beautiful. Ah was lookin at them today an seein all sorts of things.'

'Like what?'

'Well. The tree. It seems it's a hazel, so that's the hazel of wisdom that Neil Gunn's always talkin about. And the fish is a salmon. That's the salmon of knowledge with the ring of eternity in its mouth. Then there's the bell. That's the good news, ringin out. And the bird is the spirit, flying . . . soaring.'

'It's a lovely way to see it.'

'And there's other ways to look at it. Other patterns to make. And the great thing about the images is they're concrete. They're real. A bell. A bird. A fish. A tree. Things. And that's what you come back to after all the flyin about. Just the plain miraculousness of what is.'

'I'm dying to read this poem!' she says.

'All ah have to do is write it!'

'Why don't you write something now?' she says. 'I'm going to have my bath in a minute and then do the last wee bit tidying up. You could write for a while before the bells.'

'Ah'll try.' I clear a space at the table, sit down with pencil and blank sheets of paper.

'Ah couldn't really settle to it this morning.'

'If you can't write the poem,' she says, 'write something else. Just start anywhere. Write about where you are. Write about today, about the New Year.'

She goes off to have her bath and leaves me to it.

I look at the paper, and start to write . . .

Last day of another year and I sit at the window looking down over Hill Street, out across the city. Glasgow . . .

I write for a while then get up to put more coal on the fire. But before I fetch it from the cupboard, I remember I had planned on making up some ginger wine, something I've always had at New Year, ever since I was a child. I boil up a kettle and add the water to the ginger essence I bought today, mixing it up in a flagon that once held cider. Then I leave it in the kitchen sink to cool.

Passing the bathroom, I shout in. 'Are you gonnae be all night in there?'

'Won't be long!'

There is a beauty in the formality of this bathing for the New Year. Putting on clean clothes. Cleaning up the house. A ritual. A purification.

I remember my mother, scrubbing out the whole house on the last day of the year; changing the bedclothes, washing the windows, hanging up new curtains. The smell of polish and disinfectant; everything in readiness, fresh. Then there was the waiting, for the great change. The bells, and a warmth that made you want to cry. Then the drunk uncles and aunties arriving, everything bright and harsh and loud. The drink and the singing.

'Auld Lang Syne'. Uncle Billy always sang 'The Sash My Father Wore', Uncle Peter sang 'The Red Flag'. The others would try to shut them both up, afraid they might cause trouble.

'No party songs please. Give us a wee bit Country an Western, or an auld Scotch song.'

Old but it is beautiful and its colours they are fine, should old acquaintance be forgot, the worker's flag is deepest red, nobody's child I'm nobody's child, I'm like a flower just growing wild, stained by the blood, for Auld Lang Syne, we'll take a cup of kindness yet for Auld Lang Syne. Come the morning, there was always an emptiness. Glasses would be broken, food trampled into the floor, ashtrays overflowing, the smell of last night's drink. Tired and drab, a staleness. The New Year.

I heap more coal on the fire. It douses the flame, but only for a moment as it licks then leaps and flares again, and other New Years come back to me.

Crouching, in the room full of loud uncles, trying to read the Broons Book I'd been given at Christmas. The last page of the book, as always, ended with the Broons at their Hogmanay party, all misunderstandings cleared, all confusions resolved.

First New Year after my mother died, no party then, my father morose over his beer. But watching television and laughing. Duncan Macrae singing Three Craws.

> The second craw
> wis greetin fur its maw
> on a cold and frosty mornin.

Cold and frosty. Waiting for our first foot.

Jack's television set sits, alien, in the corner of our room. It is old-fashioned and bulky, a squat box. It takes up too much space; it intrudes. We should just have told Jack we didn't want it. But I'm curious to know what's on right now, so I switch it on to find out.

It takes a few minutes of droning to warm up, and what comes through is a choir that sounds like the Black and White Minstrels, singing 'In the Good Old Summertime'. There is no picture, just a flickering zigzag of lines. The song is one that touches me. I remember it from before, one of a thousand stupid songs I have floating in my head. Singing about summertime in the heart of winter.

(An old film clip, of Laurel and Hardy at a street corner, frozen. Deep in the Depression, snow falling thick. Stan plays harmonium, Ollie sings a song. In the Good Old Summertime. At a street corner. Frozen.)

My grandfather winding up an old-fashioned gramophone, cranking the handle in his big fist. Putting on record after record, old 78s in brownpaper covers. Let the great big world keep turning. When you and I were young. In the good old summertime. My grandfather the blacksmith, who came to Glasgow from Campbeltown when the shipyards closed down.

'Your bath's run!'

'Jist coming!'

She comes in wrapped in a towel and crouches in front of the fire to dry her hair.

'See if you can get a picture on the other channel.'

I switch over and we can make out the vague outline of a kilted Scotsman singing 'These Are My Mountains'.

'White Heather Club,' she says.

We watch for a few minutes, amazed. But the reception is bad. The voice is a crackle. The picture fades. The singer is reduced to a pattern, a buzzing stream of electrons. We switch off, put the television away in the coal cupboard, out of sight.

'That's better,' she says. 'Peace.'

The bath is deep and hot and I ease down into it. I stretch and soak in the warmth, muscles untensing, and drift off into thought.

And the memories come in a stream now, no order to them, a moment here, a glimpse there, random, tumbling, New Years past . . .

Walking home, in company or alone, from endless desolate parties . . . Making resolutions, making no resolutions . . . Starting diaries that never got beyond January 3rd . . . Shouting myself hoarse on the terracing at Ibrox or Parkhead, watching Rangers and Celtic try to pound each other into the ground . . . One year sleeping for a day and a night, disturbed only by the roars from the match up the road, waking through a fog, the floodlights shining on to the wall above the bed . . .

There was one year in London, stoned and raving through the crazy city night, laughing, laughing at the whole mad universe, spinning in its endless sorrow-joy . . .

There was a year we had a ceremony in Kelvingrove Park; made patterns with red thread on the hillside, left it to the weather, to be trampled, blown; let a blue thread drift on to the river . . .

There was a year I took nothing to do with any of it, made the New Year nothing special . . .

There was a year the two of us came hitch-hiking home from Europe, just making it back in time for the bells . . .

There was a year I looked out and the world was white and new, all covered in snow, everything still and perfect, in its place . . .

There was a year our neighbours' party broke up in a brawl, and outside the street was being hosed down after a car-crash, and somebody's chimney was on fire along the road . . .

There was last year when we saw the New Year in quietly, sitting together in meditation . . .

And this year that is ending will also pass from my mind, except for these moments that will come back to me, from nowhere, vivid and clear, with their own meaning, or with all meaning gone . . .

A spring day in Kintyre; crouched at the edge of the ocean, picking coral to string for a necklace; seeing, in a green and dripping cave, a flat stone painted by a saint, centuries ago . . . A horse in a field, russet in the sun . . . A smiling jade Buddha, behind a skull, in a cluttered junkshop window . . .

First days in this our latest temporary home; summer evening at the open window, listening to the sounds from the street . . . The way the sun slants across the tenement opposite; the chance shapes weathered on a gable end . . . A face. A voice. A journey . . . A tree in the park that looked golden as it shed its leaves . . . A dead pigeon in a fountain, floating on its back, its wings spread open like a bird in heraldry . . . The smile on the lips of a dead cat by the roadside, a winter day . . . The cry of my sister-in-law's baby daughter, new-born . . .

I climb from the bath, let the water run out; dry myself and put on clean clothes; I feel new.

The god of the old year is dying. His is the sadness of these last days, the dark time, the natural ebb of the year. But the solstice is past, already a week gone. The cycle is turning again towards light.

This year too we plan to meditate through the bells, and it's almost time for us to begin.

We have a little shrine set up in one corner; candles, incense, a few flowers. We sit before it and chant an ancient mantra, Aum. The seed-sound of the universe, of God the creator and God the preserver, God the transformer and destroyer. Aum.

*

The Universe, The Milky Way, The Solar System, The Earth, The Northern Hemisphere, Europe, Britain, Scotland, Glasgow, Garnethill, 110 Hill Street, Top flat right.

The Earth goes turning in space, towards another day. The tape-recorded bells of Saint Aloysius start to chime. It is the magic hour, the change. The New Year.

Further, away across the city, I hear more bells, and more, all just out of phase. Boats on the river sound their foghorns, all blending into one great drone. It sounds like an extension of our chanted Aum, and that makes us laugh. The great mantra, resounding over Glasgow!

A window is flung open and a woman's voice bellows out.

'Happy New Year Everybody! Happy New Year!'

'Wonder where this one'll take us?'

'God knows!'

The varnish has dried on my painted stone and I pick it up, feel the weight of it, solid, in my hand. The pattern has a wholeness, is harmonious, complete, and within it the lines seem in motion, interweaving, beginningless and endless, a pure energy flow.

I put the stone down and together we go to the window to look out. A few people are already out in the street. Two young couples, arm in arm, their voices laughing, go swaying down the middle of the road. An old man sits at the edge of the pavement, his head in his hands. A car passes, saluting everyone with a hoot of its horn. Two men have started to scuffle in a doorway, another two are wobbling up the hill, supporting each other and singing, happy.

For Auld Lang Syne, my dear, for Auld Lang Syne.

As a child I thought Auld Lang Syne was this old old woman, a crone, the ancient Mother. And somehow all this celebrating was for her.

There is noise from every house, television and records all but drowned out by the voices, raised.

Every window is a separate world, a little capsule of light. Here and there where the curtains haven't been drawn we can see right in; we can see a man singing; a glass raised in his hand; we can see a small family group round the TV; we can see a party, already well under way, a room and kitchen packed.

In the hospital too the lights are on and we see an old woman at a window peering out; in another ward a porter is playing a piano, and upstairs a young nurse is combing her hair at a mirror.

Further along the road there's a crash of breaking glass and a window has been broken, from the inside. One or two faces appear at other windows, curious. But nothing else happens.

'Look!' says my wife, pointing over at a house across the road.

A woman has a young child caught up in her arms and she dances with him, round and round and round. Light on her feet she spins with him, her head thrown back as they laugh and laugh.

We come in and close the window now, warm ourselves at the fire.

The incense stick has burned down. A heap of ash. Fragrance.

For Auld Lang Syne, my dear, for Auld Lang Syne.

The Earth goes turning in space. First day of another year.

Blue

Looking up, I am lost in the drift of the clouds, moving, following their own slow dance, ordered, haphazard, without end. They move to the same breeze that touches me now, the breeze I remember from before. Back it takes me; back to when I was eleven.

Like today it was a bright, clear, February day, strangely mild with that soft breeze blowing. Only a week since it had been snowing, and now there was this warmth.

The night before I had sat up late with my father, the two of us talking and talking about football. He told me his legends, of the great Rangers teams of the past. He told me of Alan Morton, scoring a goal direct from a corner kick, of Jerry Dawson, leaping backwards to make an impossible save, of Willie Thornton, face down in the mud after diving full-length to head a last-minute winner against Celtic. It didn't matter that I had heard it all before. These were the myths we shared. The fire was blazing in the hearth, and as we stared into it, my father was the teller of tales, he was the weaver of fables, and his heroes strode before me and were real.

My mother was ill, but that was nothing unusual. She had been ill as long as I could remember and the last few years she had been in and out of hospital. She had asthma and bronchitis and found it difficult to breathe. She had been in bed now for two or three days. Earlier she had been joking: 'Football, football! Is that all you two kin ever find tae talk aboot?' and we had laughed. But now she was feeling bad. She looked paler than I had ever seen her. My father went out to phone the doctor.

I had been cutting out a photo from a magazine and I pasted it into my scrapbook. It was a coloured photo of the Rangers team. The bright royal blue jerseys stood out from the grey page and from the other black and white photos in the book.

Blue was my favourite colour. The royal blue of Rangers. The pale grey-blue of the sky. The blue flame wavering in the fire when the coals were a red glow. There was a girl I liked called Maureen. She had blue eyes. Maureen was a Catholic and she had told me something special about blue. I had found a holy medal with a picture of Our Lady on it. The border of the medal was silver, but the centre part, the picture, was blue. I had given the medal to Maureen and she had told me that Our Lady always wore blue, that blue was the colour of Mary, the Mother of God.

But sometimes blue meant sad. There were songs, like 'Blue Moon', 'Singing the Blues'. I had learned the words of that one with Jim, my friend, and we sang it at the Life Boys concert.

> The moon and stars no longer shine
> The dream is gone I thought was mine
> There's nothing left for me to do
> But cry-y-y-y over you.

They were sad words, but it didn't feel sad to sing it.

By the time the doctor came my mother was much worse. He said she should go to hospital and he sent for an ambulance. When it arrived I was sent next door to Mrs Dolan's, to wait. My father went with my mother. I watched her being carried down the stairs in a stretcher. That was the last time I ever saw her.

My father came back much later and we went to bed. In the middle of the night a policeman came to the door and my father went again to the hospital. This time he came back and told me my mother was dead.

It was as if part of me already knew and accepted, but part of me cried out and denied it. I cried into my pillow and a numbness came on me, shielding me from the real pain. I was lying there, sobbing, but the other part of me, the part that accepted, simply looked on. I was watching myself crying, watching my puny grief from somewhere above it all. I was me and I was not-me.

Later, after a breakfast that neither of us felt like eating, I went out to the toilet on the landing. I still felt somehow outside myself, apart. There was a newspaper hanging behind the toilet door. I looked at it. On the back page was a picture of Ian McMillan, Rangers inside-right. I tore round it carefully.

Out on the landing I opened the stairhead window and looked out across the back courts. The breeze was warm. Everything was the same. It was very ordinary. Nothing had changed. The sun shone on the greybrick tenement buildings, on the railings and the tumbledown walls and middens, on the dustbins and the spilled ashes. It glinted on windows and on bits of broken glass. It was like something I remembered, something from a dream. Across the back a tiny boy was standing, quite still, blowing on a mouth-organ, playing the same two notes over and over again. Down below, two dogs were mating. Jim had told me that people did the same and that was how women had babies, just as bitches had pups. At first I hadn't believed him but then he had showed me a book that explained it. For a while after that I had been doubtful of my parents. There was this feeling that somehow they had betrayed me. But that had passed. It was strange to think of it, that I had been planted inside my mother and had grown there. Her life was in me, and now she was dead. That was how the life went on. The breeze was blowing through everything. It touched my cheek. It stirred the piece of newspaper clutched in my hand. It scattered the ashes round the midden. It ruffled the hair of the two dogs and the clothes of the small boy, still standing, playing his two notes. In its warmth

229

there was something gentle and soft, something infinitely tender. It touched all things and they moved to the one rhythm. It was almost sad, but behind the sadness was the faintest of smiles. I trembled on the edge of something eternal. The one flow. The warm breeze. My mother. All of it.

I closed the window and turned away, up the steps to the house. My father was occupying himself, tidying up, making the bed. I trimmed neatly round the picture of Ian McMillan and opened my scrapbook at the Rangers page. There was the coloured picture of the team. Was it really only last night I had pasted it in? My mother had watched me. I put the new picture beside it. Yesterday. Today. I turned to get the jar of paste and suddenly the flood of tears was on me again.

On the morning of the funeral we were getting the house ready for the people who would be there afterwards. My father was up on a chair, washing the windows. I was raking out the ashes from the fireplace. Dead ashes. My mother was to be cremated. She too was to be burnt, reduced to ashes, and the ashes would be scattered, spread by the wind. My father had told me not to think of the body as my mother. It was only a shell, he said, and she was gone from it. I had thought of the sea-shell, on the mantelpiece. It was big enough to cup in both hands and when you held it to your ear you could hear the ocean. I remembered listening to it when I was very small, full of wonder that something that size could contain the whole ocean, big though it was, for a shell. Depending on how you held the shell to the light, you could see different colours in it, soft browns and purples, blues and greens, colours that seemed to fade away from you, layers behind layers. It had belonged to my mother since she was a young girl. I felt the sadness again. Ashes. I turned to look at my father. He was stepping down from the chair, but he didn't look where he was putting his feet and he stepped right into the bucket of water he'd been using, soaking himself and splashing it all over the floor. It was like something from a film. The laughter swelled and burst out of me. I couldn't contain it. It took control. I laughed till I cried, and through the tears I saw that my father was laughing too.

It was after the funeral and we'd all come back in taxis. Somehow I was standing apart, on my own, across the road from our close. At the corner I could see a few of my friends. Jim waved to me and I waved back. They would know by now about my mother. I gave what I thought was a brave smile. Again I had the feeling of watching myself. I looked across at the building. Home. Soon everything would be back to normal and nobody would notice that anything had changed.

I don't know what I had expected. A sign. Jesus to come walking out of the close and tell me everything was all right. A window in the sky to open and God to lean out and say my mother had arrived safe.

I looked up at the sky, trying to lose myself in the shifting of the clouds. I focused on the shapes, willing them to change into something I could grasp. I half-closed my eyes. I could almost see a cross.

A dog barked and I looked around me. Everyone was crossing the road, going into our close. I looked back to the sky. The clouds had moved on and changed again. Through them I could see, for a moment, a patch of clear blue.

Later, after the meal, I was sitting on the floor with my cousin Jack. I told him about my father and the bucket of water and we laughed. Then I said I had a secret to share with him and I made him promise not to tell. And I told him I had seen her, dressed all in blue, Our Lady, the Mother of God, in the sky above our house.

After everybody had gone, my father sat for a long time looking into the fire. Outside it was growing dark. I closed over the curtains, shutting out the night, drawing in the room about us.

The table was littered with plates, cups, an ashtray, spilled crumbs. My father said we could clear it all up in the morning. I felt as if the day had gone on forever.

'Aye,' said my father, turning to me. 'In the morning.'